Extreme Kissing

www.**rbooks**.co.uk

Also available by Luisa Playa :

Split by a Kiss

Extreme Kissing

Luisa Plaja

CORGI BOOKS

Extreme Kissing
A CORGI BOOK 978 0 552 55681 1
Published in Great Britain by Corgi Books,
an imprint of Random House Children's Books
A Random House Group Company

This edition published 2009

1 3 5 7 9 10 8 6 4 2

The Random House Group Limited supports the Forest Stewardship
Council (FSC), the leading international forest certification organization.
All our titles that are printed on Greenpeace-approved FSC-certified paper
carry the FSC logo. Our paper procurement policy can be found at
www.rbooks.co.uk/environment.

Set in Palatino and Univers
Corgi Books are published by Random House Children's Books,
61–63 Uxbridge Road, London W5 5SA

www.kidsatrandomhouse.co.uk
www.rbooks.co.uk

Addresses for companies within The Random House Group Limited can be
found at: www.randomhouse.co.uk/offices.htm

THE RANDOM HOUSE GROUP Limited Reg. No. 954009

A CIP catalogue record for this book is available from the British Library.

Printed in the UK by CPI Bookmarque, Croydon, CR0 4TD

To extreme travellers everywhere

With special thanks to Lauren Buckland,
Rosemary Canter, Alexandra Fouracres,
Emily Gale, Caroline Green, Eve Harvey,
Kelly Hurst, Zoe Lea, Sarah Painter,
Caroline Paul, Keris Stainton,
Jennifer Taylor and Stacey Taylor

EXTREME SATURDAY: MORNING

TEEN SPICE! MAGAZINE

PRE-EXAM STRESS SPECIAL!

Are you **stressed to the max?** Need to **chill?** Or so laid back you're practically asleep? Is it time to wake up and smell the coffee? Find out now with our Super Stress Test! (You will need a pen and paper and a clock or timer.)

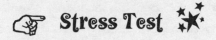 Stress Test

Shut your eyes and clear your mind. Then write down the first things that come into your head in response to the questions below. Don't let it take more than a minute – this test should be done quickly!

Name: Bethany Anne Royston Bets

Age: 16 and two months - GCSE year!!! worst luck

First thought after your mind cleared:

Whoosh whoosh, tumbleweed . . . <u>Not really!</u>
There's loads going on up there! My mind wouldn't
even clear for a second!! It's like the inside of
my BFF's designer school bag: a big old mess of
stuff, but nothing useful for actual lessons or
anything. Except that, unlike Carlota's Marc
Jacobs tote, my head is not crammed with
magazines and freebies from the covers.

**That was the warm-up! Now, write down the things
that worry you most:**

<u>THINGS BETHANY ROYSTON IS WORRIED ABOUT,
IN RANDOM ORDER</u>:

- The fact that I just wrote that title and
underlined it like it was some school thing! Carlota
would have a right laugh at that and call me
Bethany-Boffiny, or a Boring Bee or something!
What is the MATTER with me??

- Well, yeah. School. Or, actually, exams. Dad will
NOT stop going on about them. He probably
expects me to be revising right now even
though it's early on the first Saturday of the
Easter holidays, and I've been home, sick. Yeah,
probably 'cos I'm <u>SICK</u> of Dad going on about
GCSEs!

- That's not even funny, though. I've missed the last two days of school before the exams! I've missed everything! Like all the last-minute revision hints. Also the shirt-signing and the silly string and mad end-of-term vibe.
- And I've missed seeing Declan.
- And he hasn't called me.
- At all. For two days.
(Continued on next page - I've run out of space!!!)
- DECLAN HASN'T CALLED FOR <u>TWO DAYS</u>!!!!
- And he knows I've been off sick! Because I texted him yesterday, when I felt a bit better, and I told him! And he should have missed me, anyway! And, OK, I know he's not exactly the type of boyfriend to come round with overstuffed bears that have recordings of him saying 'I love you, get well soon' in their tummies - ha ha, as IF! - but STILL!
- He didn't even text back.
- I think there could be something going on with Declan.
- And I can't believe it's happening now.
- I stared at the calendar half the night last night. Me and Declan have been officially going out for seven months, two weeks and a day, and I'm exactly sixteen and two months, and I'm pretty sure it's over one month since . . . Oops, I'm running out of time. Back to the questions!

9

Something that others tell you to worry about:
GCSEs (DAD!!!)
Something that makes you feel out of control:
Right now? Everything!
An activity that makes you happy:
Singing. Yeah, right. If only!!!
A person you can talk to:
My BFF, Carlota - Lots. I need her!!! Oops, time's up. (Like I need a quiz to tell me whether I'm stressed or not.)

Now analyse your thoughts! Our expert says: instead of looking at *what* you've written, notice *how* you've written it! Give yourself a point for each time you've done any of the following: underlined a word, used more than two exclamation marks in a row, crossed a word out, used BLOCK CAPITALS, run out of space and crammed your words in, pressed so hard with the pen that you've made a hole in the paper!

Check out your score below!

☆ 5 points or more: It's official – you're showing definite signs of stress! But recognizing it is the first step to managing it. Go to our stress-busting pull-out special, designed by our *Teen Spice!* experts just in time for exam season . . . and relax!

☆ 1–4 points: You're showing light signs of stress and you

could definitely benefit from our great advice for when the going gets tougher!

☆ 0 points: Are you so chilled out that you didn't even answer the questions? Check out the final page of our special to read about 'good stress'. Stress can be a fab motivator and we all need challenges to keep us on our toes!

And before you read on, we'll leave you with the Number One *Teen Spice!* stress-busting tip . . .

Talk to someone you trust about how you feel!

Bethany

I chuck the magazine on my bed, pick up my phone again and pace around my room.

OK, 'pace' is a bit grand, really, and so is 'around' – it's more like pigeon steps, taken by a really tiny pigeon, in a straight line backwards and forwards from the bed to the window. I can cover my whole room in the time it takes to press speed dial twice. Carlota's phone's still going to voicemail.

She's obviously grounded again. Her stepdad loves doing this bargain 'two-for-one' grounding package for her – no phone, and only allowed out for school. But it's Saturday and it's the end of term, so she's a total prisoner now. Her room could fit mine in it three times over, but it's still not big enough for someone like her to be trapped in. She'll be so miserable. I wonder what she's done this time?

Well, Carlota's stepdad usually lets me see her even when she's grounded, if I go round and stun him with school-talk. He actually likes me – he says I'm a good influence. Ha ha.

But first I have to get out of here.

I slip my phone in my pocket and concentrate on filling my bag with parent-pleasing stuff to back up my case. Revision books (to impress Dad, and Carlota's stepdad) and my make-up bag (to reassure Mum – evidence that I'm 'taking care of myself' and 'making an effort'. It's all about the effort, with Mum).

My parents are nothing like Carlota's, but even so, I've just missed the last two days of school, and GCSEs are looming darkly on the horizon. I'm unlikely to get out without hearing at least a few minutes of The Chat from my dad. This is where he tries to convince me that exams are the most important thing in the universe, right up there with food, air and TV dramas about hospitals (Dad's favourite).

But I can put up with The Chat. And after that, unlike Carlota, I'll be free to go, no questions asked. Even after I started hanging around with Carlota, even after it was obvious I was serious about Declan, Dad still trusts me. He'll often say, cringe-makingly and in front of random strangers, 'My Bethany's a good girl.'

Of course, that's because I *am*.

Well, mostly.

I reach the kitchen and take in the classic Royston family scene unfolding in front of me. Dad's already in his work suit, ready for Saturday at the showroom. He's frowning at his breakfast and/or the paper. Mum's sitting across the table from him, cutting old photos into zany shapes for one of her Craft Notions parties. Craft Notions is an arty catalogue company, and the 'parties' mean that Mum's friends come round, gossip and pretend to make greetings cards while she desperately tries to sell them fancy card and cutters. (Mum calls it her 'home business'. Carlota calls it 'Crafty Nutters', especially since her ultra-glam mum shocked us all by joining recently.)

Anyway, knowing that the Crafty Nutters are coming has given me an extra reason to escape as soon as possible. I'm in no mood for all those mums sizing me up and telling me how much I've grown and how far I've come since the Great Potty Training Incident of Fourteen Years Ago.

Dad rustles his paper at me. 'You're early.' He pats his paunch meaningfully. 'How's the gut today? Are you up to some breakfast?'

'No, yeah, I'm fine. But no, thanks.' I've been better for a whole day, really, but I still don't feel like eating. 'I've got to go out for a bit.'

'Well, as long as you're not going all faddy on me! All rake-thin like Trixie here.' Dad stabs at the paper – a grainy picture of a skinny pop star getting out of a limo. 'It's not healthy!'

'Not healthy,' Mum echoes absent-mindedly, even though she's always trying out some celebrity diet she doesn't need to be on.

'Your Trixie needs a decent meal.'

'Trix,' I correct him, fighting the urge to roll my eyes.

Dad calls her *my* Trix (or Trixie, which isn't her name) because I'm always warbling her songs when I think no one's listening. They're so big and anthem-like, and they sound particularly good with the echo from the tiles in our newly done-up bathroom. Carlota keeps telling me I should sing in front of other people. As in, people who aren't family, my best friend or my singing teacher. But that's *never* going to happen. I keep chickening out of taking singing exams, and if I can't even do them, there's no way I could sing in public. I'd die of embarrassment. In fact, my stomach's churning just thinking about it.

Or am I going to be sick again?

Uh-oh.

Maybe I shouldn't go out. Carlota's house has

a cream-coloured carpet.

But I'm aching to talk to her, and going round is really the only way.

Dad's in joke mode. 'Course, I'm on a seafood diet, myself.'

Mum smiles at him. I do not understand how she can put up with, let alone *encourage*, Dad's so-called humour. But I'm not going to roll my eyes – not today. With Dad in this happy mood, I might even make it out of the door without The Chat!

Dad wields his spoon at me triumphantly. '*See food* and eat it! Seafood! Ha! And – listen to this – I eat it every day. It's a *cereal!* A cereal, every day – get it?'

Mum laughs heartily.

Oh, save me. Still, I've got to keep Dad happy.

'Good one, Dad.'

Mum peers at me. 'You *sure* you're better, darling? You look a bit pale. Would you like a hand with your make-up?'

Oh, no. I should have groaned! I've totally drawn attention to myself. If I'm not careful, Mum will abandon her craftwork and attack my face with a make-up brush instead. She was training as a make-up artist before she met my dad and 'settled down'. I sometimes let her practise her skills on me and it can be sort of fun. But I don't have time right now.

'Oh, yes,' I mumble. 'I'm definitely well enough

to go and, er, revise with Carlota.'

Well, now I've said the magic word – 'revise' – which will set Dad off, but what can I do? It's the best way to avoid any more questions.

Sure enough, Dad puts down his spoon like he means business. 'I'm glad to hear that. But I hope your friends don't distract you, Bethany. I hope you don't just talk about fashion, boys and pop music when you see them.'

I fight the urge to say, 'Da-aad!'

'Marilyn Bloom told me that Becca's coursework has suffered since she got obsessed with boys,' Mum backs him up.

Now my eyes are hurting from the effort of staying unrolled. Marilyn Bloom is Becca's mum, and Becca is one of my oldest friends – I always hung around with her and Baljit before Carlota came along. And it might be true that Becca's replaced a chunk of study time with boy-obsessing time, but it doesn't stop her doing miles better than me at school.

I realize Dad's already quite a way into The Chat. He's reached the 'exams are a serious matter, just ask your brother' stage.

I'd never ask Rowan anything like that. The fact that I'm having to listen to this at all is completely his fault. My parents were far more laid back before my big brother took off on a sudden trip round the world the day after his last A-level exam. They thought he wasn't coming back for uni, but he did, at the last minute, all tanned and extra smelly. So now Rowan's miles away doing Boozing Studies or whatever, and The Chat is focused on me. Grr. When Rowan comes home for the holidays, I'm planning to beat him up on the Wii again to make up for this. Anyway, Dad should relax. I could never do anything wild and sudden and Rowan-ish. I'd worry far too much. I definitely inherited Dad's stress-out gene.

He keeps worrying at me. Blah-di-stress-di-worry-blah. 'When I was your age I used to think I could get by without exam passes. I used to think my guitar was all I needed – my ticket to fame and fortune, you know?'

I resist the temptation to say, 'How could I possibly know? I've only heard this a million times.'

'You're a chip off the old block, ha ha, with your musical ambitions.'

I shift about a lot. They're hardly *musical ambitions*. A few large white tiles and a warbling sixteen-year-old. I'm certainly nothing like my grandad's idol, the man who's about to turn up in The Chat right about . . .

'You know, John Lennon had something to fall back on.'

. . . now.

'As your grandfather always said, *John Lennon had his O-levels*. That's GCSEs to us youngsters, of

17

course, ha ha. But the point is that John Lennon passed his exams at sixteen. It's the smart thing to do, Bethany. And even that's not enough. You need a degree to make burgers nowadays!' Dad celebrates the impending finale of his speech by shaking more cereal into his bowl. 'But I know you know that, and I trust you to put the work in.'

There's a silence.

Dad looks at me expectantly, waiting for my comment on his words of wisdom.

Well, it's not like I don't get the message. Whatever I do with my life, right now only four letters matter: G. C. S. E. Zzzzzz. OK, five letters.

But, actually, I don't want to think about The Future. I mean, *at all*. Apart from getting to Carlota's house.

'Your father's right,' Mum says. That's when I give in and allow my eyes a good roll. She didn't even pass many exams herself – she just loves agreeing with Dad. It's her second favourite hobby after cutting up photos. She probably wasn't even listening.

But then she says, 'Mind you, one thing you don't need exam passes for is producing cuties like these!' She holds up a star-shaped photo of a toddler princess gazing up at a little Superman. (It's me and Rowan – cringe!) And she laughs.

'Anne, I really don't think that's appropriate. Oh, you've put me right off my breakfast.' Dad's face is contorted in cereal-choking appalledness. 'Bethany has prospects!'

It makes me uncomfortable when he says things like that because it sounds like he's saying to Mum: *unlike you*. But today it makes me feel positively . . . sick.

Mum shrugs and picks up another photo.

A *baby* photo.

I don't mean to knock the cereal box over or shout, 'I'll be revising! Bye!' so loudly that the door-bell kind of rings, but I can't get out fast enough.

It's like they know.

But they don't, of course. Not even Declan knows. Not even Carlota knows, because I only figured it out myself last night.

No, that's ridiculous. I've just had a stomach bug, that's all. Plus there's all the worry and stress.

Dad's stressing me out with The Chat.

Declan's stressing me out by not answering my texts and calls.

I'm stressing myself out by stressing. I have *stress* stress.

Teen Spice! always says that stress can delay periods.

Anyway, Declan and I have been so safe and sensible.

Well, mostly.

TEEN SPICE! MAGAZINE

PRE-EXAM STRESS SPECIAL!

Stress Test

Name: *Lots*

Age: *nearly 16*

First thought after your mind cleared:

Today! Today! Today!

That was the warm-up! Now, write down the things that worry you most:

no point in worrying

Something that others tell you to worry about:

Bets does all the worrying for me!

Something that make you feel out of control:

Yres nothing

An activity that makes you happy:

snogging (!!) mwah-ha-ha

A person you can talk to:

Carlota

OK, I'll love *Teen Spice!* for ever, it's my favourite mag and a source of infinite wisdom and everything, but . . . that stress test was a waste of time!

I mean, anyway, stress? What's that? Nothing's worth getting worked up about! Ever! You just *deal*! It's easy.

I keep trying to tell Bets this, but she's practically an Olympic stresser and she doesn't listen to me. She can't help herself.

I throw the stress test behind my back and it lands on top of a huge pile of magazines. I've got them spread out all over my bed, covering the designer lambskin bedspread Veronica chose for me without even asking me whether I liked it. Which I don't. As if she cares.

What she does care about is me calling her 'Veronica' instead of 'Mum', though, and she definitely cares about me calling my stepdad 'The Diplomat' instead of – ugh, ugh, ugh – 'Dad'. So I do it whenever I can. Mwah-ha-ha.

Anyway, the bedspread's not so bad when it's completely coated in fabulous copies of *Teen Spice!*, the magazine that has the answer to everything.

Yeah, never mind a list of worries – I'm going to think of a list of things I'm NOT worried about, thanks to *Teen Spice!*

For example, right now I'm trapped in my massive room like a grounded princess in an ivory tower. And it really is – ivory, I mean. When we moved in, I was in a bit of a Goth phase, but Veronica did up my whole room in pure pure white – the walls, the carpet, the bedspread, even the flat-screen telly she bought me (without asking if I wanted it, which I didn't) – they're all white. I used to hate it.

But, thanks to *Teen Spice!*, I've reclaimed the white. I've made it mine! They did this fashion special about a year ago called 'White Is the New Black'. It was a double-page spread with all these smiley dark-haired models (like me, only thinner!) wearing white clothes from head to toe. It got me thinking. So I've worn as much white as possible ever since. I call it the Reverse Goth look, and it's definitely catching on. I've seen groups of Year Eights in the shops on Saturdays, parading around all in white, not caring whether their bums look big or not. It's exactly what Reverse Gothdom is all about.

Another thing *Teen Spice!* has sorted for me is what to do while I'm bored out of my mind waiting for Bets to arrive and get me out of here, which I know she will as soon as she can – any minute now.

But in the meantime, I've started this new thing. It's like Bets's mum's Crafty Nutters, only cool. It's . . . Knitting!

According to *Teen Spice!*, it's a craze in America, where they have knitting clubs for teenagers, for stress relief. Not that I need stress relief, of course, but apparently all the A-list stars do it. And, after all, I have the mind of an A-list star, trapped inside the body of a fifteen-year-old girl, trapped inside her bedroom by her wicked stepfather. Mwah-ha-ha!

So that's what I'm doing right now. Knitting. I've

got needles and wool from a *Teen Spice!* giveaway, and rusty skills my grandmother taught me back in Spain, when I was little and Veronica hadn't married The Diplomat and taken me to Brussels yet.

And, wow, I hadn't met Yves yet. That's weird to think about. I look at the mark on my otherwise spotless white wall – the place where the photo of us together used to be. I took it down ages ago, a few months after I left Brussels, when I gave up on him. Not that I ever *really* gave up – I think I always knew deep down that Yves had to have a good reason for not getting in touch with me after I left.

Well, *Teen Spice!* has finally given me a likely explanation for that one too. There was a True Life Story about a girl whose dad blocked emails and messages from a boy who fancied her, using some clever computer trickery. Every message he sent her – *bam!* – blocked, gone for ever. She found out by accident, months later, when the boy's mate made a joke about his unrequited love and the unanswered messages, right in front of her. But it was too late for her and the blocked-message guy – he was too hurt, or something. Or he was over her.

I only read the story yesterday – I don't know how I missed it before – but it explains *everything.* The Diplomat 'monitors my computer usage', as he puts it. He could have done it – he *would* too. It's him all over! It makes me hate him even more. How could he do that to me?

It doesn't have to be too late for me and Yves, though.

I keep knitting, flicking through another magazine, thinking about today and hoping I can make it work. I got my plans from the stress-busting issue, weirdly enough, well before I tried the stress test. It was an article about a thing called Extreme Travel – all about freedom, risks and fun. You're supposed to travel around any-old-where, doing silly random challenges and stuff, and enjoying living 'in the moment', which the stress expert says we don't do enough of in this day and age.

It's just what we need, even if my plans aren't entirely random.

It's the reason I'm not worried about Bets and Declan.

Or rather, *Becca* and Declan.

Shudder.

Because I think it can make everything OK. I'm going to use it to show Bets that there's life away from Declan. Soften the blow. Maybe even find her another boy. Definitely show her she has real friends.

You know, people who aren't Becca.

I knit another row. There's a big hole in it now but I keep going anyway.

I've never trusted Becca. I mean, I hang out with her and Baljit. I call them the Boring Bees for a laugh – they don't mind, they know they're total boffins! And I act as if I like them. But I do it for Bets, because they've been her friends since for ever. Though really it's only because I wasn't around until two years ago so it's not like Bets had much choice.

Bets has got some kind of loyalty to Becca, though, because their mums are friends or something.

Well.

Now I've found out what kind of 'friend' Becca really is.

And I just have to stop Bets from getting hurt.

I found the answer to that in *Teen Spice!* too. I read the problem page on Thursday night, practically right after it happened.

BEZZIE BETRAYAL! it said in huge letters. Then, smaller, *I saw a mate snog another mate's boyfriend – what do I do?* Underneath was the sensible part by Dr Boffin-face. After a bit of waffle, it said, *Who would benefit if you did tell your best friend what you saw?* Then it said there's no point in upsetting everyone by blurting it out, especially if you suspected it was a one-time thing. But you could confront the people involved. You could tell them what you know, scare them maybe, make sure it never happens again.

Then your mate never needs to know and get upset. The idea is, she naturally grows apart from the cheating boyfriend, or you kind of steer her away gently, and it all works out for the best.

It makes sense, I suppose. I thought I'd try it.

So yesterday at school I explained it to Declan. It was incredibly awkward and weird, but I did it for

Bets, you know. He seemed to agree with me. He stared at the ground for ages and eventually he said, 'I wouldn't know what to say to her anyway.'

But Becca, a bit later, was a nightmare. She looked horrified and she chewed like crazy on her cuticles, and then she said, without looking at me, 'I don't know, I don't know. I think telling her might be the right thing to do.'

Appropriately enough, the same magazine had an article about 'Frenemies' – people who pretend to be friends but are really enemies in disguise. People who get a kick out of upsetting their so-called friends.

People like Becca.

Because, OK, there's nothing to worry about. I'll make sure of that.

But, honestly. Breaking my best friend's heart could not *possibly* be 'the right thing to do'.

Bethany

Even though I'm in a mega-rush, it's probably a bit early for Carlota on a Saturday morning. She might be too sleepy to sort out my life. Or I might disturb her stepdad and he might stop me seeing her.

So I dawdle a bit past the shops on the high street near Baljit's house. The chemist is open and I can see the outline of Baljit's mum at the counter, tidying rows of tubes and bottles.

I hesitate, but then I move away from the door before she sees me, because there's just no way I could go in and ask for—

I can't even *think* it, let alone say it.

I bet Carlota would. I bet she'd walk in and ask for one, just like that. She'd probably shout it. 'A pregnancy test, please, Mrs Kaur!' She's not scared of anything.

I have to get her un-grounded. And preferably to a different town.

I pass the chippy that me and my friends always go to – or at least we did in the days before Becca got funny about Carlota.

You'd think Becca and Lots would be friends – they live near each other, with Becca's flat diagonally across from Carlota's house, and they're both friends with me. But they've never really got on. I think it's Harrison's fault. He's Becca's on-off boyfriend and he always flirts with – and sometimes even snogs – other girls right in front of Becca. She just puts up with it and spends loads of time stressing about whether he likes her or not. It's awful. Carlota can't stand it and keeps telling Becca she should get off with someone else and see how *he* likes it! It might sound a bit extreme, but sometimes I really wish Becca would do that.

Then I get worried. What if Declan's like Harrison? They're good mates, after all. What if he's been doing a Harrison, and I don't even know it?

But I don't think he would. Declan's always been kinder, nicer, more of a laugh than Harrison. More reliable too. OK, he ignores me sometimes at the club bar, but only because he wants to talk about football, and I don't care anyway, because I always have Becca to talk to. She's my football-club friend.

I realize with a hot rush of guilt that I haven't called Becca back. She called me three times yesterday and I was so full of my worries, and so desperate to speak to Carlota, that I let the calls go to voicemail. To be honest, I sort of expected Becca to go on about Harrison, Harrison, Harrison, and I didn't feel like dealing with it, not when my head was full of Declan, Declan, Declan.

Well, it still is, and I still don't. But I should at least text her.

I settle on a bench near the newsagent, wondering what to write and wishing I could talk to Lots instead. That makes me feel even guiltier. I've been friends with Carlota for two years, ever since she started at my school, but Becca's been my friend since we were tiny. Our mums are friends. We went to toddler groups together, started school together, and even met Harrison and Declan together, at a brilliant party at the end of the holidays last summer.

Well, it was thanks to Baljit, really – she was the one who got talking to the Nearly-Year-Thirteen football crowd, as she has insider knowledge, being a fan. And it was thanks to Carlota too, even though she wasn't there because she was grounded. As usual. But she had been giving me Boy-Snaring lessons, and she suggested trying it on a random 'practice boy' that night. So I did. And it worked.

First me and Becca stood by sipping cups of punch as Baljit talked football to the guys. She'd done that before, but they'd never looked twice at us, not really, not in *that* way. We're not that sort of girl, you know. Well, we weren't before that night.

Harrison has completely changed Becca. She obsesses about him the way she used to about coursework – it's like she's studying for a GCSE in Harrison Studies. She'd definitely get an A star for it too.

I think I also changed that night. I was the one who made the first move with Declan. The whole thing went like this:

BALJIT: Offside offside goal kick free kick.
RANDOM BOY: Yes yes ref-er-eeeee we was robbed.
BALJIT: Relegation new season premiership.
RANDOM BOY: Transfer deal league table.
BECCA: *mad flicking of hair*
HARRISON: *eyes attracted by flicked hair and wandering all over Becca*
BECCA: *flirty eye contact with Harrison*
HARRISON: *moving in on Becca*

BOY NEXT TO HARRISON: *smiling at me*
ME: Hi, I'm Bethany.
RANDOM BOY: Game of two halves sick as a parrot!
BOY NEXT TO HARRISON: I'm Declan. *more smiling* What's the punch like?
ME: It's OK. Want to try? *moving closer to Declan*
DECLAN: Yeah, all right – whoa! Mmmgh!

That last bit was me brushing my lips on his, which I know is not a normal way of letting someone try your punch. But I was trying a Carlota trick, being ultra-confident. And, you know what? I didn't care! By the end of the night we were snogging, and three party snogs later, he asked me out, and that was seven months, two weeks and a day ago.

Harrison never exactly asked Becca out, even though they get together all the time for what Carlota would call 'Kisses Etcetera'.

Becca's always moaning to me, saying she wishes she had a proper boyfriend, one like mine – the kind that talks to you at school and buys you Valentine's cards and replies to texts. She goes on and on about how lucky I am to have Declan.

And I know I am. Declan's brilliant. When I do magazine quizzes about boyfriends, he always comes out as the perfect one, Mostly Bs, the one with just the right balance of whatever good-boyf qualities the quiz is testing. Right from the start, he took me out to all these great places in his dad's car – proper dates and stuff, to restaurants and faraway country pubs and everything. And he used to text me every night to say goodnight. It was so sweet.

OK, he hasn't done anything like that for a while. But that's natural, isn't it? I mean, I'm not even sure how long ago the goodnight texts stopped – they just sort of fizzled out, and I didn't mind. It's because we're so comfortable together. When you've been with someone a while – and mine is practically the longest relationship in our whole year – it's OK to take each other for granted a bit. It doesn't mean you don't still love each other. He's still my gorgeous, sexy, trustworthy boyfriend.

Who hasn't called. Why hasn't he called?

I make myself stop daydreaming because it's getting later and I can go to Carlota's now and talk about all this and she can make everything all right!

I write to Becca, R U UP? But she will be. She'll be either a) revising or b) obsessing about Harrison or, more likely, c) both.

She replies straight away. I knew it! She writes, YES. ARE YOU OK? Becca never uses txt-speak.

I write, YEAH, ALL BETTER NOW. WHAT R U DOING 2DAY?

She replies, USUAL SATURDAY BABYSITTING. BALJIT'S COMING ROUND TO REVISE LATER.

Becca looks after her little sister while their mum

drives her taxi, mostly in central London. Becca's mum is really cool – sometimes, if little Leah is at a friend's, she gives us lifts to TopShop in Oxford Street on Saturdays. Carlota's never allowed to come with us, so I haven't been for ages because I feel a bit mean going without Lots.

I type, HAVE FUN!

I'm thinking that's probably the end of the conversation – phew, no Harrison stuff – when she writes back, HAVE YOU SPOKEN TO CARLOTA?

I type, GOING ROUND NOW. This makes me feel a bit guilty, so I add, WANT 2 MEET L8R?

I don't know *when* later – I might need all day to talk to Carlota; I have a lot to talk about. And I always go to Declan's on a Saturday night – always.

Becca's reply takes ages to arrive. I'LL BE IN THE CHIPPY AT 6. MEET ME MAYBE?

I squint at it. That's a slightly weird message. I shrug and text back a quick, OK. BYE. XX.

Becca can be strange sometimes. That's probably what happens when you're a total brainiac for fifteen years and then you suddenly lose a large part of your mind to a boy who doesn't deserve it.

Anyway, I now have a great excuse to text Declan again without seeming clingy, even though he hasn't replied to my previous six messages. I write, FEELING BETTER, BUT CANT MAKE IT 2NITE. SEEING BECCA. And I don't add my usual kiss.

There. That has to get a reaction. He'll think it's

weird, he'll text me back, and I'll tell him that I can see him after all, when I've seen Becca. And all this will be after Carlota's sorted my life out, and I'll know what to do and what to say to him.

Me and Declan haven't had a Saturday night apart for the whole the seven months, two weeks and a day we've been together. And Saturday night is *our* night – the night his mum and dad go out and we have the house to ourselves. Declan will text me about that message, definitely. He's not like Harrison. He wouldn't mess me around; he's a proper boyfriend.

I walk up and down the high street three times before I turn into Becca and Carlota's street.

My inbox is still empty when I reach Carlota's house.

Carlota

I explained to Becca again all about why she shouldn't tell Bets. I quoted the mag and everything.

'After all, we both know it was a *one-time thing*,' I stressed, giving her a serious, warning look in case she got any ideas. 'So she really doesn't need to know.'

Becca's voice was shaking. 'But what if she finds out? It's horrible when you're the last to know.'

I knew she was talking about herself and Harrison,

and I had to stop myself groaning. She probably thinks she's teaching Harrison a lesson in some warped way – using his friends to get at him. But she shouldn't be dragging Bets into it!

And I hope she's not even going to *try* comparing this with what happened between me and Harrison, which was ages ago anyway. I didn't know she was serious about Harrison at the time, but she knows for *sure* how Bets feels about Declan! Anyway, I did exactly what she's talking about doing now – I was honest with her, I told her that me and Harrison snogged, and she's never really forgiven me! Has she forgotten about that?

The magazine's right. Being overly honest about this stuff just hurts everyone, and you'd think Becca of all people would know that.

But she finished on her cuticles and moved on to chewing her lip. 'What if she suspects something? What if she *asks* me? I can't lie to Bethany. I have to tell her. I should have told her already.' Chew, chew. 'Oh God, she's going to hate me.'

I took a deep breath then, the third time Becca refused to accept the magazine's wisdom.

I didn't want to – I don't owe Becca anything – but for Bets's sake, I said, 'Listen, if that's the way you feel, *I'll* tell her. I'm her best friend, and I can help her through it.' I ignored the look on Becca's face, which was a mixture of relief and disgust, because I swear part of her still wanted to argue that *she* was actually

Bethany's best friend, even now when she seemed so intent on hurting her. Incredible.

Straight away my brain was racing, thinking of ways to break it to Bets and ways to protect her and show her that she didn't do anything wrong, that Declan's not worth it anyway, and that she deserves more.

Becca said, 'All right.'

So at least that was something.

Then she looked panicky. 'But she always sees Declan on Saturday night. What if he pretends everything's OK and nothing happened?' She attacked her cuticles again.

Well, that was likely, because at least *he* listened to me when I told him what it said in the magazine.

'It's . . . it's wrong. She needs to know before Saturday night.' Becca put her head in her hands. 'So if you don't tell her, then I will – I'll have to . . . I can't keep a secret like that from her. I . . . I wouldn't feel right.'

'Yeah, Becca. It's all about *you*,' I said nastily. But I said it after she'd walked off. I'm not sure why. I'm not scared of her.

So it's Saturday, and Bets has to be over her weird bug by now. And when she comes over to free me from The Diplomat's evil clutches, we're going out. Who knows where, though I've got some pretty great ideas. Me and Bets are going to have a day we'll never forget. I'll show her who her real friends are, and I'll make sure that by the time I tell her, she doesn't even care any more. We'll get through this.

There is nothing to worry about.

Bethany

I pause for ages at the door, practising my most innocent smile for Carlota's stepdad, who she calls The Diplomat and I call Mr Peters, if I have to call him anything at all. He's usually really nice to me, even when he's in a total mood with Lots, which is most of the time. I've got Good Girl power.

But when the door opens, it's Carlota's mum standing there. She fixes me blankly and says, 'Yes?'

I've never said this to Carlota, but I think her mum is even scarier than Mr Peters. At least you know where you are with him. I have no idea what Carlota's mum thinks of me, or, right now, whether she knows I'm not just some random door-to-door loon.

'It's, um, Bethany,' I say, trying to make myself look as sane as I can manage under the circumstances.

The reason I can't tell what she's thinking is that she only has one expression. Her features are etched in permanent, though beautiful, disapproval. Take now, for example. I don't think she's annoyed with me – why would she be? – but that's how it comes across.

'I know who you are, Bethany. I'm going to your house shortly, for your mother's Craft Notions club.'

She says 'you' and 'your' with a 'j' at the beginning like a proper Spanish person. She looks so Spanish too – all dark and glossy-haired, like she could be dancing flamenco with a rose between her gritted teeth. She looks exactly like Carlota, really.

Except that Carlota is miles curvier and her face has a lot more expressions.

Well, anyway. I'm good at talking to adults – Dad taught me some tricks when I did work experience with him in the car showroom.

Trick number one: flattery.

'Oh yeah, you go to Craft Notions. My mum says you made some excellent cards last week.'

'I was unable to go last week.'

Oh, right. 'Sorry, I meant the . . . other time you went. Or whatever.' OK, moving swiftly on to trick number two: politeness. 'Well, I'm sorry to disturb you, Mrs Peters—'

'Ms Del Rey Peters,' she corrects me, still no trace of a smile.

Duh, of course, like Carlota's surname, even though she hates the 'Peters' bit because it's her stepdad's name. But Spanish people don't have just the one boring surname, they make a whole list.

Trick number two (a) is to get people's names right.

'I'm sorry, Ms Del Rey Peters. I need to see

Carlota about . . .' I glance at my rucksack, where my books are poking out at the top and helping my cause. 'Stuff to do with her school. Our school, I mean. Exams. Could I speak to her for, like, a second? And then I'll go. I promise.' I feel a desperate need to babble at her about French and history, but I manage to stop myself.

Trick number three: if you want to sound honest, don't say much. The more you talk, the more it sounds like you're lying.

'It's about her *school*, is it? Well, not for much longer. You may as well come in, I suppose.' She steps aside to let me in.

Weird. What did she mean by 'not for much longer'? Carlota's not leaving. We're both down for A-level courses in September, taking over from Declan and Harrison in the sixth-form wing. Oh, God, I'm going to miss Declan so much.

I race up the stairs and burst into Carlota's room at long last, dying to see my best best friend in the whole wide world, who is—

Knitting.

O-*kay* . . .

I don't know why I'm surprised. This is just like Carlota. She's all about the shocking and the Reverse Gothdom.

But instead of tearing the needles out of her hands and happy-screaming at her about seeing her against all grounding odds, I find myself staring at the white wool and mumbling, 'Hi, Lots.'

She doesn't even look up, she's concentrating that hard. And this is massively *un*like Carlota. Apparently, at the last parents' evening, Ms Harris told Carlota's stepdad: 'Carlota demonstrates the concentration skills of a butterfly with ADHD.' And Ms Harris does *not* have a sense of humour. She must've *meant* it.

I try to get her attention. 'What's going on?'

'Why?' She says this to her knitting, because she's still not looking at me.

'Well, because you're . . . knitting!' Maybe Carlota has decided to be like her mum. I can't get over the fact that Ms Del Rey Peters goes to Craft Notions.

I feel better when I notice that whatever Carlota's making is an odd shape and full of holes.

She frowns. 'You should try it, Bets, for stress relief. It's totally relaxing!' Then she swears loudly. 'I dropped a stitch!'

Oh right, it's the kind of stress relief that gives you a coronary embolism,' I tell her. Dad always says me and Rowan give him those. He watches way too many hospital dramas.

She rests the white creation on her lap and looks at me. Finally!

'You're here! At last! Were you really sick or did you fancy some time off?' She doesn't wait for a reply. 'Don't blame you! I wanted to fake some illness yesterday so I could have the day off to look for

39

my phone, but I decided to have a search in the night instead. I didn't find it, though.' She calls her step-dad loads of names and then laughs it off. 'Anyway, you didn't miss anything. School was the same old . . .' Then her face twists strangely. If I didn't know her better, I'd think she looked worried.

I sit next to her on the bed. 'Lots, what's the matter? Is it to do with why you were grounded? What did you do this time, anyway?' I think of her mum's bizarre words. 'It's about school, isn't it? Your mum said something weird just now. Is that it?'

She shrugs a bit and then she nods vigorously and says, 'Yeah, that's it! The Diplomat says I have a bad attitude and our school isn't helping. Veronica's talking about me doing A levels some-where else.'

No wonder she's acting weird. This is terrible! My life's just getting worse and worse! 'Carlota! No! You can't leave!' Sixth form's going to be bad enough as it is, with Declan gone and . . . Oh.

Will I even be at school next year?

I mean, depending . . .

And what about Declan? Will he still go to uni?

I haven't thought this through at all. This is way beyond worrying. It's earth-shattering. It's unreal.

'Don't worry!' She sounds completely upbeat. 'It's just a threat, something Veronica and The Diplomat are holding over me to make me behave.' She picks up her knitting again and growls at it.

I lie back in relief, pushing magazines out of the way to make space. But I still feel weird – uneasy and wobbly. I'm holding my breath, thinking about Declan, Declan and more Declan.

I watch Lots move the needles and mutter.

I want to tell Declan I can see him tonight after all, because I miss him and I wish I hadn't cancelled our date. I can see Becca before I go to his house; there's time.

But first I need Carlota to tell me everything's all right and I'm worrying about nothing, and then I can breathe again.

I sit up. 'Lots . . .' I pick at the magazine next to me. I don't know how to say this.

'You look stressed! Here, have some knitting.' She holds it out to me.

I shake my head and push it back at her, laughing through the knot in my stomach. 'No way. You look fifteen going on eighty-five!'

'Hey! All the Hollywood A-listers knit!' She pokes an open copy of *Teen Spice!* with a knitting needle. 'It's in there.'

I wish I could solve all my problems with magazines, like Carlota thinks you can.

'Magazines don't have the answer to everything, you know.'

'You're wrong. They do!' She puts down her knitting and hands me the issue with the Pre-Exam Stress Special, the one I was looking at this morning.

'I've got this one,' I tell her. 'I did the quiz. It told me I was stressed out. Like I didn't already know.'

She bounces on the bed as if it's good news. 'Great! So you've read the thing about Extreme Travel then?'

'Extreme *what?* No, I . . . Listen, I need to talk to you. Really talk.' I sigh. 'About Declan. And me. Because . . .' I can't say it. I'll start small. 'Declan's ignoring my texts!'

She loops some wool around her needle. She's so calm. I wish I could be more like her.

'Well, he's probably caught up in A levels and stuff, isn't he? You know what he's like – he's worse than you in the boffin stakes. He's even worse than Becca – I mean, Baljit.' She kind of shudders. 'Exam central. He's a total girly swot.'

I laugh. 'Shut up.' I girly-swat her on the head with the magazine. 'We can't all be butterflies with ADHD that only have to flap an exam paper to get a B! Declan's . . . committed. He'll die if he can't go to Loughborough in September and do that course about bandaging footballers' legs or whatever.'

September . . . how long is that? It always seemed so far away, before. 'Oh, no. Six months. He's going away in six months!' This is terrible!

'Bets, seriously. Read the article.'

'But something's happened . . . or rather, hasn't happened . . .'

'Carlota!' a voice booms from downstairs. It's her

stepdad. 'I need you to come here – now!'

Carlota motions frantically at the door. 'Bets, you've got to talk to him for me. Use your special dad-pleasing powers. You have to get me out of here.'

'Why? Where do you want to go?'

'Extreme travelling, of course. With you.'

I look at her.

'I'll explain later.'

'CarLOTa! NOW.'

'Please?'

I sigh and stuff the magazine in my bag. But really, it's the least I can do for her, when she's about to sort out my whole life. I hope that's included in Extreme Travel, whatever it is.

Carlota's stepdad is at his computer, his office chair creaking under the mass of his standard-issue dad-paunch.

He's actually smiling at me. 'Ah, Ms Royston, nice of you to join us,' he booms, posh and commanding, but also sounding like he means it.

'Nice to see you, Mr Peters,' I say.

Carlota smirks at me.

Her stepdad taps his desk. 'Well, if you'll excuse us a moment, Bethany, I need to talk to my daughter.'

'If she leaves, I leave.' Carlota stares at him with pure attitude. My best friend is her own worst enemy.

I try to smooth things over. 'Mr Peters, it's just

that Lots . . . Carlota and I need to go somewhere right now.'

He looks at me sceptically.

'It's' – I pat my rucksack full of books, which is proving very useful today. It looked better when I didn't have a magazine sticking out, though – 'about exams. I need Carlota to help me with . . .' Less is more when you're lying! 'We have to go' – *think, think* – 'to the library. To use the computer.'

Now they're both staring at me. Carlota's lips are curling slightly. She'd better not make me laugh.

'You see, I'm having trouble with French.' Yes! That should do it. Carlota once told me that her stepdad really struggled with French, even though he needed to be fluent for his job. She used to love embarrassing him when he made mistakes. I'm proud of myself for mentioning *le français*.

But he looks suspicious. 'French? On the computer? At the library?'

'*Oui.*' I think I should give up now.

'I see. Well, that's appropriate. I was about to address Carlota about not using my computer ever again.' He swivels the screen so that it faces us. It's counting down in skinny white numbers on a bright blue post-crash-like screen. It's got the computer-crash blues, waa-waa-waa.

'And Bethany, please explain to my daughter that the "no phone" rule includes no Spacebook or My-Face or whatnot when my back's turned. I could have lost *important files.*' He turns to Lots. 'I hope you've quite finished with whatever you were doing, sneaking around on my computer.'

'Yeah I have, thanks.'

Honestly, she's so unsubtle. I can't imagine her ever keeping a secret of any kind!

Mr Peters opens a drawer in his desk and takes out a key. 'Well, I must say, Carlota, apart from this unfortunate incident, you've displayed unchar-acteristic maturity since your latest punishment, largely staying in your room and not complaining.'

I stifle a laugh. Carlota displayed 'uncharacteris-tic maturity'? How did she get her stepdad to think *that*?

'If you can keep up this behaviour, I might be prepared to talk to your mother on your behalf – maybe rethink those boarding-school plans.' He taps a pile of brochures by his desk. The top one features some glossy-looking girls in neat green uniforms, and various props arranged around a fancy crest. I spot a violin, a flute, a book and a tennis racket. It reminds me of one of Rowan's computer games where you have to collect the magical objects in order to complete your quest. I imagine the girls saying things like, 'Lady of the Flute, you may progress to Level Two if you throw down the Enchanted Tennis Racket.'

But no one mentioned it was a *boarding* school! It's even worse than I thought. She can't go! She can't leave me! Of all my friends, she's the only one who'd understand. I *need* her! Especially right now! And in the future. She's got to help me – I can't ask anyone else!

And I know she needs me too, though obviously she doesn't have reasons like mine. But she always says I'm the best friend she's ever had. So why doesn't she seem more worried about this? Her parents are so strict – they could *make* her go!

As if to prove it, Mr Peters says sternly, 'I'll give you one more chance to earn my trust, and your mother's.'

He unlocks another drawer and takes out a white mobile phone with albino animal charms hanging off it. Carlota snatches it from him and starts pressing buttons. If she's checking her messages, this could take a while – I think she has at least thirty from me.

Mr Peters nods. 'So. You may go to the library if you promise to stay with Bethany at all times and promise to return by five, not a minute later—'

'Six,' Carlota mumbles without looking up. She just can't stop herself.

'By five thirty—'

'Six thirty.'

'I said I'd meet Becca at six,' I mumble.

Carlota goes quiet.

'By five!' Mr Peters triumphs. 'And you come straight home, no dallying around chip shops, good behaviour at all times. It's in your interests . . .'

Carlota's dad waffles on, but the main thing is I've done it! I've managed to get Carlota un-grounded. So at least one thing has gone right today, which has to be a good sign.

Carlota

I knew Bets could get me out of there! Now I've just got to calm her down. At least it's obvious that Declan hasn't spoken to her. (Phew.) And she's not seeing Becca till six. (Aargh.)

All the way to the bus stop, she asks me millions of questions about Veronica and The Diplomat's plans for me. Where's this boarding school? Wouldn't they *make* me go? Will she ever see me again?

I reassure her that there's nothing to worry about. There's no way I'm starting another new school, especially one without my best friend in it. It was bad enough leaving Yves behind before. I don't tell her that bit, though. I don't usually talk about Yves much – I used to think there was no point, when all I got from him was silence. I didn't want to go on about him like a saddo, so I made sure I kept it all in my head. But now . . . well, wow. Even thinking his name makes my insides fizz today.

Anyway, right now I've got to get Bets away from the subject of *me* and focus on *her* and the plans for today.

I've decided to start with a *Teen Spice!* quick quiz called 'Is Your Boyfriend Good for You?' I want to plant the idea in Bets's head that Declan's not as perfect as she thinks he is. Then we can do the Extreme Travel thing and she can stop thinking about him altogether while we have a wild and fantastic time. And by the end of the day she won't care about him at all any more, so she won't feel hurt when she hears what happened. I'll make sure of it.

At the bus stop, I lie back on the bench and read the questions out to her while she leans against the glass and scratches nervously at some graffiti.

'*Question One*,' I announce in my best, booming quizmaster voice. '*Does he buy you unexpected presents when it's not even your birthday?*'

'You know the answer.' Bets goes a bit red.

This might be a bad idea, making her think about him at all.

I pretend to look annoyed so she'll take it seriously. 'Yeah, but you're doing a quiz! Come on! So is it: A) Yes, he's always showering me with gifts I don't really want, for no reason, B) Occasionally he'll buy me unexpected treats, or C) Never, or only when he wants something from me?'

'But, Lots, it's obvious I'm supposed to say B. A is going to be the freaky stalker boy, C is the love rat who doesn't care and B is just right. It's like Goldilocks and the Three Bears for boyfriends. It always is.'

Now I really do feel a bit annoyed. 'See, Bets, this is why magazines don't help you. Because you won't let them! Just answer the question.'

She sighs. 'OK. B, then.'

If she's not going to be honest, though, this isn't going to work. *Now* what should I do?

'*How* is it B?'

'What do you mean?' She goes an even deeper red. 'You know he buys me a lottery ticket every Saturday. It's really sweet. It's our thing.'

'But it's not unexpected, is it?'

'Maybe not, but it's closer than the other two answers. Why, which one do you think it is?' She looks even more worried now. 'He's definitely not a freaky stalker boy. Are you saying you think Declan's a love rat?'

'No, of course not!' Or not yet, anyway – she's not ready to hear it. I make my voice as casual as I can manage. 'OK, B it is.'

Maybe I shouldn't have started this. Besides, I know Declan's a C, but Yves is probably a C for this question too. Although I always used to go to burger places with him and we'd get kids' meals for a laugh, and I'd steal his free toy when he wasn't looking, and he'd always let me. It was a joke between us. So that's practically a B. Not that I'm trying to second-guess the answers or anything, like Bets is.

'What's the next one?'

I smile. 'I knew you'd get into it! Right. Question

49

Two. *How many times a week does he call you?'* She shouldn't be able to lie to me – or herself – about this one. *'Is it A) I've lost count – he rings me constantly and gets upset if I don't answer, B) A few times, to make plans or if we're not going to see each other for a while, or C) Rarely or never?'*

I wait. Yves was . . . well, a C, but he didn't *need* to call me, because we were together every day. Oh, I miss those days so much. I glance at the Mostly Cs result, though, and Bets is right. It's not good.

Now I'm starting to think that Bets has a point about this quiz.

It also seems to be making her increasingly miserable. It takes Bets ages to say, 'B. At least, it used to be B.' Her expression is as empty as the street she's glancing down. 'I'm not even sure when it stopped being B. Is it my fault? Do I take him for granted?'

Oh no! I wanted her to realize Declan wasn't perfect but I wasn't prepared for this! She wasn't supposed to blame *herself*!

I decide the best thing to do is move quickly on. *'Question Three. Does he ever give you compliments? A) All the time, in front of everyone – it gets embarrassing, B) Sometimes, or C) No, never.'*

Yves . . . didn't. He didn't have to. He told me in other ways how he felt about me. I was never really in any doubt about *that*.

'Well, that's definitely a B,' Bets says slowly, like she's not too sure.

I close the magazine. I give up. The second part of my plan, the Extreme Travel, *has* to be more success-ful than this.

There's a rumble in the distance. Perfect timing. Fate, even.

'Here's the bus!'

I spring to my feet, waving my hands about. It's the bus driver's lucky day. He's about to stop for *us*!

'That's not our bus,' Bets says as it lumbers towards us.

I nearly groan. I should have known she would get it into her head that we were actually going to the library now. She probably thinks we're going to revise French on their computer too. It's like as soon as she tells a lie, she believes it!

Of course, in a way, she's right. It's not our bus. I've never been on it before, and it certainly doesn't go anywhere we normally go. But we're on an extreme adventure now, even if I do have a fair idea where we're going, and now my fizzy insides feel even more shaken up.

Then I realize she hasn't even read about Extreme Travel yet. The magazine's poking out of her rucksack.

'Just follow me,' I say. 'And read that article on the bus!'

She stares at a random red-faced woman who's heaving a screaming baby off the bus with one arm and a pushchair with the other. 'I can't . . . I need to talk to you . . .'

I skip onto the bus, wafting my Oyster card about and speaking in a silly voice to the driver, who doesn't laugh. Honestly, some people have no sense of fun. And then they moan about having miserable lives!

'But Lots . . .' Bets is still whining, although she's following me up the stairs. 'Where are we going?'

'Who cares?' I call from the back seat.

The bus lurches.

'The point is,' I tell Bets as she hurtles towards me and lands awkwardly on the seat in front of me, 'there is no point. It's extreme! It's a way of life!'

'It's GCSEs next month.'

Argh! 'Exactly why we need this. Didn't you say Rowan does some extreme thing? For his uni stress? That's practically the same thing.'

Bets has this ordinary-looking brother who suddenly seems a lot more attractive when you hear that his hobby is ironing clothes up mountains and filming it to put on YouTube. No, seriously. Imagine that! Risking your life to iron a pair of socks? It's wild! I looked it up on The Diplomat's computer once, when I was on one of my nightly Yves cyberstalking sessions. I needed a break from examining page twenty of the Google results of a search on 'Yves van der Meyer'. I found a website completely dedicated to Extreme Ironing. It's like an international sport or something, and it's madly cool.

'Lots, I wouldn't copy anything Rowan does. Really.'

'Why not? It's so cool.'

'It's so *deranged*.' Bets does a vigorous twirly-finger madness sign at her temple. 'Plus Rowan still expects Mum to do all his normal ironing in the holidays.'

'But it's nothing to do with ironing. It's not even anything to do with travelling. The journey isn't the point – it's just the backdrop, the excuse for a thrill. It's about freedom. Risks. Avoiding real life.' I swing my legs onto the seat. 'That's the plan.'

Bets kind of sniffs. 'Are we still talking about my brother's socks?'

'Extreme ironing, extreme travelling. Same thing. Rowan's got the right idea, if you ask me. We need it, Bets! Trust me. Read it! Plus I think we should set challenges!'

'I'm not ironing any of my brother's crap clothes.'

'*Travelling* challenges. Random things, like it says in the magazine, but done our own way.' Which is how I think people should live their lives, really. There's a lot of sound advice out there, but you've got to adapt it to suit your situation.

'What do you mean?'

I sigh. Bets is being so Bets-ish! 'So if we open the magazine on a fashion page, we could go shopping. Or on a beauty page, we could get makeovers. And all the while we travel. Just anywhere.'

She's still all serious. 'OK. We could go to another town or something – somewhere we don't know anyone. But just for a little while, though. We can't take off on some totally random journey.'

'Why not?'

'Well, for a start, we told your dad we'd be in the library!'

I can't help myself, even though I told myself to be extra-lovely to her today. I give her a look and she caves straight away.

'You're right, you're right. I sound pathetic. Why don't I just give up now? I can join the Boring Bees in a Saturday morning sponsored revise-athon.'

'Yeah, Bethany-Boffiny,' I say, but nicely, you know. Bets isn't like the other Boring Bees, anyway – she never has been. She has so much more to her. 'Listen, it says it's like a holiday from your normal life. It's the ultimate stress relief. It's exactly what we both need right now. You've got to admit I'm right.'

She sighs. 'OK. You're right. Give me that magazine.'

She's so spacy today! 'It's in your bag – you put it there. Go on, read it. You'll see how right I am.'

She gets the magazine out, finds the page and starts reading, like the ace friend she is.

I open my white leather bag. My phone's on the top – at last, I've got it back! The Diplomat is so annoying. I can't believe he hid the key in the drawer this time – I didn't even think to look somewhere so obvious. Well, at least he doesn't lock his computer. I've got the printouts with me. Today is going to be amazing, for both me and Bets!

I take out my knitting and focus on the stress relief.

TEEN SPICE! MAGAZINE

You don't need to go far to have a stress-relieving adventure . . .

EXTREME TRAVEL – HOLIDAY IN YOUR HIGH STREET!

It's the latest craze! Extreme Travel is the name given to random travelling, where anything goes and the journey is the whole point. But it doesn't involve going to the other side of the world. Far from it! Here are some of our fave Extreme Travel ideas:

☀ – Shut your eyes and point to a square on the A–Z of your town. Grab some mates, go to that square and swan around pretending to be an A-list celeb, with your mates asking for autographs. See how long it takes for a crowd to gather!

☀ – Borrow your granny's clothes and visit the trendiest shops in town, remarking loudly on how fashions have changed nowadays.

☀ – Set random challenges from the pages of *Teen Spice!* For example, if you turn to our Fitness 4 U page, find a ball and do a Wayne Rooney around the park. (Bonus: Who knows what fit guys might kick the ball back to you!)

Come up with your own variations and relax as you learn to live in the moment! But remember the basic rules of safety: **Never travel alone.** No talking to strangers or getting into their cars. Always tell an adult exactly where you are and when you'll be home. Make sure your mobile is topped up, working well and with you at all times.

Oh, one last rule . . . have fun, even if you don't leave your local high street!

Bethany

 Lots is knitting away, lost in concentration, so after I read the Extreme Travel thing I flick through the rest of the magazine. I didn't get beyond the stress quiz earlier today.

I skim an article called 'Is It Lust or Love?', a checklist called 'You Know He's the Guy of Your Dreams When . . .' and a quiz called, 'Is Your Boyfriend the Cheating Kind?' Then there's a true-life story called 'Dumped by Text' (lucky her – *her* boyfriend actually texted her), and one called 'Baby Shock', about a girl who got pregnant before she even started having periods. (*I wouldn't*

be without Amelia now, I read before I quickly turn the page.)

At last I find the safe pages, the ones that talk about movie stars and fashion. *SUPERSTARS SPLIT!* they scream at me. *CELEBRITY BETRAYAL! CHECK OUT LINDSAY'S POST-BREAK-UP MAKE-UP!*

Oh no. This whole magazine's talking about me and Declan!

'Are you still reading it?' Carlota calls over to me.

For a second I think she means 'Baby Shock', but of course she means the Extreme Travel article.

'Yeah, sounds cool,' I say.

'It's going to be the coolest!' She beams at me.

But I don't manage to smile back. I think about being pregnant, dumped by text and wearing terrible make-up as a result.

Or what if I'm never officially dumped at all? What if Declan just never gets in touch again? Could it happen? Surely not – he's a proper boyfriend! But I've got all sorts of doubts in my mind, especially since that quiz I just did with Carlota.

He used to ring me a lot. I used to ring him a lot too. He used to text me every night. I used to send kisses back. He used to surprise me. I used to get butterflies just thinking about him. When did it stop? I don't know! *Why* don't I know? Is our relationship in danger?

But it can't be – not *now*! And, anyway, we're so sure of each other. I mean, there's no way that can be a bad thing. We don't ring each other much because we don't need to. We know where we're going to meet. We're in tune! We have set dates: Mondays and Wednesdays at the football club bar after practice, Saturday night at his house. And I see him at school if he's not too busy being an aloof sixth former.

And I *always* get a reply if I text him. Especially if I'm breaking a date.

Although, honestly? I've never actually broken a date before.

It's a test.

He's failing.

Well, it can't be that we're drifting apart, or anything like that. We're *not* drifting apart. We're happy. I was with him last Saturday, I saw him on Wednesday, I *know* we're happy.

There must be something else . . . some other reason he's suddenly not replying to my texts.

But why now? How could I have all these doubts . . . now?

This is torture, all this worrying.

I watch Carlota in knitting-land, counting under her breath. I wish I could be more like her. She'd never get upset about a boy. There's only one boy she's ever cared about: Yves, an ex-boyfriend she left behind in Brussels, and who she says was the fittest boy in the world. But even though she still talks about him occasionally, she completely got over him in about five seconds. Now she has millions of male admirers queuing up to be the latest candidate for what she calls 'Kisses Etcetera', and she doesn't think twice about any of them. She gets these angry boy texts that say things like, L SEZ HE SAW YOU WITH R. SO F U, and half the time she doesn't even know who they're from.

But I can't imagine going out with anyone else, ever. *Ever*, even if Declan never speaks to me again. I can't imagine kissing another boy. And as for 'etcetera' . . .

Carlota waves from her seat. 'Oi! Stop thinking about Declan!'

My face goes hot. 'I wasn't.' Well, not exactly.

She shakes her head at me.

I stare out of the window. I don't recognize the roads any more.

The bus screeches to a halt in the middle of nowhere.

'This is *perfect!*' Carlota jumps up.

In the distance there's a sign for a station – proper trains, not tubes. It's not a line I know.

'Hey,' I say as I follow Carlota off the bus and towards the quiet station. 'Let's not. Let's go back. I need to . . . tell you something.' My heart goes all swooshy in my ears.

'Tell me on the train,' Carlota says, running onto the platform. 'Or the plane. Or the helicopter. Or spaceship! We're extreme travelling!'

No, no, no. I can't take off on some random adventure!

I drag myself over to Carlota, rehearsing the start of a big speech in my head. 'Look, Lots . . .' My eyes prickle. 'I'm sorry. I can't do this because I have this . . . problem and I need to—'

'Course you can do this!'

'No, I can't. Because. I . . .' Deep breath. 'I've only got a fiver to last me the Easter holidays.' Why can't I say it? This is stupid. Although it's also true that I've only got a fiver.

'No problem!' Carlota digs in her bag for a second. 'Look!' She waves a Burberry purse at me and grins. 'I've borrowed Mum's wallet!'

My big speech flies out of my head. 'Carlota! That's stealing! Your mum will go mad!'

'Nah, she won't care! She'll just get more cash from the Bank of Diplomat! And besides, I'll pay her back or something. OK, let's take the first train that comes and see where we end up.'

'I don't know, Lots.' It's one thing to be distracted from my problems, but I don't want a whole set of new ones. 'I think we should go home.'

Then two things happen at once. A train pulls in, and my phone beeps.

Declan.

DECLAN! At last!

Carlota pulls me onto the train as I open my message.

Carlota

☼ I want to tell Bets not to read it, whatever that message is, whoever it's from. Oh, God, is it from Becca? Is she checking up on whether I've told her yet?

The train moves away from the Nowhere-land station. We're going Somewhere now. I don't want anything to spoil this.

But Bets's eyes are shiny and she's just staring at her phone.

I manage to swear in my head without yelling any of the words out like I really want to.

'Who's it from?' I ask. I hope I sound casual! Oh, why aren't I a better actress? Bets always says I wear my heart on my sleeve. I've never cared about it before. Take me or leave me, you know. It's your problem if you don't like me!

But it matters now. I shove my hands into the pockets of my white jacket and try again. 'Are you OK? You look upset. Can I see it?'

She blinks a lot and hands me the phone.

It's from Declan.

I hear my voice, all flat, reading it out. '*Need to talk.*' Well, it actually says, ND 2TLK. He couldn't even be bothered to break her heart with vowels.

Bets does this sickening sniffle thing.

'It's not that bad,' I tell her, hoping I sound normal.

What is he doing, sending her this message? He promised! At least he hasn't said anything, not really.

Not yet. Has Becca told him she's going to tell Bets? Has she talked him into saying something? Maybe they're going to tell her *together*! Urgh, this is horrible.

Bets turns her teary eyes at the sky. 'He's going to dump me. That's what "need to talk" means. That's what it always means. I'm not stupid!'

Help!

'Lots . . .' She takes a big breath. 'Do you think there's any way . . . I know it sounds crazy but . . . Do you think he could be cheating on me?'

Oh God, how do I answer? Now I know why the knitting is so useful. I wish I had it in my hands now, instead of stuffed in my bag. I want something to stare at so I can avoid the look on her face, which is just agony. Then her expression changes, like she's worked something out.

'He *is* cheating on me!'

My stomach does an impression of the bus we were just on, revving up and lurching about. I have to calm it down by thinking, *She can't possibly know.*

Omigod. Should I tell her now? 'Why d'you think that?' I say quietly.

'I've seen the way Harrison gets with Becca, all hot and cold! When he avoids her, it's because he's snogging someone else! And Declan's definitely avoiding me. He's never taken so long to answer my texts before.'

'Bets—'

'It's Lauren Smith, isn't it! I've seen him talk to her! And they both do science. Biology and chemistry. They *have chemistry* together!'

I can't help it then. I giggle. Maybe it's the relief of her going off-track, or her joke. Only Bets can be so upset and still be funny! 'Bets, stop it! There's no way Declan's interested in Lauren Smith.'

'He talks to her chest! I've seen them outside the labs!'

'All boys talk to Lauren Smith's chest. Where else can they look?'

I stick out my boobs, Lauren-like, although I haven't got as much as her. But it's how you use it, of course!

Bets half-smiles, glancing around the carriage as if she's worried about being told off.

'Ah, see?' I tell her. 'They're luring you.' I make my voice spooky. 'You feel the pu-uuuull – the pull of the incredible inflating boobs!'

She laughs. Phew phew and triple phew.

'Now,' I continue in the mystical voice, 'imagine you're a boy. You're more controlled by your hormones, more highly pathetic. You're going to look— No – you're going to *ogle*. It doesn't mean a thing.'

'Lots, seriously—'

'You're not imaaaagining it!'

'OK, OK.' She turns her head back to where I'm doing the whole pneumatic-glamour-model

63

impression. She covers her eyes with one hand in mock shock.

'Admit it. If you were a boy, you'd be drawn to my chest!'

'OK, OK! Now, put them away!'

'Told you.'

Our adventure train pulls into a station and a muffled voice announces, '*The train on platform two, tissue-tissue-boxcar.*' The doors close and the train moves on.

'Lots, seriously, where are we going?'

'Anywhere. It doesn't matter!' But even though I couldn't make out the announcement, I do know where we're headed. Bets was too busy with her phone to notice, but there were only two platforms on the station, and I followed the sign that said: TRAINS TO LONDON.

Bets stares at her phone and looks worried again.

'Stop thinking about it. Who needs him, anyway?'

She sighs and mumbles, 'Not me.'

It's a start. 'Exactly. We're extreme travelling. Anything could happen! But the main thing is, we're carefree today! It will take our minds right off Declan, guaranteed.'

She's looking totally unconvinced, so I add, 'Everything will turn out fine, Bets. I promise.'

Bethany

After a few minutes I recognize the names of the stations and it's obvious we're heading for central London. So I'm not exactly venturing into the unknown, even if I usually go in Becca's mum's taxi and not on some random train.

'I should tell Mum and Dad I've gone out,' I realize. 'They think I'm revising at yours.'

Carlota shakes her knitting out, tutting exaggeratedly. 'You just can't stop being a Good Girl, can you? Yeah, OK. Tell your mum you're on a wild adventure and you'll be back in time for tea.'

I type a quick message: GONE OUT WITH C FOR A BIT. WON'T BE LATE, PROMISE WILL TRY TO REVISE. XOXO. There: no real lies, not much information, and I feel better. As long as I avoid looking at my inbox again.

Or my calendar.

'All sorted, Daughter of the Year?' Carlota watches me put my phone away.

I nod. It's all right for Carlota – she hates her stepdad, and she hates her mum for marrying him. But my parents can be sort of all right, if you ignore the way Dad nags me and the way Mum has no backbone and agrees with everything he says. I don't want them to worry about me.

'OK! Time to spice things up.' She hands me a *Teen Spice!* from her bag. 'Choose your destiny.'

'What?'

'The magazine is our destiny.' Carlota gestures at *Teen Spice!* as the familiar arch of Wembley Stadium appears outside the train window. Yep. We're headed for London all right. 'Pick a challenge.'

'How?'

'Open it at random, or pick a page with a significant number, like your birthday.'

'You do it first.'

Carlota shrugs. 'OK. My birthday.'

'Page twelve?' I leaf through and work out which one it is, because it isn't numbered, though pages fourteen and ten are. 'Top Ten Tips for Hot Snogging'.

'Great!' says Carlota. 'So the first challenge is to snog a fit boy today.'

'It's supposed to be a challenge,' I say. 'You do that every day. You've snogged a whole boy alphabet just this month. Anwar, Baz, Carl—'

'Snogging a boy alphabet each would be a good challenge!'

I look at her.

'Too much?'

I nod. That's putting it mildly.

'A boy alphabet between us?'

I shake my head.

'All right. Two boys each. Fair?'

'No! I'm not snogging *anyone* today.' Not even Declan, the way things are going. I stare out of the window to stop my eyes from filling up again.

Carlota's looking really concerned about me, so I try to smile. 'I'll pick another one. Page twenty-one for *my* birthday.'

I flick through quickly, suddenly desperate to change the subject. The magazine's full of snogging, shopping and slebs, so I really don't understand how this challenge thing is going to work. Well, maybe apart from the shopping. 'I don't get it, Lots. Do adverts count? There's a huge one here for a games console. What would we do, pretend to be Lara Croft?'

'Yeah, good idea.' Carlota does the puffed-out-Lauren-chest thing again and then uses her knitting needle to pretend-shoot a cross-looking old woman sitting at the end of the carriage. 'Nah, we'd go to one of those Soho games places and chat up some boys.'

Boys again! Carlota just can't stop.

She glances at the magazine. 'And if you pick a Tampax ad . . .'

I flinch.

She puts on a new-age guru voice. 'We'd goooooo with the flooooooow!'

The old woman Carlota pretend-shot frowns at us then, which makes me laugh. This crazy idea of Carlota's might even work. I'm already starting to think less about Declan and my problems. Except by thinking that, I'm thinking about it. I stop laughing.

I wave the magazine at Carlota, trying to get back

into it. 'We still need to pick our first proper one because we're not doing the snogging thing or the games arcade, right?'

Carlota gives me a 'why not?' look, but she says, 'All right then. Pick another page – a challenge for me.'

'OK. Eighty-five, because that's how old you look when you're knitting.'

She play-shoves me a bit and I play-shove her back and hand her the mag. She opens it and flips through the pages, saying things like 'Ooh, look at those pecs' and 'Yum'. Then she stops turning and goes quiet.

'What is it?'

She turns the page quickly.

'Hey, you cheat! Turn back to where you were before. Don't try to wriggle out of it!'

The look on her face makes me laugh. 'It was your idea to do this!' I remind her. 'So what was it?'

She stuffs the magazine into her bag. 'It was . . . er . . . the main problem on the problem pages. It was about . . . keeping secrets from mates. Whether you should tell friends everything or not. So we should, um, tell each other a secret.'

Oh.

So. This is the challenge?

I pull out my phone, scroll quickly to the calendar and check the date again. I've been doing that all morning – it's a new habit I've developed.

Well, great. I'll tell her now.

Carlota

I've got loads of magazines. Loads! Why did I even bring this one? Sometimes I drive myself crazy!

But who would have thought Bets would pick that page? *The* page – the one with the problem about seeing your friend's boyfriend with another friend. The one that got me into awkward conversations with Becca and Declan! I can't believe my bad luck!

Still, I think I dealt with it pretty well. I'm not ready to tell her the real secret and she's not ready to hear it, but in the meantime I'll think of some random innocent thing to say.

Or I could tell her my other plan for today – the one that involves Yves. But I sort of haven't even admitted that plan to myself yet. I can't bear the thought that it might not work out. I feel excited and terrified just thinking about it. Yves is the most incredible boy in the world.

And that's when I remember that I've never told Bets the truth behind the why-I-left-Brussels story. It's not exactly a secret; I've just let her go on believing the rumours that started spreading the minute I arrived in England. I've heard all sorts of variations about what me and Yves were actually doing when we got caught, and I've never denied a single one. I laugh and let everyone think what they want.

Because, to be honest, I quite like the rumours. I don't mind being seen that way. I sometimes wonder if Bets would have made friends with me in the first place if I didn't have a reputation like that attached to me. I think she was attracted to the danger in me, mwah-ha-ha!

But now I need a secret, and this should work. Hearing the truth shouldn't matter now we're such good friends, should it? She'll probably just find it funny.

Anyway, it's better than telling her what I know about Declan.

The train creeps to a full stop. Euston Station. The doors open and the people around us flood out, pretending to be important.

'OK, Bets, I'll go first!'

She's fiddling with her phone, paging through the calendar. 'No, wait—'

A guard pokes his head in and yells, 'All change!'

She sighs and stands up. 'We should get off the train. Where are we going now, anyway? What's next? What are we . . . ?' She carries on babbling for a bit in a very Bets-like way.

'I don't know,' I manage to interrupt her. 'We'll let the magazine decide! But what were you going to say? Before, I mean. The secret.' I can't believe Bets has got a secret! It's probably to do with school, like she's decided to change her A-level subjects or something.

'Nothing. What were *you* going to say?'

'I was going to tell you' – I lower my voice and tug at her sleeve to make her sit down again, so I can get close and make it sound like a proper secret – 'the truth about what happened in Brussels, the stuff before we left.' I look at her meaningfully, like I'm about to tell her something truly juicy.

But she already looks unimpressed. 'But I know! The whole school knows.' She puts on a bored, list-making voice. 'You got caught, you know, *with* some guy in a disused science lab at your posh school, the teachers went mad, you got kicked out and your stepdad left the country in shame and made you go to a normal school with no Euro-brats in it.'

I still think it's funny that Bets knew all this before she even met me, and I only told one random boy on my first morning at my new school. Boys are such gossips, even though they pretend not to be. They can't keep their traps shut when it comes to behaviour they see as 'slapperish' or whatever ridiculous double-standard word they come up with. Like, duh, I wasn't all by myself in that lab!

'Aha, but' – I'll start small – 'The Diplomat was about to get a new job anyway! I didn't get kicked out, I left! What happened with Yves just speeded things up a bit, know what I mean? And—'

'All change!' The guard sticks his head in and calls to us. 'Ladies, you need to leave the train now unless you want to spend the day in the service depot.'

'Yeah, yeah, whatever,' I say, but as soon as he's

71

moved up the platform, I grab Bets by the arm and pull her off the train. 'Come on! I'll tell you later! Let's find our next destination!'

There's no way I'm spending our extreme day stuck in some smelly depot, and anyway, the secret's not important. Not like the real secret I'm keeping. I've got to keep focused today – got to remember it's all about de-stressing Bets and making sure that by the time she hears it, she's ready.

It's also about finding Yves again and taking my whole life off hold, where it's been since we were torn apart.

Bethany

I didn't tell her! I couldn't!

And Lots just came up with some unthrilling twist on that old tale about that ex of hers, Yves – the story I overheard in the corridor on the day I first met her! She doesn't have any proper secrets, of course. She'll blurt anything to anyone and she doesn't care. I wish I could be as open as her.

I'll tell her later. Or maybe I'll pretend nothing's happening, for ever.

I say casually, to cover up my thudding heart, 'So, what's next?' I think I've already asked her that at least ten times – when I'm nervous, I just can't shut up.

She laughs, all carefree and Carlota-ish, and pulls me to one side. Some people push past us. Everyone here is in a hurry, apart from a group of boys with backpacks who look like they're worshipping a huge information screen. We stand next to them. Carlota cranes her neck like the backpackers.

'We could go anywhere!' Carlota reads the screen. 'Glasgow Central? Manchester Piccadilly? Liverpool Lime Street? Hey, I think the Eurostar to Brussels leaves from down the road. I could show you all the places me and Yves used to hang out!'

'Lots, no! We can't go to Brussels!' My voice is all whiny. I can't help it! 'We have to be back by five!'

She laughs. 'Relax! I haven't got my passport. The Diplomat keeps it locked away.' She frowns as if going abroad for the day would be a real possibility if it wasn't for that small detail. 'Your face! Anyway, I was only showing you what's out there. But we should stay in London and get you chilled out. That's what today's all about!'

She turns to the backpacker next to her – a stocky boy with a red face and sandy hair. 'Where are *you* going?'

'Lots!' I hiss. I should have known she'd try something like this. She can't resist boys, any of them!

The boy looks round and then at his mates.

'Sorry?'

'Where are you going?' Carlota repeats, as if it's a perfectly normal question to ask a total stranger.

'Er, home,' he says, going even redder.

'Is it somewhere in London?'

'Not really. Uh, Hertfordshire. Tring.'

Lots makes a face.

'We're just back from Holyhead – we've been orienteering in Ireland,' the boy adds hopefully, but Lots is already pulling me away.

'Never mind, let's get on with the extreme challenges,' she says. 'I'll find you a boy later.'

'Lots, I don't want a boy!' Well, apart from Declan, my boyfriend of seven and a bit months. What crazy ideas has Lots got into her head now? I thought I'd vetoed the snogging challenge.

'Don't worry, I was going to chat him up *for* you.' She looks disappointed.

'Choose another challenge,' I suggest.

'OK,' Carlota says, to my relief. She pulls out another magazine and checks the front. 'Forget the number thing – we should do this randomly.' She makes a great show of opening it.

'What is it?' I peer over her shoulder.

'People have written in with their embarrassing stories. Falling about and showing their knickers to the wrong people, that sort of thing. This one says she saw someone she fancied when she was shopping for tampons, and she got so nervous she held up extra-ultra-absorbent ones and waved them about in front of his face. Actually, that's a bit pathetic. There's nothing embarrassing about tampons!'

74

Yeah. Not if you're Carlota, there isn't.

She looks around. 'I know what we should do. Let's buy something really cringe-making.'

There's a tie shop, a big newsagent and a chemist nearby, among some cafés and snack bars.

'You mean, like a ridiculous tie or a magazine about stamp-collecting?'

Carlota grins. 'Is that the most embarrassing magazine you can think of?' She points to the chemist. 'How about glow-in-the-dark condoms, or massive incontinence pads, or—'

I blurt, 'A pregnancy test?' I can't look at her.

But she laughs. Of course – why would she think I meant it? 'Yeah, or pile cream. You coming with me?'

I'm frozen to the spot, willing myself to tell her, *It's not a joke. Carlota, please will you buy me a pregnancy test, because I need one and I'm too scared to get it myself.*

But she's halfway to the shop already, saying, 'Suit yourself. Back in a sec with the embarrassing loot!'

I watch her wandering up and down the aisles, pausing to ask a shelf-stacker about a huge pack of pads she's picked up. She looks very serious, like she's contemplating a major decision. If I didn't feel so terrified, I'd laugh. This isn't a challenge for her at all, and she's not remotely embarrassed.

'Got it!' She comes back holding the plastic bag

open to show me the contents: cream for piles, a breath spray, foot odour lotion and a small box with blue writing. 'I didn't buy the incontinence pads. Too bulky. And I had to ask for the pregnancy test at the counter, but it was easy.' She sounds disappointed. 'I should have sent you in to do it.'

I gaze at the test. I could tell her now. She could help me – we could try it out right now. And then I'd know.

'Did it cost a lot?' I say instead, stalling for time.

She shrugs. 'Didn't really notice. Veronica's been to the cashpoint recently. Don't look at me like that! I said I'd pay her back, didn't I?'

I'm not sure I exactly believe her, and anyway, maybe *I* should pay her back – at least for the pregnancy test. But I don't say any more because Lots is shoving another magazine at me, saying, 'Your turn for a challenge.'

I take the magazine and wonder if it will help – if it will give me something I can use as an opener with Lots, like maybe that article about Amelia, even though I know this is a different magazine. This is crazy – why can't I just tell her? But it feels too huge, like if I said it out loud I would make it real. Right now it's safe, hidden in my head.

I open the magazine at a shopping page – a spread full of left-handed accessories and gifts called 'Go Left!'

I show Carlota and say the first thing that comes

into my head. 'OK, it says "go left". So let's turn left out of the station.'

She doesn't look too impressed at my first attempt at being extreme. 'Is that your challenge? That's even less *challenging* than what I just did.'

'Yeah, but let's keep turning left. Who knows where we'll end up?' I try.

Her face brightens. Phew. 'OK. But I'm definitely choosing the next one! You're hopeless!' She swings the embarrassing bag at me. 'Come on then!'

We weave through people and suitcases. Outside the station, to the left, huge grey buildings swamp us. The pavements are wide and empty. The cars that swish past us on the huge main road are all dark blue and black and expensive-looking.

As we trudge along, I realize no one knows exactly where I am. I could be anywhere – or nowhere – in this huge city space. My problems seem far away, like they're shrinking. Maybe Lots is right about this Extreme Travel – it *is* freeing. I wonder if this is anything like the feeling Rowan gets from his crazy ironing trips.

Suddenly Carlota gasps. She grabs my arm and jumps up and down. 'Bets! Look! Look!'

I look at the big modern building across a large courtyard in front of us. The sign says: THE BRITISH LIBRARY.

'We have to go in,' I tell her.

'I know, right? Then we can honestly tell The

77

Diplomat we've been to the library! Who says I'm a liar?'

'No, I mean because . . . I need the loo!' And I do, suddenly, desperately, and a library of this size would definitely have one. Also, from what I know about pregnancy tests, I could take the test at the same time, couldn't I?

Except that means asking Lots for it.

I hesitate in the large foyer, next to a rack of tourist leaflets. There's a feeling of museum-like calm inside, despite the crowds. There are people milling around statues and pillars, stopping to look at framed pages from old books on the walls.

'Hey, GCSE-worrying dad-pleaser,' Carlota teases me. She picks up a few leaflets, glances at them and starts fanning herself dramatically. 'You must be in library heaven!'

'Lots, can I borrow . . . have your . . . ? Listen, I need—'

'Yeah, course. Help yourself,' she says distract-edly. Then she points to a sign. 'Ooh! There's a café! Now that's more like my kind of library!' She puts the leaflets back and swings her bags onto her shoulder like she means business. 'Meet me in there when you've finished!'

She breezes away without a care in the world. And with the test.

Carlota

☀ We sip our lattes and I look around. The café is kind of open plan and there are all these colourful language-school-backpack groups arriving and leaving in waves. It's like a tide of talent in a sea of hot boys, and still none of them match up to Yves.

I used the time Bets was in the loo to flick through a few magazines until I found the perfect pages for the next challenge. It was the leaflets that got me thinking. I'll pretend to Bets that it's still random, though. It isn't really cheating – I'm just making the most of my resources.

Bets fidgets like crazy with some sugar sachets.

I tear myself away from talent scouting and focus on cheering her up, though really I was looking for boys for her, so it's the same thing. 'So we're in the library, huh? In a minute you'll have me revising.'

She gives me her shy Bets smile, the one I happen to know guys love. I had to teach her to use it more, back when I was giving her Boy Snaring lessons – the ones that worked too well, because she ended up with Declan. I'm too good a teacher!

Bets goes, all serious, 'Well, maybe we should look at some books – you know, while we're sitting here.'

My face must be totally betraying what I'm think-ing, as usual, because she adds quickly, 'Becca and Baljit are revising today. And I promised Dad.'

I'm not even going to reply to that! I just shake my head. Then I say, 'God, I hope your Good Girl thing's not catching!' and I'm glad I said it because it makes her laugh.

Course, I know it's not catching, or I would have caught it by now. That first day when I saw her with Becca and Baljit, sitting on a fallen tree trunk at lunch time, I was thinking, *I wonder what it's like to be them.* They seemed like girls whose parents weren't constantly, totally, completely, utterly disappointed in their embarrassing let-down of a daughter. Not that I care, you know.

But I started hanging around with Bets that day – and Baljit, and Becca (worst luck). I've been Bets's friend ever since and, nope, nothing's changed for me. If anything, I've corrupted her instead! Mwah-ha-ha!

But I know that's not true. People don't *make* you do things. You usually want to do them anyway and you're just looking for an excuse. Well, I don't mind being Bets's excuse!

My first day at school in England, the day I met Bets nearly two years ago, was pretty eventful. For a start, I narrowly escaped being given a detention just before lunch. I was in a boring lesson and decided it would be fun to add my number to some random boy's mobey – you know, make a start, even though he hadn't asked for it. (Yet!)

So I helped myself to the phone sticking out of his jacket pocket on the back of his chair. I was punching in the numbers when this beaky-faced teacher towered over me, took the phone (the boy's phone, of course, so, like I cared?) and kept me behind to squawk at me about school rules, until I played the New Girl card and got away with it. (I found that technique pretty useful for at least a term.)

I was only slightly late for lunch, but by the time I'd got myself some revolting food-related cereal bar thing out of the vending machine, all the girls were settled in cosy groups and I couldn't see any interesting boys to flirt with. So I wandered towards this field where I was surely more likely to find fit boys, and that's when I saw them: the neat girls with the regulation, non-adapted, ironed uniform. One had loads of pink clips in her long dark hair, one had a perfectly tidy, mousy ponytail and the other had blonde, wispy chin-length hair. But they all seemed to match somehow.

I walked a bit closer until I could make out what they were talking about, which I can't remember now, though it was definitely school-related. I do remember getting this sudden ache in my stomach – probably hunger, come to think of it, but at the time I had this crazy thought that it was because I wanted to be like them: the kind of girl my parents wanted me to be.

And I thought, *Why not?* I could do that – I could worry about school and grades and all that crap; I could be a born-again Good Girl.

So I climbed up and squashed in next to them and

I vaguely tried, but within about two seconds I was being my same old self. I couldn't help it. I said hi and they said hi and then I said the first thing that entered my head, which was, 'So, you know, I'm new in town. Who's worth doing around here?'

There was a silence and then the one chewing a strand of her long dark hair said, 'Mostly we hang around at each other's houses.'

'You live in my road, on the posh side,' the neat ponytail one added seriously, giving me a suspicious look. 'There's a good chip shop in the high street round the corner.'

That was Becca. I didn't know she lived in the same road as me – girls like her were invisible to me. Usually.

'I didn't ask *what* was worth doing, I asked *who*.' I threw my bag on the ground and they all watched it land. '*Who* is worth doing.' Then I nearly choked with laughter. I also felt a little bit like running away.

That's when I saw the wispy blonde girl was smiling behind the hand she'd clasped to her mouth.

'What's your name?' I asked her, swinging my legs.

'Bethany,' she said, and her voice sounded small and shy but I knew straight away that she was pretending. She was like me, only she hadn't had the opportunities I'd had. Yet.

'I'm Baljit and this is Rebecca,' the girl with the pink clips said.

I didn't ask you, I thought.

'Becca,' the serious girl said.

I remember thinking, *Oh, how cute.* That's why they matched – their names! They were all Bs – Boring Bees. Buzzzzzzz.

Except that Bethany looked all right.

I stretched out my arms and yawned. 'So, Bethany – *Bets*, who's worth doing around here?'

Bethany giggled and looked straight into my eyes, like a challenge, so I knew I was right about her. 'Well, there's always the football team, Carlota,' she said.

I hadn't actually told her my name, I hadn't told any of them, but I found out later she'd been hearing those rumours about me and Yves all morning.

'Lots,' I told her.

So then *our* names matched and she wasn't one of them any more, not really, not ever again.

So, you know, take that, Becca!

Bloody Becca.

Yeah, I've got to stop daydreaming and find Bets another man and make her forget Declan. Because even though the day's only just started, we're running out of time.

Bethany

This should be the perfect time to talk to Lots about it, but she seems to have drifted off into some world of her own. On second thoughts, she's just doing her usual thing of eyeing up anything vaguely male within a sixteen-mile radius. Right now she's staring at a nearby wall, where two scruffy-looking, unshaven men are leaning, deep in conversation.

'I'm studying,' she laughs when she catches me looking at her. 'Libraries are places of learning, aren't they?'

'You're studying?' I read a poster filled with pictures of stamps on the wall she's been staring at. 'Philately?'

'Fit boys, silly.' She nods at the men.

'Carlota, they're not.' Ugh. 'They're *men*!'

'Boys, men, whatever. They're sexy, don't you think?'

'No.'

'Which one do you like best? I mean, you know, if you had to choose.'

'Out of *them*?!' Oh, please! The things I do for my friend. 'Why would I ever have to choose one of *them*?'

She perches on the edge of her seat and says efficiently, 'Don't worry, I'll have a chat to both of them for you and report back. OK?'

She doesn't wait for me to reply. She just gets up and sashays over to them, smoothing back her dark hair and switching on her sex appeal. Carlota in action is truly amazing. I've tried to copy her moves but they look ridiculous on me – I look like a child trying on her mother's oversized shoes. I'm actually four months older than Lots. It's not fair.

I almost can't look, but I also can't resist.

'Hi, guy-sh,' she says, in her put-on 'esh-panish' accent. Carlota does all accents perfectly. When she does impressions of teachers at school she has everyone in stitches. I think it's the main reason most girls at school like her, even when she does unforgiveable things like looking effortlessly drop-dead gorgeous in her school uniform, and leaving trails of broken hearts behind her as she snogs her way through the male half of the school.

'Can I borrow a cigarette?' I hear her asking, still with that Spanish lilt.

The men look at each other and one of them looks disgusted, as if she'd asked for money or something. But the other one, who has a thin crescent beard that puts a permanent extra, slightly creepy smile under his mouth, says pleasantly, 'Shouldn't smoke, love. It's bad for your health.'

Carlota wrinkles her nose. 'You are eh-so right,' she says. 'So can I borrow a cigarette? Actually, two?'

The smiley-beard man laughs as if she's just said the funniest thing in the world, then does a loud smoker's-type cough and winks. He takes out a packet and hands a couple of cigarettes to Carlota.

'So, are you Spanish?'

'How you know I am eh-Spanish?'

The man smirks a bit. 'Lucky guess. What is your name?'

'I call myself Carlota!'

The man nudges his friend. 'Well, I call myself Ash, and this is Connor.'

Connor frowns at Carlota by way of a greeting. Carlota doesn't seem to care. She just shakes her hair back and does her Lara Croft/Lauren boobs-out thing, which makes Ash's beard extra-smiley. I try not to laugh, even though I'm thinking, *Carlota, stop it!*

Carlota puts her head to one side. 'Are you tourists too?'

Ash smirks at his friend. 'Are we tourists? No, we're not tourists, but we *like* tourists, don't we, mate? We hang around 'em whenever we can.'

Connor just grunts and turns away.

A noisy family crowd forms by my table, rowing loudly about expensive coffee and where to sit. The group includes a toddler in a Thomas the Tank Engine coat. He's staring at me, which really can't be a good sign.

Now I can't see or hear Carlota any more but I can make out one of the men – oh, no – glancing over at me. What has she told them?

'Are you a mummy?' the little boy in the Thomas coat asks.

Argh – he's talking to *me*! 'What? No! No way! I'm still at school!' Which doesn't necessarily make any difference, does it, Bethany? Argh!

'I like school,' he tells me. 'We sing songs.'

And he begins a lisping rendition of a song about the days of the week and how he loves them all.

Instead of thinking anything sensible or normal then, like, *Aw, cute, you small person,* or *Excuse me, but I can't hear my unhinged friend chatting up strangers now,* I find myself thinking, *Why doesn't he mind singing in front of people?* If he can do it, why can't I? I've had singing lessons and I bet this little boy hasn't! He can't know the first thing about airflow, resonance and diaphragmatic breathing, allowing your stomach to expand so that you look almost . . . pregnant. Argh. My thoughts are driving me crazy.

'Freddie, come on!' One of the arguing people yanks the little boy's arm.

'Bye, lady,' he says as the family clear off in a flurry of 'I told you' and 'No, I told *you*' and general loudness.

Then they've gone (phew) and that's when I realize that so has Carlota, and the men.

I spot her in the distance, wandering away from the café with Ash. I can't see his friend. Carlota glances back and does this flat-palm gesture at me, which either means she'll be back in five minutes, or she's stopping traffic. Either way, I don't need gesturing at twice. I'm not going anywhere with those dodgy lads and neither should she! I try to shake my head at her and beckon her back towards me, but she's gone.

I wrap my hands around my coffee cup, wondering what to do. Should I go after her and keep an eye on her? I think she needs a babysitter! But what if she's planning on snogging Ash or something . . . and creepy Connor expects me to snog *him*? Ick! No, a whole world of ick doesn't cover it!

I decide to wait and hope she's not up to anything too loony.

I feel a bit weird sitting on my own, so I take out one of my school books at random. *GCSE French Revision Guide Part 1*. See, Dad? I'm revising!

It only takes a couple of snoozesome words to make me slam the book shut and turn to Carlota's stuff.

The plastic bag with the pregnancy test in it is right next to me. I reach over and pull the handles apart, but I don't take the box out. What if someone sees? Should I take the test right now? Is five minutes long enough? The writing says: *Results within three minutes*. Three minutes to decide my future!

I can't do this on my own. I need Lots. I wish she was here. I'll tell her as soon as she gets back.

I scrunch the bag's handles together and reach over to her leather bag for a magazine instead.

The first one I pull out seems to have a bookmark in it. I glance at it. It's a computer print-out of some holiday thing – there's a grainy photo of a hotel. It's on official-looking headed paper, so it must be something to do with Carlota's stepdad. Anyway, I fancy doing a quiz so I flick past the print-out, and reach a Quick Friendship Test. I already know I have the best friend in the world – if only I could tone her down a bit and stop her disappearing with strange men – so I decide to try the test with Declan as my friend.

I get Mostly Bs and the magazine declares that Declan's a reliable and good mate. So what does he 'need to talk' to me about?

I take out my phone again and read back over months' worth of Declan's texts. I've kept loads. The oldest ones are sweet, even slushy, with loads of kisses and stuff at the end, especially when he was saying goodnight. Then they get a bit rude, but in a nice way. I remember how much they made me laugh at the time, and ache to see him. The last month or so has fewer messages and they're all pretty simple – things like: U 2. C YA L8R, which was last Sunday when I texted that I loved him. He's never said 'I love you' back to me, but he does say U 2 in texts, and 'You're gorgeous' when I'm with him. Or sometimes 'You're effing gorgeous'. And once, when we were kissing a lot, he said, 'I've never felt like this before.' I know it's his way of saying he loves me – after all, boys don't say those exact words. It's not in their vocabulary – it's just not a boy thing to say.

Carlota doesn't agree with me. That's why sometimes it's brilliant to have Becca to talk to about

Declan. Becca understands what Declan means by 'You're effing gorgeous', and she says all the things I want to hear – like she wishes she had a boyfriend like Declan. Whereas Carlota just gets out her magazine to make her point. Well, she did once, anyway.

Teen Spice! has this regular page called: *'Boy Talk: What Boys Say and What They Mean'*.

She showed it to me. 'Here. It's got "You're gorgeous" and "I've never felt like this before" together.'

So I said, 'Well, yeah. They're both good, aren't they?'

But under *He says: 'You're gorgeous, I've never felt like this before'* the magazine had, *He means: 'I fancy the pants off you, how about jumping into bed with me right now?'*

Carlota's magazine addiction can be so annoying.

'So? He's my boyfriend. He's supposed to want that.'

'Yeah, maybe.' She didn't look convinced.

I said to her, 'Look, if you don't like Declan, why don't you just say so?'

She went all innocent-faced. 'I never said I didn't like Declan! I'm just warning you he might not mean what you think he means. And it's not the same thing *you* meant when you said the L-word. That's all.'

But I'm not even too sure about that. Maybe we *do* mean the same thing. Sometimes I'm not sure about 'love' – it seems like a big word – but I definitely fancy him. And I was the one who took things further between us a couple of months ago. Declan and I were alone in his room on the Saturday night after my birthday. He said, 'Hey, I've got something for you, now you're sixteen,' which sounded a bit slimy. So before he could say anything even more cringey, I shut him up by kissing him, and then I got more and more lost in him, going further and further, till he asked, 'Are you sure?' and I said, 'Yes.'

Well, why not? We'd been getting closer to it every week. I knew it was only a matter of time. I'd even brought condoms (I found a whole load in Rowan's room, which is slightly icky but I tried not to think about it). To be honest, I'd been wanting to do it for a while. Everyone thought me and Declan already were, anyway, so what was the difference? And Carlota's been doing this stuff for years. I actually asked her before if she thought I should do it, and she said, 'Of course, if you want to,' like it was no big deal. Which, really, it wasn't, even for a worrier like me.

Afterwards, Declan told me what he'd actually meant was that he'd bought me a lottery ticket, but it was obviously his lucky night anyway. He's been buying me lottery tickets every week ever since. It's like a tradition between us now; it goes with our Saturday nights together. It's what we do.

I stare at today's text from Declan for ages. ND 2

TLK. I can't make it mean anything good. What am I going to do now? My life's a total mess.

Then I realize that loads of time has passed and there's still no sign of Carlota. It's definitely time to worry about her.

I quick-dial her number. She's got this new Trix ringtone that Baljit downloaded for her last week – a dance track based on an ancient Doris Day song. The title is Spanish and Carlota says it means: *Whatever will be, will be* – not worrying about the future, that type of thing. The original song is some kind of Del Rey family thing that Carlota says her nan used to sing to her when she was little. The dance version is brilliant – great beat, with Trix's fab vocals. I'm always singing it when I'm sure no one can hear me.

The ringtone song goes round and round in my head as I gather up our stuff and go in search of Carlota.

Wait. It's not in my head. I can hear it, really faintly! It's definitely Carlota's phone!

I hurry towards the sound.

There's a dark corner under a nearby stairwell, slightly hidden from view. The dancey plinky-plonking gets louder as I rush towards it.

And there's my friend Carlota with Ash, the revolting total stranger, and she's holding something – a bit of card or something. He's probably just given her his phone number. I don't care! I was *worried*!

She could have *called* me to say she'd be longer than five minutes! She could have answered her stupid *phone*!

I cannot believe my friend!

Carlota

'Bets! Hiya!' Amazing timing!

When I told Ash about Bets and her singing, he said he'd just got some great tickets that would be perfect for her. He said he'd go and get them to sell to me – you know, at a good price. He and Connor got up, with Connor grunting something about going to work, and how Ash should be 'getting busy' too, or some work jargon like that.

Bets was busy chatting to some little child. I decided to follow the boys – after all, I wanted the tickets to be a surprise for Bets, for later. I couldn't buy them in front of her.

Connor walked off in a different direction, so I followed Ash to this dark corner where there were some lockers. He unlocked one and spent for ever sorting himself out, pulling out about a million bags and things and stuffing them back in . . . gawd, I thought *I* was messy!

Then he saw me standing there and jumped about a mile.

I laughed. 'Hi!'

He slammed the locker shut. 'Tickets,' he said, not

smiling, and sounding a lot like his grunting friend. He handed me two large pieces of card.

I glanced at the swirly foil on them. 'This is fantastic!'

I kind of forgot to act foreign, I was so excited. My phone started ringing, but I ignored it.

'Twenty quid each,' Ash told me, twitching a bit and not noticing my sudden fluency. 'You can't get them anywhere else. They're very exclusive.' He sniffed. 'Have you got the money on you?'

'Yeah, I've got my mum's – I mean, *my* wallet.' I reminded myself to sound Spanish. 'I have much money and much credit cards of gold and platinum. My friend and I are wealthy, like practically members of the Spanish royal family!'

I checked for signs he was suspicious, but Ash just said quickly, 'So where is it, then? Your money.'

I realized I'd left all my stuff at the café. 'Oh, yes,' I said. And that's when Bets appeared, holding my stuff! Perfect!

Except that she looks like she wants to kill me.

'I was worried sick about you!' she says, glaring at me, and then Ash.

Knowing her, she probably thought I was in some kind of danger. I've never met anyone who could blow up a situation with worry quite as much as Bets – she always takes everything to its worst possible conclusion. These past two days when she's been off school with a sick bug, she probably thought she was dying or something. And now she still sees an axe murderer where I see a beardy bloke making her dreams come true. It's Bets all over.

'You're here!' I say, because I'm not sure how to react. I mean, to be honest, she's reminding me of my stepdad right now, and it is so not a good look for her.

I hold the tickets behind my back. How am I going to get the wallet off her and hand over the money without her noticing?

'Ash, is it OK if I meet you later?'

Bets looks daggers at me. 'Oh, don't mind *me*!' she says, and then she storms off. *With* my bag.

'You want to meet me later?' Ash looks me up and down with a greedy kind of expression in his eyes. Honestly, guys make it so obvious they fancy me.

Mind you, I suppose it might have sounded like I just asked him out.

'Yes, I mean meet me later for the paying of the tickets.' I give him a vague smile while I wonder what could be wrong with Bets.

Ash keeps staring at me. 'I need the money now.'

'Oh, my friend has it.' I shrug, folding the tickets and shoving them in my pocket. 'She walks off with it. I go and find her.'

He does that nervous twitch again. 'I'll come with you.'

I spot her marching towards the toilets in the distance. 'Uh, no. It's, how you say it? The troubles of girls. Back in a minute. Wait here.'

As I'm leaving, Ash calls, 'You'd better bring me that money! You've got the tickets!'

I turn and give him another smile to melt his heart. 'Don't worry, I will.' And just for fun, I add, 'The money is nothing to me, you know – I have the mountains of the stuff!'

When I get to the ladies, she's standing in front of the mirror looking like she's going to cry.

'Bets?' I try to hug her.

She flinches away from me.

Oh, no. What happened? Did Declan ring her?

There's a long pause while I wonder whether to ask her. Then she says, 'Honestly, Lots, you didn't even answer when I rang!'

Oh, is that all? Phew!

'I thought it might be my Stepdad!' I tell her. Which isn't exactly true. I didn't really think at all – I just ignored it because I was busy with Ash. 'Sorry, Bets. Next time I'll check the caller ID.'

'No, next time you won't run off and snog some random stranger!'

'I didn't snog him!' Oh, no, is that what this is about? Does Bets fancy Ash? I'd almost forgotten I was supposed to be finding her a Declan distraction boy, I got so involved in the ticket thing. But it's played right into my hands! Bets can go to the show and have the man! 'Ash is all yours, I swear. I didn't go near him.'

Her face goes all weird. Uh-oh, she's still angry.

No she isn't. She's creasing up. She starts practically howling with laughter.

'What?'

She keeps laughing like a loon.

'What?' I don't get it. 'What's so funny?'

She wipes at her eyes. 'You are!'

I find myself laughing, although I've no idea why.

'OK. Why?'

She does a terrible impression of my voice. *'Ash is all yours!'*

'But Bets, it's true! You can have him!'

She laughs even harder, clutching her sides.

'You can snog him for the challenge!'

She's starting to hiccup now.

'He's waiting for us right now. Just let me go ahead and speak to him for you a second.' I can give him the money, and warn him not to tell her about the tickets. 'And then you can come and speak to him yourself.' I pick up my bag from the counter where she's left it.

She grabs my arm. 'Lots, stop! I don't fancy Ash!'

'Oh. Connor, then? Maybe you can ask Ash for his number.'

'No! No! They're revolting! *Hic!* Both of them!'

Oh? 'Really? You don't like either of them?' I should have known! Bets is really choosy. That's part of the problem – the reason she stuck to Declan the Practice Man for way too long. She can't see male talent the way I can! It's everywhere – in the most unexpected places, not just the obvious ones, like the school football pitch.

'No *way*! Seriously! *Hic!*' She creases up again. 'Hold on, I need the loo again!' That seems to stop her laughing.

She disappears into a stall.

I unfold the tickets as I pull them out of my pocket. I can't get over how great this could be! I turn them over in my hand. On the back it says, *Complimentary tickets. Not for sale.* Wow! Ash must have got it wrong – these aren't expensive tickets! They're free! They're also perfect.

I find the magazine that has my print-out as a marker.

As Bets washes her hands, I open the magazine at the right page and move the print-out quickly to the back.

'Look! I *randomly selected* our next challenge!' My voice sounds weird. I'm such a bad liar. It's lucky she's making faces in the mirror and not listening too closely.

'What is it?'

I show her the page. It's called '*On the Road*' and it's about this boy band on tour, travelling in Eastern Europe or something. There's a great big picture of the bus and the whole focus is on *touring*, and seeing the sights of a new city.

'So what's the challenge?' Bets asks, pushing open the swing door.

'An extreme bus tour, of course!'

She gives me one of her doubtful looks, but she follows me into the main library area.

I can see Ash frowning by a pillar in the distance, waiting for me to give him that money. He doesn't seem to see me. I could go over and explain about the tickets, but there isn't much point.

And besides, I've got to put my other plans in motion!

I do a gangster sort of voice at Bets. *'Let's get outta here!'*

Bethany

Outside, Carlota points into the distance.

'Over there! I saw a leaflet about them on the way in. And they're painted white. They even match my clothes!'

I try to work out what she's talking about as I follow her. There are three double-decker buses parked in a row, all white with TIP TOP TOURS written on the side. The bus at the front has a couple of people sitting on the open-top deck, studying a map. A bored-looking overweight man is spilling over the edges of a picnic chair next to the bus. He's holding a newspaper and has a cigarette hanging out of his mouth. Beside him is a sign that says, TIP TOP'S LONDON MUSEUM TOURS. The tour leaves every half-hour and costs £16 per person, which seems like loads of money, but I know by now that it isn't going to put Carlota off. It's going to take her months to pay her mother back at this rate. And I suppose I need to pay for my share. Like for the coffee, this bus tour and . . . the pregnancy test. I half wish I'd never got Carlota un-grounded and we'd never left her bedroom.

Carlota says, 'OK, let's prepare for the great *Teen Spice!* extreme bus tour challenge.'

'Why do we need to prepare? Can't we just get on the bus?'

'Nah, we've got to do this properly – no more of your "turn left" crap, Bets! Getting on a bus isn't *extreme!*' Carlota nudges my rucksack. 'You got a notebook in among all that boffin kit?'

'Erm, yeah. So we're *not* getting on the bus?'

'You'll see. Something to write on – quick!'

I rummage past Carlota's magazine and pull out the 'revision organizer' Dad gave me last week, which is actually an accounts book from his work. I had to draw up a revision timetable on the first page and show him – urgh.

Carlota takes it and turns to a blank page. 'And a pen.'

I find a pen.

She shakes her head. 'A red one.'

I roll my eyes.

'I know you've got one.'

I sigh and find my pencil case, avoiding Carlota's eye. I just know she's giving me that triumphant

'Bethany-Boffiny' look as I hand her a red biro.

'Great. Come with me.'

'Lots, what are you doing?'

'What are *we* doing! Ssh!'

Carlota approaches the bored man in her usual bold way. No – bolder.

'George!' she says. She sounds like she's doing an impression of Ms Harris, our English teacher, on the rampage. She looks instantly at least ten years older – not that Carlota ever looks fifteen anyway.

The man shifts his bulk slightly. He coughs and narrows his eyes at Carlota. 'It's Steve.' He sounds wary, but you can sort of see cogs grinding slowly in his head. 'Who are you?'

Carlota tuts. 'Who do you *think* I am, Steve?' She raps my pen significantly on my notebook and then uses it to point. 'And put that out at once!' Now she really sounds like Ms Harris. And it works, because Steve totally acts like a Year Ten who's been caught smoking in the toilets.

He stubs out his cigarette on the ground and grumbles sulkily, 'I'm having a break.'

'There are no breaks! You're reflecting the image of Tip Top Tours at all times.'

I put my hand over my face to hide my smile because that's what Ms Harris says if she catches us 'loitering at bus stops'. Although about the image of the school, obviously, not a tour company.

'Now! Who's in charge of this bus?'

'I just drive the thing.' Steve makes a huge effort to shift one bulky arm to a chunky-looking phone strapped to his belt. 'Delphine and Tom just popped to the . . .' He swallows the last word. 'I'm taking care of the punters for a few seconds. No one warned me the gaffer was coming. Bloody typical, that is. Are you from head office?'

Carlota pretends to consult her notebook. 'They went *where*?'

Steve sighs, looking trapped. 'The Arms. To use the toilet. You don't provide proper—'

'The Arms? Is that a *public house*?!'

That's when I snort-laugh – I can't help myself.

Carlota glares at me. 'Excuse my trainee.' She lowers her voice. 'Work experience, you know.' Then she does her Lara Croft breast-jut thing, and Steve's eyes look like they're going to pop out of his head.

'Start the tour without them. I'll take it from here.'

Steve doesn't take his eyes away from Carlota's chest but he makes a great effort to tap his phone and mumble, 'I'll tell them.'

'No need!'

He huffs to his feet very slowly. 'But they . . . we need a guide—'

'I wrote the tour script!' Carlota announces. 'Your job is to drive the bus. I'll do the rest. Come with me, Miss Royston. It's time to learn from the best.'

Steve heaves himself onto the bus and into the driver's seat. He hands Carlota a microphone headset and goes, 'Here, miss.'

I can't believe he called her 'miss'!

We go up to the top deck and collapse laughing on the front seat as the bus rumbles into action.

Then I notice there are people staring at us. Tourists, expecting us to be tour guides.

Carlota

☀ I try not to think about where we're going, and how, if my plan works, I might get to see Yves again. Thinking about it makes my insides fizz like crazy.

Bets, giggling like a loon, helps me put on the microphone headset thingy provided by the slightly thick driver, who totally fancies me. Then I stand at the front of the top deck and go 'One two, one two' like a real expert, and my voice echoes around as I address our tour customers. Luckily there's only two of them and, judging by their clothes, they're foreign. Hopefully they won't understand a word of what I'm about to say.

Er . . . what *am* I about to say?!

Well, how hard can it be?! You just stand there and blether about landmarks and British stuff like Union Jacks and Shakespeare, right?

I make a start. 'OK, thank you for shopping at Tip Top Tours!'

The people – a man and a woman who look a little

bit alike but I think are a couple, because they're holding hands over a map – stare at me like I've got five heads.

The bus moves off and I take a deep breath. I'm not scared, anyway! 'If you look to your left you'll see a road . . . and several other roads coming off it.' Bets is smirking, but I don't care. I'm doing really well! My voice is ringing out loud and clear and only a bit crackly! Besides, so what? 'And you'll notice some buildings. Tall ones. Very tall!'

'Lots, Steve's going to chuck us off the bus at this rate,' Bets says quietly.

I shush her with my hand. 'People working in that building make a lot of money. And they spend it at Harrods or something.'

See, it's easy! Bets doesn't need to worry. The bus turns down a busy dual carriageway and I add, 'Note the cars below. There are blue ones, red ones and white ones. Those are the colours of the British flag.' That's sure to be a tourist-pleaser. 'The dirt shows more easily on white ones, which I can relate to because I wear a lot of white clothes. I'm a Reverse Goth.'

Bets puts her head in her hands.

What? I'm giving my tour a personal touch!

The couple whisper to each other and laugh at some private joke. Well, they definitely haven't understood then. I'm safe! I just have to keep sounding confident. I'm good at that – confidence was the first rule I tried to teach Bets for Boy Snaring. It's the number one requirement, whether you're looking for a snog or a Saturday job, or even trying to out-smart some teacher or your annoying stepdad. Bets could still do with a bit more of it, which is part of what today is all about.

'To your left is London Bridge, and Big Ben – he's the man down there with the bald head and the tragic green mac.'

Bets says, much louder this time, 'Lots, everyone knows Big Ben is a clock! And we're nowhere near London Bridge. Or any bridge! Where's the river?'

The customers titter. That's weird, considering they don't speak English.

And now I'm starting to get the uncomfortable feeling that maybe they do understand after all.

Ah, well, never mind. I haven't said anything that bad. I've kept it clean and everything! 'Just testing you, Miss Royston. Of course, Transport for London recently moved all the bridges because of . . . er . . . pirates. You still get pirates nowadays, you know – they're not all Johnny Depp-type ones – you get common thieves and stuff. It's not funny. What now, Miss Royston?'

'Nothing,' Bets goes, with her teeth kind of gritted.

'Thank you. To your right is the famous pub where Shakespeare used to drink . . . vodka and orange. If you show them your Tip Top Tour receipt and quote a line of Shakespeare at them, they'll give you a discount off a Shakespeare Special.'

There's a station in the distance and I can't make out its name. Help, I'm feeling really twitchy now. I think we're getting close, but my knowledge of London isn't brilliant and I'm not sure. I can't even bring myself to make anything up, I'm suddenly so twittery inside at the thought. I need to get a grip!

'Miss Royston, quick test! Where are we now?'

She gapes at me. 'You're asking *me*?'

'You're my trainee.' I desperately try to communicate with my eyes, along the lines of: *And you're the only one who ever has a clue about anything.* I need to get this right! It's all part of my plan! But, of course, she doesn't know I have a plan. This is supposed to be random, after all.

I was right to rely on her, though.

She's leaning over, smiling at the couple. 'I'm so sorry,' she says in that voice that makes The Diplomat melt. 'Can I borrow your map? It's my first time and I haven't learned the route yet.'

I give her an approving, boss-like nod.

'Uh, yeah, I guess,' says the man in pretty good English, but with a slight German accent. I'm still in with a chance of his foreign-ness, then.

'OK, over to you, Miss Royston. Don't be scared – it might seem a bit extreme, but all our trainees have to start somewhere.' I collapse into a seat.

'Lots, you've got the microphone!' Bets hisses at me.

'You've got a loud enough voice, Miss Wannabe Singer.' I don't have the energy to get this headset off right now.

'Errrrr,' says Bethany, frantically looking around, and then at the map. Her voice is tiny and wobbly. Oops – maybe I'm expecting too much of her. 'The next stop . . . on our tour . . . tour stop . . .'

Oh, Bets, I'm sorry!

'Is . . . Madame Tussaud's.' Bets goes thoughtful and quiet, but then she picks up. 'This is a waxworks museum where former Prime Minister Tony Blair and film star Tom Cruise might give you a fixed grin . . .' She does this perfect deadpan pause, pulling a face. 'Well, that's if they happen to be visiting. You'll find wax versions of them there all the time.'

Omigod! That's a joke worthy of Bets's dad! She's somehow tapped into her inner Mr Royston!

Our audience break into appreciative laughter. Hold on! I didn't get any laughter with my nonsense, and that was pretty funny, wasn't it? Obviously not compared to Royston humour!

'Speaking of wax, does anyone know how long it takes Madame Tussaud to light a candle?' Bets does the comedy timing thing again. 'About a wick! And what did the big candle say to the little candle?' Perfect pause. 'I'm going out tonight!'

And she keeps going like that, with the jokes getting worse and worse, and the tourists are loving it!

The bus pulls in at the Tip Top Tours sign and the

German man walks towards me. *Achtung!* He's going to have a go at me about my terrible tour!

I can deal with it, of course.

I gather my stuff, ready to run.

But he says, 'Great tour!' He glances back at his girlfriend, who's giving me an embarrassed smile, then he looks at Bets. 'You sure made this wax sound interesting. Hope we see you on the way back!'

Bets looks like she's going to have a heart attack, probably at the thought of 'the way back'. But she did brilliantly! See, I've always told her she was a superstar, and she never believed me!

'Gretchen?'

The man's girlfriend – Gretchen, good German name – stands up and walks over, holding out a note. I glance at it.

It's a twenty-pound note!

It's official. Tourists are insane!

'We can't accept this,' Bets says.

I glare at her. Not that we need it, but still. We totally deserve it!

'No please, take it. You have earned it. We believe in tipping where we come from.'

'Oh, Germany?' I ask.

The man gives me a strange look and says, in a German way, 'Lewiston, Idaho.'

Well, it practically sounds like 'lederhosen', the way he says it!

'We emigrated to the USA from Eastern Europe but

we've completely lost our accents now.' He looks at the money in Gretchen's hand as if he wants to keep it himself now that I've insulted his English.

'Oh, yes, completely.' I eye the money.

'Tipping – is that a place in China?' Bets mumbles, looking shocked at herself and her final descent into her dad's humour.

Gretchen and the Lederhosen Man crack up laughing again, clearly forgiving me my accent-bashing sins.

The money finally makes it to my hand, and I hear them saying, 'What a great tour,' and, 'So funny,' to each other as they leave the bus.

Something's bugging me. Something Bets said before I got distracted by twenty-pound notes. Oh yes. 'Bets, where did you say we were?'

'Madame Tussaud's. Baker Street.'

'Baker Street?' I was right! Omigod. This is IT!

There's this huffing sound and the bus shakes and for a minute I think I'm having a heart attack because I can barely breathe! But then I realize all the heavy breathing and trembling is Steve tackling the stairs. He appears at the top looking like he'd be really angry, if only he had the energy.

'Look, I don't know what you're playing at, but—'

I chuck the headset at Steve and then, as an after-thought, I go up to him and press the twenty-pound note into his hand. Then I remember the cigarettes Ash gave me, so I fish them out of my pocket and give him those too. He sort of stares at me with his mouth half open.

'Thanks, Steve,' I say. 'That's your bonus. You passed your assessment – well done! Now you'd better get hold of Delphine and Tom.'

Bets follows me down the stairs. 'Lots, where are we going now?'

Well. Only to see the love of my life again. Yves, after all this time.

'Follow me.'

Bethany

I can't believe I'm doing it again! Trudging down the road after Carlota, holding all our stuff! Maybe this is what Extreme Travel and/or Extreme Ironing is really about. I bet every time Rowan goes up a mountain to iron a shirt, he has some willing mug of a mate with him, staggering about behind him with a flowery-patterned ironing board.

I've given up asking Lots where we're going because she's in some kind of daze. After a while she stops outside a large building and gazes at the awning.

I wonder if she's playing one of those tricks again – the kind where you stare at the sky and try to attract a crowd of nosy people to join in with you. She did that once outside the staff room at school, staring at the ceiling with this angelic expression on her face. It was brilliant – by the end of lunch, the whole of Years Seven and Eight and even some teachers and the caretaker were crowded round her, craning their necks.

I stare at the awning with her.

Something's familiar about the sign, but I can't think what. It says, L'ANDRÉ HOTEL BAKER STREET and there's this logo that I'm sure I've seen before.

Carlota looks pale, a bit like she's about to throw up. That must have been what I looked like yesterday and the day before. I'm the worst friend in the world because for a second I tell myself, *Yay, if she's ill, that means I definitely had a bug and no other reason to be sick*, but then I tell myself off and say out loud, 'What's the matter, Lots?'

Her voice is very quiet. 'What's the time?'

I take out my phone and try not to think about the message from Declan as I tell her. 'Time for another challenge?'

'No. Yes. Not yet.' She stares a bit more. 'Yves should be in there right now. Well, here or one of the other places. But I think he's supposed to be here first.'

'Yves? You mean *the* Yves? Your Brussels ex?' Wow. It seems weird now, thinking that Carlota has an ex-boyfriend. Carlota and Kisses Etcetera, yes. Carlota going out with someone – nuh-uh. She did talk about Yves a lot when she first arrived at our school, but then she stopped. I thought she'd

111

forgotten all about him, especially judging by the number of other boys she was seeing.

Her voice is that completely un-Carlota-ish near-whisper again. 'Yes. I read some of his Bebo messages. He was messaging his cousin about working at his uncle's hotel chain. I don't think it's the first time he's come to London since I left Brussels. But it's the first time I decided to find him.'

Wow. This is huge. Then I remember where I recognize the logo from. It was on the print-out in her magazine – the one I saw in the library café!

Hey! Carlota had a print-out of information about this hotel.

But today was supposed to be random. How did she get us here?

I feel this strange prickle of irritation at Carlota, like I did when I caught her with that Ash in the library. I thought she was taking me out for the day to distract me from my Declan worries. But she's been planning this! It's been all about *her* after all!

Not that it should matter. I mean, she *has* distracted me, hasn't she? I've just led a bus tour, for a start!

'Lots' – I try to keep my voice casual – 'did you *plan* to meet Yves today?'

She stares at the ground. 'No! Not exactly. But I was doing all these searches last night. Well, early this morning when The Diplomat was asleep.' Her voice gets even softer. 'I do it a lot – look for

Yves. I can't help it.'

Wow. She doesn't sound like herself at all.

'And then I found the message to his cousin, and I looked up his uncle's hotel chain – I remembered the name – and I'd read the Extreme Travel article and I knew you needed cheering up and I thought . . . Maybe we could do the travel thing and see Yves too.'

'But we nearly didn't go to London today. We took the first bus, the first train . . .' Didn't we? I try to remember. I'm already starting to forgive Carlota, because she looks so weird for her – sort of sad and . . . hopeful. I want her to be happy. It sounds like she's been thinking about this Yves a whole lot more than she's ever let on.

'I just had a feeling this could happen today.' She shrugs as if that explains it.

'But since when have you been' – I nearly say *spying on Yves* – 'reading Yves' messages?'

She fiddles with her bag. 'Well, probably since I met him. But I've done it more since . . . well, since I've been here, and The Diplomat started blocking his emails to me. I'm sure he did, Bets.'

I think, *Oh, no, my friend's a stalker*. She's *Freaky Stalker Girl, Mostly As*, from the quiz we did earlier.

But then I think, What would *I* be like if Dad told me I could never talk to Declan again? I'd be curious about him, wouldn't I? And he's not even the love of my life or anything, not like it suddenly

113

seems that Yves is to Carlota.

Wow, did I really just think that about Declan?

Not the love of my life?

Where did *that* come from? Especially now, when there's all this stuff going on?

Carlota fiddles with her bag, pushing her knitting and magazines deeper into it.

'Going for another challenge?'

'Um, no.' She holds up the plastic bag of embarrassing things, the ones she bought at Euston. 'It's just . . . If he's here . . . What if he sees these? I don't want him to think I need them.' She digs in her bag. 'I need to bury them.'

'No, wait,' I say, feeling kind of dazed and shocked at this all-new Carlota, who cares what a boy thinks of her. But I'm also thinking fast. 'I'll take them. You never know when foot-odour lotion will come in handy, ha ha.' I find my make-up bag, which is a large sparkly sequin-studded old-fashioned purse thing. 'We can hide it all in here.'

'Thanks,' Carlota whispers.

I do up the clasp. Well, now I've got the pregnancy test. I just need to find the guts to use it.

Then Carlota stops me thinking about it any more because she sort of braces herself, doing the Lara Croft thing with her boobs, and she says, 'OK, I'm going in. Stay with me, Bets.'

'Course,' I mumble.

Everything inside is marble and leather and

hushed, with a few suited men milling about looking serious and macho, even though the newspapers they're reading are pink.

Carlota heads for the front desk. I'm not quite sure what to do with myself, so I hang back near the leather chairs and read a laminated poster on the wall. It says, *L'André Hotel can accommodate your every need for a luxury stay in London over three prime locations.*

Wow, I'd sort of forgotten that Carlota's Brussels friends were all loaded. Apparently after the whole caught-with-Yves-in-a-science-lab thing, Carlota's stepdad made a big deal of sending her to a 'down-to-earth school' to 'teach her real values'. Sometimes I wonder if he regrets it, now he's seen how rubbish our school really is.

'I'm here to see Yves van der Geezer,' Carlota tells the receptionist, her voice wavering slightly. Well, she doesn't say 'Geezer', but I have no idea what she does say. How weird. I don't remember her ever telling me Yves' surname. In fact, I don't know much about him at all, because Carlota has barely told me anything. Not like me and Declan. I must have bored her silly about him.

The receptionist says, 'And your name is?'

'Omigod! You mean he's here?' Carlota almost jumps up and down. 'Bets, did you hear that? He's here! He's really here! Omigod!'

'Is Monsieur van der Geezer expecting you?' asks

the receptionist, sounding oily and patient (and obviously not saying 'Geezer' either).

Carlota stops squealing and her voice goes tiny. 'Um, no.' She almost sounds worried, like she doesn't think he'd want to see her.

I need to tell her she's being a nutter. A boy not wanting to see Carlota? That would never happen. And especially not Yves. I heard all about what was going on between them in that science lab even before I knew who Carlota was, back on her first day at our school! There's no way this guy is anything less than totally smitten with her.

She says, 'Tell him it's . . . an old friend. Um, from Brussels,' but at the same time a male voice says,

'Carlota? Carlota Peters! Is that you?'

I turn away from the poster in time to see Lots jump – surprise-jump, I mean, not excited-jump. She actually looks terrified. A film-star-gorgeous boy is leaning languidly on the counter next to her. And beside him is an even hotter boy who looks similar but taller and thinner with longish wavy hair. His features are sharp and his eyes dark. He's the kind of person you look twice at because you think he must be famous.

Normal Carlota would give the first boy an earful for calling her by her stepdad's surname and leaving out 'Del Rey'. She *hates* that.

But this new Scaredy-Lots just says in this half-whisper, 'Yves.' She looks all swoony and ridiculous.

'Omigod. Yves.'

'Carlota! This is amazing!' He holds her shoulders and does this French-style cheek-kissing – left, right, left; one, two, three. 'Are you staying here? London is such a big place and yet I'm always running into people I know! Hey, this is my cousin Zacharie. Zac. Remember? You met him that summer?'

'Oh, yeah, after the funeral.' Carlota does the kissing thing with the hot boy too. I mean, with Zac.

'I'm sorry about your mother. Er, again. Even though it was a really long time ago now and every-thing.'

Zac frowns slightly but he says, 'Wonderful to meet you again. Excuse me a second.'

I only realize I'm totally staring at him when he looks straight at me, smiles and walks over. 'Yes? Can I be of any assistance?' He sounds all business-like and confident, like he owns the place. Which – gulp – I suppose he does.

I stand there like a speechless idiot and I'm so glad when Carlota steps in. 'That's my friend Bethany.'

'Oh! You're together?' He loosens his tie. 'Hello, Bethany.' He pronounces it '*Bet*-a-nee' even though he barely has an accent the rest of the time. It sounds so exotic. He holds out his hand and I hesitate before I take it, almost disappointed that he doesn't do the French cheek-kissing thing with me. But his hand is lovely – warm and strong.

God, what am I *thinking*? I'm catching Carlota's boy-madness! Except that she looks dreamy and besotted, staring at Yves the way she's probably seen me stare at Declan a thousand times.

I tear my eyes away from Zac and mutter some generic 'pleased-to-meet-you' thing that I hope doesn't make me sound stupid.

Zac looks at his watch and gives me a hugely apologetic look. 'I'm so sorry – I'd love to offer you both a drink but my father needs us at the South Bank hotel. We were on our way right now – you only just caught us. If you're staying here, perhaps we'll see you later?'

'No way,' I mumble like an idiot. 'We're not staying here!'

'That's too bad. Great to see you again, Carlota,' Yves says.

Carlota looks desperate. 'No, wait!' She *sounds* desperate too. 'Can we come with you? We're on an extreme adventure.'

I can't believe she said that!

Yves laughs as if he's used to Carlota spouting nonsense. 'You're on a *what*?'

'Me and Bets. We're doing this new thing where you travel randomly, doing challenges.' She touches his arm. 'I can explain it to you on the way. You could join in.'

Yves shakes his head, smiling. 'Sounds like a laugh, but we can't. Can we, Zac?'

'My father wouldn't like it.'

Yves shrugs at Carlota. Her face falls about a mile and goes splat on the marble floor.

Zac fiddles with his tie. 'But, well . . . he's expecting us in an hour and if the traffic's good . . . we've got a little time.'

Yves widens his eyes at his cousin as if he can't quite believe what he's hearing. 'OK then. Looks like we're in!'

We stand on the pavement waiting for – what? A bus? I doubt it. A taxi? More likely. I wouldn't be surprised if it was a horse and carriage, though, or a helicopter, the way things are going today.

Carlota's gone all silent and pathetic again, which is beyond weird. It's like, all of a sudden it's up to me to do all the talking. I'm not used to this! I try to think of something intelligent to say.

I turn to Zac, avoiding his eyes because I can't risk thinking the things I thought the first time I looked at him. 'So which of the hotels are you staying at?'

Before Zac can answer, Yves laughs. 'Zac lives in London.'

Oh, right. Well, *excuse* me, Mr Love of My Best Friend's Life. Where have you been for the past two years while she's apparently been pining for you (ahem, by snogging every boy in sight)?

I laugh as if I knew that about Zac and I was just trying to make a hilarious joke.

'I live with my dad in Muswell Hill,' Zac says

pleasantly as a massively long and sleek black car pulls up beside us. 'And Paris. Ah, here's the limo.'

I don't feel like laughing any more.

And *Paris*?

'The *limo*?'

Oops, I said that out loud!

Zac sighs. 'Dad's forcing me to use it. He likes to know where I am at all times.'

The *limo* – yes, the sleek black limo – door opens and a driver in a suit gets out and frowns at Zac. Then he opens the passenger door for him.

This is mad! I can't believe this is happening right in front of me, as if it was completely normal for boys our age to ride in a car like *that*.

And for us to go with them.

As the boys climb in, I suddenly feel iffy about the whole thing. I hiss to Carlota, 'We shouldn't get into a *car* with *strangers*.'

She stops being a love-muppet for a second and stage-whispers back at me, 'It's not a *car*, it's a *limo*. And Yves isn't a stranger. I've known him since I was eleven. I started going out with him when I was thirteen.'

'Well, OK, but in any case, most sex crimes are committed by people you know,' I mumble. I read that once in Dad's *Daily Scare*.

'Well, good. I feel like committing a sex crime.' Carlota smiles smugly at me.

'Lots!' I pretend to be shocked, but I'm not really.

It's typical Carlota.

'He's gorgeous,' she breathes, all dreamy-faced again.

We get into the limo. I settle into a huge, sleek, leather-scented space. Carlota pushes past me and Zac to sit next to Yves, forcing me closer to Zac.

I edge away. I'm finding Zac unnerving. He's unbelievably gorgeous. He's like some kind of poster from the back of the *Teen Spice!* Lad Special. I didn't know guys like that really existed. Mum told me once that magazines use tricks to alter photos and that's why girls need to wear lots of make-up, to get closer to that airbrushed perfection. Mum adores make-up – she loves blotting out her imperfections and she's always encouraging me to do the same. Mum calls make-up 'nature's helping hand'.

But there's no way Zac's wearing make-up. He's naturally perfect.

Ooh. I'm sure I should *not* be thinking like this.

The sights of London flash past the black-tinted windows. I sit up very straight and try to look like I'm used to this. If I was with Becca and Baljit on one of our shopping trips and we saw this limo, we'd be trying to guess which famous person was inside.

Zac's staring out of the window too. I wonder what he's thinking. He's wearing a suit and he looks all grown up and professional – not like someone who'd ever consider doing mad challenges from a magazine.

He notices me looking at him. Oops.

He smiles and says, 'So what are these travelling challenges? Is it for school?'

Yes, our geography coursework is to ride in limos with hot boys. 'Er, no. It was a thing Carlota wanted to do to get away from . . . life and stuff.' I sit on my hands. I'm not sure what to do with them. I feel like reaching up and touching the yellow lights on the ceiling, because I've never seen anything like them in a car before.

'Sounds like a good plan. I don't get away much.' He gestures to our luxury surroundings. 'My main break is taking the car to another hotel. I'm always working. My father's constantly stressing out about my future.'

'Oh, I know the feeling,' I say, as though being forced to use a chauffeur-driven limo compares to getting daily lectures about John Lennon's exam passes.

'Yeah? Does your dad hassle you too?'

'Yeah. About GCSEs,' I explain. Then I'm distracted by the sight of Carlota and Yves kissing – and it's pretty full-on! How did that happen so quickly? They haven't seen each other for years, since they were cruelly torn apart. Surely they have a lot to talk about?

Well, obviously not.

Zac raises his dark eyebrows at me. My stomach does a flip. Then it does a flop and then a full pair of designer flip-flops.

What if he thinks I'm like Carlota, ready to get entwined with him at the drop of a hat!

What if he *does*? He's really pretty nice.

No! I can't believe I thought that!

'So . . . Bethany?' Zac says in that lovely French way. He doesn't look like he's about to pounce at all – which is a relief, right?

Right.

I kind of nod in a bit of a weirdo way.

But Zac doesn't seem to mind. He starts asking me about school stuff, like where I go and what GCSEs I'm doing. He tells me he's doing this thing he calls 'the Bac', which he says is like A-levels. Which means he's the same age as Declan. If Declan could see me now, would he be jealous of Zac sitting so close to me? If he was jealous, would that be a good thing? I decide to push my thoughts away. Those worries belong to some other Bethany, the one sitting at home revising for GCSEs. I'm Extreme Bethany, the tour guide and limo rider.

'My father drives me crazy,' Zac says. He sounds so normal. I could be chatting to a boy from my school, if that boy put on a slight French accent and sat in a posh car. 'He has my life all mapped out for me in detail. I'll be taking over one of the hotels at some point whether I like it or not.'

Oh, and apart from things like that. Although it's not so different from me, in a way. My parents have my life planned out too. Well, Dad does. He wants me to do GCSEs, A-levels and a degree, get a safe office job and pursue a weekend singing hobby. Mum basically agrees with him (as usual) but would add settling down with a nice boy and having 2.3-recurring kids.

Though not yet, obviously.

The limo turns near Oxford Street, where Becca's mum usually drops me, Becca and Baljit off for our Saturday shopping days.

Carlota comes up for a snog break and some air. Phew – I was starting to worry about her survival skills.

'Hey, Bets, have you told Zac all about Extreme Travel?'

Hey, Lots, are you *insane*? 'Um, not exactly.'

'Because I think it's time for a challenge.'

'With them?' I ask. I don't mean to sound rude but . . . they're really going to think we're crazy.

And, you know. They'd probably be right.

Carlota grips Yves' arm as if to show that now she's found him, she's never going to let go. She's lost that timid look since the snogging, though. She's back to her abnormal self. 'Yeah,' she says, as if it was obvious.

'But they can't!' Now I sound even ruder. I turn to Zac to try to make it better. 'I mean, we don't want you to get into trouble with your dad and stuff.'

Zac grits his teeth. 'Well, you know what,' he

124

says, 'I think I want to escape for a bit longer. How does it work?'

'We'll show you,' says Carlota. 'Bets, pick a page.'

Carlota

☀ Omigod omigod!!!!

It has really happened. My crazy almost-random plan worked. I can't even think straight, I'm so happy.

I'm finally back with Yves!

He hasn't changed much, not really. He's older. Hotter. Kind of different from how I remembered him, but also the same. He still does that thing where he puts his head on one side and considers things and then just totally laughs like a lunatic.

Yes, I sort of planned this. Bets is right. But I also sort of didn't. Because I really didn't think it could happen. I thought we might maybe find the hotel, but he wouldn't be there. And he nearly wasn't – he was on his way out. It was fate that brought us together.

Also I don't know why I bothered with all that man-hunting stuff earlier. Because Bets – super-choosy, picky-pants Bets – seems totally taken with Yves' cousin. I don't know why I didn't think of it before! Zac always had this reputation for being the sensible one, the one who showed Yves up and got his dad saying, 'Why can't you be more like your cousin?' Zac never smoked or took stuff or got into trouble at school. He's perfect for Bets.

And Yves, of course, is perfect for me.

I was a bit awkward with him at first. I didn't know how to be around him. Everything felt a bit different. But when I sat beside him in the limo, well, he smelled the same. So I decided to go for it, take up where I left off, pretend we hadn't been apart for two years. And I kissed him.

It was easy.

And it's AMAZING! He's mine again! I should have done this long, long ago. I should have run away from home and gone to Brussels to see him, all those times I thought about it. Why didn't I? Why did I stay in London snogging all those English boys? I'm mad, that's why! And, yeah, The Diplomat locks my passport away. But I could have worked it out somehow. What was I afraid of?

Well, never again! We've found each other now and This Is It!

Everyone stares at the four of us as we get out of the limo. I hear some nearby girl say to her friend, 'It's Hayden, I'm sure it is.' They have to be talking about Bets, since I'm way more dusky and curvy than Hayden Panettiere. I'm more of a size sixteen Vanessa Hudgens, you know. Only without the innocent expression! Mwah-ha-ha!

Anyway, I nudge Bets and say, 'Did you hear that? They think you're Hayden!' It would give anyone a confidence boost, being compared to a glamorous actress. But she shakes her head and says, 'No way.'

Argh! She drives me crazy. I've just got to keep building up her confidence today and show her she's a superstar and Declan doesn't deserve her. Zac could help out with that too!

We go into this huge shop near Piccadilly Circus which Zac calls an 'entertainment superstore'. Bets's random magazine page was the music, book and film review section, and Zac suggested coming here. The limo driver grumbled like mad about the change of direction – he waffled on about his job and Zac's dad, but then he cranked up the in-car techno surround sound and drove us here anyway.

I wrap myself around Yves, sniffing his beautiful (expensive) aftershave, the one I never thought I'd smell again. I used to find department store testers just to get a whiff of it, but it was never the same when it wasn't mixed with him. And now it is! Genuine Eau de Yves!

He gives me a smile that makes my insides melt and says, 'Zac and I are heading over there, to the books. Manga and stuff, you know.' He looks a bit embarrassed – cute or what?! 'Do you mind?'

I laugh at his expression. 'Mind?' I say. 'We'll come with you. Bethany loves books. Don't you, Bets? You've been dying to read books all day.'

She makes this funny noise at me but the boys have already split away from us anyway. It looks a bit snorey where they're headed, so I stop at the pop-star biographies shelf and leaf through a book about Beyoncé Knowles.

'She should wear more white,' I tell Bets, who has stopped beside me. The glam black sparkly outfit looks all wrong on her. The sooner I spread the Reverse Goth word, the better!

'Yeah,' Bets says like she's not really listening. She's staring in the direction of the boys and shifting from foot to foot. 'Lots, can we talk?'

'Yeah, sure.' I follow her gaze. 'Didn't I tell you Yves was wonderful?'

'Yeah, once or twice.'

'He's amazing! And Zac's nice too, don't you think?' She shifts a bit more. She seems nervous. Uh-oh! Why didn't I think of this? She isn't giving herself *permission* to like Zac! I should have known my loyal friend Bets would be like this! That's probably why she didn't like Ash either, or Connor, or that dodgy backpacker from Tring who I didn't even bother chatting up for her.

'Bets, you're allowed to fancy other guys, you know.'

'No, I'm not. I'm . . . I've got a boyfriend. And also . . . well, it's just wrong.'

Honestly, sometimes I forget that Bets's cute 'n' innocent act is, well, not an act at all. She's really like that! 'So? Declan's not here. Have some fun!'

'Lots, I can't!'

'Course you can!'

'I can't. I shouldn't even be here.' She stares at the floor.

Oh, I can't stand seeing her like this! I take a deep breath. 'Bets, stop worrying. We're female, remember? We're totally in control.'

She doesn't look convinced, even though she's heard me say all this before. But I have to try again – I can't have her standing there worrying about some stupid boy not ringing her. I mean, how nineteenth century is that?

'Bets, remember what I told you? Men – boys – want you to think that they're the boss, but they're not. Not unless you let them be. That's why they always have to beat their chests and act all loud. To remind us they exist. Because they know we don't need them. We have the power!'

'Maybe we have the power,' she says, looking in the direction of Yves and Zac, 'but they have the limo and the hotel.'

I shake my head. 'This is about more than money. It's like The Diplomat – he thinks he rescued Veronica with his high-powered job and sending me to Euro-brat school. But deep down, he knows he needs her more than she needs him. She was doing perfectly well before he came along! And that's why he always resorts to shouting and throwing his weight around. He feels like he has no balls.'

This is serious stuff, but Bets starts giggling as soon as I say the word 'balls'. And The Diplomat thinks I'm the immature one out of me and Bets!

'It's not funny! I'm Spanish, remember. Balls are very important to us,' I explain. But that sets her off even more.

Well, I can't talk to her when she's in this mood, but at least I've cheered her up. Anyway, she knows I'm right. I'm always right about everything to do with boys. I don't know how it happened, but I am definitely some kind of boy expert. It's a talent I was born with, I think. I can judge them straight off.

All except Yves.

Bethany

Just as Carlota stops talking about balls and goes all spacy-Yves-faced again, the whole shop darkens.

I look up but the lights are still on. Weird. I glance at my mobile but it's not very late. Oh, God, am I going to faint? Is this a pregnancy thing? My heart pounds.

I try walking a bit, to see if it helps. I walk round the bookcase Carlota's leaning on. A flashing light blinds me for a second and I see red dots in front of my eyes.

This is it! I'm going to pieces! The stress has driven me mad!

Then, through the red dots, I notice people climbing over each other in the shop window. Grown men with cameras.

Paparazzi. That's who they are. They're crowded at the window, taking pictures of me.

Of *me*.

What's going on? My first thought is that they think I'm Hayden Panettiere, like Lots said outside, but honestly, that's ridiculous. I mean, my clothes are from Primark. I look about as LA as a full English breakfast with extra black pudding.

And yet there they are. Loads of scruffy-looking men in puffy waistcoats with long-lens cameras, snapping away at me.

I want to run away but I find I can't move. I'm caught in the flashing lights. Carlota pokes her head round the bookcase, but she's no help. She just sort of gasps.

The scruffy men in the window gesture at me with their hands as if they want to shove me aside. Then I notice that a shop assistant, a man with a small tufty beard, dressed all in black and actually looking a lot like Milo Ventimiglia, is looking at me with a sardonic smile on his lips.

There are also two giant men towering behind me and a tiny woman looking at some sheet music. They don't seem to notice me or the photographers. It's so strange that no one else is bothered by the flashing lights.

I finally find my voice. 'What's going on?' I ask the black-clad Milo-lookalike assistant.

'Trix is in the shop,' he states simply. He nods in

the direction of the tall men and the tiny woman.

I look at him as if he's mad. 'Trix? *The* Trix? How's—?' *How's that possible?* I'm thinking, but I turn and see her, and say, 'TRIX!'

I say this right in Trix's face.

And it sounds like I just said, '*How's tricks*?' to her, which has to be an unspeakably cringey thing to say to a famous singer whose name is Trix.

It's definitely her, anyway. She's the tiny lady. Seeing her close up like this, well, I'd almost say she's nothing special to look at. But she's got this presence, or whatever it is. She sort of shines. I stare at her.

The tall men on either side of her stand like stone pillars. Bodyguards, of course. I can't believe I didn't notice it before: that these huge men had gone shopping with a little lady but they weren't actually looking at anything in the shop. Or, you know, moaning about the little lady taking too long, and wanting to wait in the pub or the bookies, like my dad does if he ever goes shopping with my mum.

Trix smiles at me and lowers her dark glasses. 'I'm good. Hi there,' she says. Says TRIX to ME. Her eyes twinkle. I can practically see a little spark in one eye, going, *Ting!* like in a cartoon.

'Hello,' I mumble. I don't move. I want to tell her I'm a huge fan of hers, but as soon as I think the word 'fan', a Dad joke pops into my head. I'm *this* close to saying, *What do you call a man who used to worship farm machinery?* Luckily I don't say that, or add, *An ex-tractor fan.* It feels so weird standing near a real-life famous singer. It's like she has Carlota's confidence multiplied by a million. It's overwhelming. She must need it, though, to sing in public. That must be what it's all about.

Why are my thoughts waffling on while I'm staring at Trix? She must think I'm crazy.

'Well, bye,' I say because, after all, she's just a person, isn't she? Which doesn't explain why my legs feel shaky.

'Bye.' She pats her glasses back into place and goes back to her shopping.

The men's eyes dart around in all directions, taking everything in. One of them looks towards the back of the shop, where Yves and Zac are obliviously leafing through comics.

The photographers keep snapping me. I imagine my picture in *OK!* magazine. *Mysterious Hayden Panettiere not-lookalike gets in the way of perfectly good shots of Trix that could have made starving paparazzi some cash.*

When the flashes die down, I dart round the bookcase, where Carlota is waiting for me. She looks totally star-struck.

'Oh my God, Bethany,' she whispers. 'You just talked to Trix. People took pictures of you with Trix!'

'I know,' I say, feeling a bit special, which is pretty

stupid really, but there it is. 'Why don't you come over and say hi too?'

'I want to but my legs won't move.' Carlota leans against the bookcase and sinks to a sitting position on the ground. I flop down next to her and we watch the Trix-and-bodyguards party heading for the staff area, maybe to leave the shop through a back entrance. The photographers stop blacking out the windows and the sun streams in. It's like the end of a total eclipse.

Carlota and I sit in silence for a while. I pick up the nearest book, which is a biography of my grandad's favourite group, The Beatles. I flick it open at a photo of John Lennon.

Ah, noooooo! Dad's voice echoes spookily in my head with lines from The Chat, like a film voiceover. *John Lennon had his O-levels, Bethany . . . You need something to fall back on . . . You need a safety net.*

All my worries pour back: I should talk to Declan, I should use that test, I should be revising.

And that's when a paragraph from the page opposite the photo catches my eye: Liverpool Art College . . . *Despite Lennon failing all his O-levels the headmaster made a special recommendation . . .*

I nearly drop the book.

'Oh my GOD, Lots! Look at this.'

'What?' Carlota glances over. She sounds weak. 'Don't tell me John Lennon's here. I couldn't take seeing a ghost as well.'

'It's bigger than that.' I wave the book at her. 'John Lennon didn't have any GCSEs, or whatever. He failed them. All of them.'

Carlota reads it and looks at me open-mouthed. 'Wow, Bets. Hasn't your dad been pushing John Lennon's exam passes at you since you were tiny?'

'Yep.' I gaze at the book. 'My dad's based all his lectures to me and Rowan on a total lie.'

'He must think it's true.'

'He did. My grandad told him. To stop him trying to be musician.'

'Wow.'

'I know.' This is huge.

It's like I've been given a licence to stop stressing. Life happens whether you worry or not. People become megastars whether they have a safety net or not. Girls get pregnant whether they use contraception or not.

Oops, that wasn't a good one.

Well, still. It won't change anything if I worry right now. I want to be reckless and free like Carlota. No, I want to *be* Carlota, even if it's just for the day.

Just one thing, though. I'm going to tell Carlota about my pregnancy scare. Right now. Because, you know what? I think she's going to tell me I'm over-reacting. I think I *am* overreacting. I always *over* think everything. I'm just going to tell her calmly – it's too late now anyway, isn't it? I just need to *deal*. Like a grown-up. I need to stop running and hiding.

'Carlota' – I'll say it quickly – 'this might sound stupid, but—'

'Hey,' says Yves. Zac is behind him, holding a small plastic bag. He must have bought some books from the sardonic Milo Ventimiglia. Well, that's the end of my confession to Carlota.

'You two OK?'

'Help us up,' Carlota moans next to me.

Yves offers Carlota a hand. He keeps holding her hand once she's up. Her face lights up in a huge smile.

Zac holds his hand out to me. I take it. It makes me go all dizzy inside. It feels like the beginning of something.

Not to him, though. He lets go of my hand as soon as I'm standing up. I almost crash back down to the ground in disappointment.

'Let's do another challenge. Let's go somewhere else,' I say. Somewhere, anywhere, to freedom.

Carlota

☀ 'So you see what Extreme Travel is all about?' I tell Yves and Zac, back in the limo. 'It really works! Bets chose her destiny and she ended up meeting a real-life star!' I push myself close to Yves. It's hard to think straight when he smells so yum.

He hesitates for about a second and then puts his arm round me.

Bets, beside me, gives Zac a shy smile. I think meeting Trix has helped her understand what I've been telling her all along – it's all about confidence. If you're confident, boys want to snog you, girls want to *be* you. Even *I* felt in awe of Trix just now – she had this special air about her!

And Bets has also found a fact in the Beatles book that makes her dad's lectures disappear into dust. It's like instant chill-out! I was so right about Extreme Travel! *Teen Spice!* always has the best advice. I just need to keep this going – I'm not far off being able to tell her what I know about Declan and Becca, and her not caring at all!

'So, who's next? Zac, Yves, you want to have a go?'

The limo driver moans at Zac – something about his dad phoning and expecting Zac at work. Yves' uncle sounds like he'd get on well with my stepdad.

Then Zac sighs and punches some numbers into a teeny-tiny clam-like phone. He starts speaking French, pleading with his dad for time off, saying he's run into some old friends. I try not to smirk – 'old friends'? I've only met Zac once before, and Yves is way more than a friend! It seems that, when it comes to parents, we're all liars.

But they drive us to it! Parents, I mean. When people don't let you be yourself, you're forced to lie. What choice do you have?

'My father says we can have another hour or so,' he announces, clipping his phone shut.

'It's your life. You mess it up,' the driver grumbles, but he starts the engine. 'OK, where to, boss?'

'As if! We're colleagues. We both work for my father.' Zac gives a dry laugh. Then he turns to me. 'How do I do this?'

Great! I hand him the magazine. 'Just open it any-where. Or you can choose a page number that means something to you.' I wait as he follows my instruc-tions. 'What did you get?'

'Er . . . horoscopes.' Zac shows us a page filled with swirly astrological pictures.

'Well, that's a pretty obvious challenge!' I snuggle into Yves. 'You should find a fortune-teller or a palm reader or whatever. Some mystic gypsy type to see into your future.' And I can find some magical corner to be alone with Yves. 'Anyone know where we can go?'

'My mum used to go to this little place that's pretty central,' Zac says. 'A tarot reader.'

Yves pulls away from me slightly and asks Zac, 'You OK?'

'Yeah.' His eyes go a bit shiny, and I remember when his mother died and Yves was busy with family stuff for a while and I missed him like crazy. 'Mum used to say it was better than counselling. And Dad said it was a load of nonsense, like counselling.' Zac gives an embarrassed laugh and says over-brightly, 'Should we find it?'

There's a bit of a silence and I'm sort of wishing I

138

hadn't suggested fortune-telling after all, since we've obviously brought up painful memories for Zac.

Then Bets says, natural as anything, 'Yeah, let's go.'

She beams a smile at Zac. I just know she's made him feel better. I want to hug myself about how well things are going between them. This is what it's all about!

Zac gives his driver instructions and tells us, 'I don't know the exact address, but I know it was on that road somewhere. Dad drove her there once and I sat outside listening to him complaining. It's in a shop that sells crystals and new-age stuff.'

I can just imagine this tarot reader. 'Ooh, I bet she'll be really mystic. Like, with big earrings and a head-scarf, and called something like Madame Zorastra!'

'Lots!' Bets laughs. 'I'm sure she'll be totally normal.'

It turns out Bets is more or less right. The shop smells of joss sticks, but mixed with frying oil, probably because it's opposite a huge chain burger place. It looks pretty ordinary too, despite the jangly new-age music that's playing. Also, the person behind the counter looks like Ms Harris from school, all curly hair and trouser suits. Only she looks less mean and she's wearing about a hundred bracelets.

I idly pick up a crystal and turn it over in my hand. Madame Zorastra, or whatever her name is, looks right at me. There's something in her eyes, like a knowingness. I suddenly panic. Just how psychic are these people? I don't really want someone looking into my deeper soul! What if they discover I don't actually have one, mwah-ha-ha!

'Malachite,' says Madame Zorastra, nodding towards my crystal. 'It's interesting that you picked that up. It represents unburdening. Are you a Capricorn?'

I put the stone down quickly, as if it had burned my hand. I exchange a glance with Bets. 'No, but she is.'

Freaky.

'Aquarius cusp,' Bets mumbles.

'Interesting. You girls have a strong connection, don't you?'

I stare at her. This was a terrible idea. Madame Zorastra really seems to know stuff!

She smiles kindly. 'So are you here for a reading?'

Zac answers, muttering something about his mother coming here. I'm glad he doesn't say anything about magazine destiny, because now that we're faced with the real thing, it's freaking me out.

'Oh, she would have seen Julie. I'm really sorry but she isn't here. I've been learning from her, though, and I can do you a cut-price reading if you want one.'

'Julie. That was it,' Zac mumbles.

Julie, huh? It doesn't sound all that mystic. Mind you, if this Madame Zorastra is just a trainee and she's spooking me out big time, I don't think I'd like to meet Juju-Julie.

Madame Zorastra jangles her bracelets. 'Did all of you want readings?'

No, no! Not me! And Bets shouldn't have one either! What if Madame Zorastra tells Bets everything before she's ready?

Or Yves. What if she tells him I've been stalking him?

I try to beam thoughts into Madame Zoroastra's head: *Not us! Only Zac!*

'Only, I'm so sorry to have to say this,' she says, 'but you do have to be over eighteen. It's policy.'

I laugh with relief. 'That's only Zac, then!'

Yves does that adorable puffed-out-chest thing he does when he's affronted. 'I'm eighteen . . .'

'In your dreams!'

'. . . in May!'

I laugh and kind of pull him aside. I love the way he acts like such a baby – I'm surprised he didn't say he was 'seventeen and a half and three quarters'! I also love being reminded that I'm almost exactly two years younger than him – I've always thought it was the perfect age gap.

Well, I hope Madame Zorastra isn't reading my mind now, because what I'm thinking about is *getting him alone.* 'Yves, you didn't want to do this anyway, did you?'

His chest un-puffs. 'No, not really.'

'Well, I'm hungry. Fancy taking me to the burger place, like old times?' I give him my flirtiest smile,

141

which is saying something.

'Um, yeah, OK.'

He glances at Zac and says, 'Will you be OK?'

Zac nods.

'Bets will stay with him,' I announce, and she squirms but not exactly in an unhappy way. This couldn't have worked out better if I'd planned it, although I suppose I did plan it, a bit.

I reach for Yves' hand. 'Are we going to get kids' meals?'

'Yeah, all right, but you'd better not steal my toy when I'm not looking!'

He remembers! I rest my head on his shoulder and laugh as we leave. Those years we were apart? They've vanished into nothing.

Bethany

'Does your girlfriend want to be present for the reading?'

I don't know where to look. She's obviously not very psychic if that's what she thinks.

Zac must feel as awkward as I do because he mumbles, 'Er, no, she's not . . .'

I stare very hard at the board that advertises TAROT READINGS WITH JULIE, ADV. DIP. ASTROLOGY, AND KATH. FOR ENTERTAINMENT ONLY AND NOT EXPERIMENTALLY PROVEN.

So the psychic's name must be Kath, and she's

clearly not as good as Julie, because she has no letters after her name. Not that I think that matters any more, now I know that I don't really need GCSEs to cook burgers or be a pop star, despite what Dad's been telling me for years.

'We're just friends,' I tell Kath the trainee tarot reader.

She doesn't seem embarrassed by her mistake – unlike me and Zac, who haven't managed to look at each other since. 'Well, friends are welcome to sit in on a reading too, if it's OK with the client.'

Zac says, 'Er, well, yeah, OK. If you want to, Bethany.'

I'm not sure if I want to, but Lots is off with Yves and I don't want to stand on my own looking at crystals, and besides, I'm curious. About tarot reading, but also about Zac. I wouldn't mind knowing a bit more about him. Just, you know, out of interest.

'I'll get things ready. Wait here a minute.'

After Kath has gone, Zac and I stand about in silence.

'It's weird to think this is where my mum used to come,' he says eventually. 'Things were really different then.' He says this so easily, I can't help but be flattered that he doesn't mind talking to me like this.

'I'm sorry about your mother,' I tell him.

'Thanks. It was a few years ago now. I was ... you know. Younger.' He frowns like he's concentrating

143

hard. 'I mean, don't feel bad. It's a bit strange being here, but I'm enjoying myself right now. Really. And the best thing is that I've got away from my father for a while.' He smiles at me.

'Do you think your dad keeps a tight rein on you because he's lost your mum, and he's scared of losing you too?' I ask, and then I kind of kick myself, because I'm sure I shouldn't be trying to psycho-babble-analyse a total stranger. But it feels natural somehow, talking to him like this.

'Maybe.' He shrugs. 'He did get a bit worse afterwards. But mostly it's just what he's like. A control freak. I'm a bit like that too – like father, like son.' He picks a piece of fluff off his immaculate suit, as if to prove it. Then he catches me looking at him and laughs. 'See what I mean?'

'You missed a bit,' I joke, finding a piece of fluff on the arm of his jacket and picking it off for him.

'Thanks.'

We both go quiet again.

I get this sudden impulse to giggle at him, Becca-with-Harrison style, but thankfully Kath appears and tells us she's ready.

She leads us into a small kitchen with a round white table and some chairs in the middle and a row of freshly washed mugs lined up by the sink. Everything looks clean, basic and functional. In fact, it looks a lot like the kitchen at Dad's work, except that the rota pinned to the wall lists CHAI, ROSEHIP

AND CAMOMILE rather than TEA, COFFEE AND SUGAR. I think Carlota got to me with all her talk of Madame Zorastra, and I was expecting crystal balls and broomsticks, or something.

Kath sits down and motions for us to join her. She talks for ages about the process and how it's a two-way thing, and Zac should relax and clear his mind and tell her if he has any worries, or a specific question for her. She hands him a large deck of cards and tells him to hold them and think peaceful thoughts. I'm so glad it's not me doing this. My thoughts are racing. I keep wondering about Zac, wanting to know more about him, amazed that he'd want to go through something like this, and in front of me too. It feels, well . . . intimate. I also feel like holding his hand – just to reassure him, you know.

Kath tells Zac to hold the cards and then choose as many as he wants. He chooses three and Kath studies them.

'Do you have a question?'

Zac glances at me. 'Er, I don't know. Just the usual. What's in the future, I suppose. I didn't really plan on doing this today. Or, um, ever, really.'

Kath studies the cards.

Zac picks at the knees of his trousers.

I whisper, 'Do you want me to go?'

He shakes his head.

Kath makes clucking noises that are oddly soothing. 'OK, this card. The fool – this is about new

145

beginnings, but it could also be a warning.'

Zac kind of shrugs, looking at the door as if he's had enough and wants to escape now. 'That's appropriate. My father's going to think I'm a fool for doing this,' he says quietly.

Kath runs with it. 'Hmm, yes, I can see you're very sensitive to your dad's needs, which is admirable, but you're possibly *too* sensitive. It could be time to break away, strike out alone. This card suggests a need for change in your relationships. Especially because you've chosen this one too – the queen of cups. This signifies a woman in your life . . . your girlfriend?'

'Well, I suppose it could be . . .' Zac shifts in his chair. 'My girlfriend . . .' His eyes flit briefly over to me. 'Never mind. That's interesting.'

I nearly insist to Kath again that I'm not his girl-friend, but then it occurs to me that they're not talking about me. He probably does have one. A girl-friend, that is. Someone who's not me. Because, obviously, I'm not remotely his girlfriend. And why shouldn't he have a girlfriend? It's none of my business!

'Well, there are issues around this person, this woman who's relatively new in your life. The way this card came up suggests growth, or a new life, which could be a challenge, emotionally, but could ultimately . . .'

Growth? *A new life?*

146

I don't want to listen to this! What am I doing here?

I wish I could disappear without saying anything, and definitely without making that horrible scraping sound with my chair that makes them both stare at me.

'Oh, um, sorry. I, er, have to go.'

Zac looks worried. 'OK, Bethany.'

Kath says calmly, 'A reading can be an intense experience.'

I hurry out of the room and don't stop walking until I'm outside the shop. Which is where I see Yves, speaking into his phone, laughing and saying, 'No, definitely wear the black one. You look so hot in that.' And before he notices me, he says, 'Miss you too, babe.'

For a second I even stupidly think he's talking to Carlota. But she's in the burger bar, of course. She's sitting on a high stool facing outwards and she waves happily at me. So why would he miss her?

The answer is obvious. Yves is talking to his girl-friend.

Yves and Zac both have girlfriends.

Of course they do! Why am I even surprised about that?

Carlota is going to hate this. It's so obvious that, for her, Yves isn't like those millions of boys she snogs at school. He means something to her.

But what's Yves doing, getting entwined with

147

Carlota all morning when he has a girlfriend?

Yves gives me a guilty look and wraps up his conversation with a 'Bye, Aimee-cakes, love you.'

Well. I can't help the way this makes me feel. It's so wrong!

I think Yves is reacting to the look on my face when he says, 'Um, listen, I wasn't exactly expecting Carlota to walk back into my life today.'

That's not the point, I think. He didn't have to kiss her.

'Well, you should at least tell her about *Aimee-cakes*,' I say. 'Or I will.'

And suddenly it doesn't matter how chilled out I felt before, back in the bookshop. Because now I'm stressing for England again. I'm worried about Yves breaking Carlota's heart, even though I think she should know the truth.

But I'm also worried about this other girl. This Aimee. Yves is messing around behind her back, pretending there's nothing wrong.

He's making a fool of her, the way Declan might be making a fool of me.

Carlota

☀ Back in the limo, I lean my head on Yves' shoulder but he pulls away with an odd expression on his face. He always was mysterious, my Yves. Even when we were together, he'd be all

148

over me one minute and then all distant the next. It drove me crazy! I nearly forgot about that side of him.

Bets is acting funny too – Zac keeps asking her if she's OK and she keeps insisting she is, but I'm not convinced. I wonder if Madame Zorastra freaked her out with her psychic powers. Old Zo-Zo probably told Bets and Zac they were meant for each other or something! Well, I must be more psychic than her, because I can see it without a crystal ball.

I nudge Yves. 'It's your turn to choose your destiny.'

'Aw, Carlota, I don't know.' He looks at his cousin. 'Zac and I need to get back. If I don't stay in Uncle André's good books, that'll be the end of my stay in London.'

Zac waves a hand dismissively. He seems a lot more chilled than before we visited Madame Zorastra, so she must have told him something good. 'If there's a problem, I'll sort it out.'

'Go on then.' I press the magazine at Yves.

He makes a face and just opens it any-old-where, which I know is the whole idea but I can't help feeling disappointed that he isn't putting more effort into this.

'What did you get?'

'It's an advert for a games console.'

'Ah, that one!' I laugh and do my Lara Croft impression at Yves. That should perk him up a bit. Mwah-ha-ha! 'Great! We can all go to Soho!'

Bets catches my eye and says quickly, 'Lots, I don't know.'

'Why Soho?' Zac asks me.

'To a games arcade,' I say, even though Bets's eyes are going: No, no.

'Cool!' Zac says. He leans in towards Bets. 'What do you play?'

She blushes and shifts away from him, making it so obvious she fancies him while trying not to, being Bets. Well, it's obvious to me, anyway.

She starts babbling – another sure sign. 'I don't really play. I mean, I do sometimes, but not in arcades or anything. It's Carlota who wanted to go there – she said so before.' She takes a deep breath, which I'm not surprised she needs, the way she's squashing all her words together. Honestly, she desperately needs another of my Boy Snaring lessons! 'My brother Rowan is an *Instant Kombat* fan – you know, that cult version of *Street Fighter* – and he said he could never be beaten by a girl, and when he's home from uni I want to prove him wrong.'

Phew, she's stopped.

'Mordor Mayhem's better than Soho for gaming,' Zac says. 'Er, I've heard.'

Yves smiles a bit at last. 'Gaming geek.'

Zac grins. 'Speak for yourself, *Grand Theft Auto* slave.'

'Mordor Mayhem's a cool name,' I tell Yves, and Bets's mouth hangs open like she can't believe I said that. At least she doesn't speak any more, though.

Zac gives the driver instructions. The driver

grumbles, drives, grumbles and drives. They must be his two main skills.

Mordor Mayhem is darkly lit and filled with *Lord of the Rings* posters and figurines, as well as shelves of games consoles and cartridges. It's more of a shop than an arcade. But never mind – it's still filled with males. They're sitting at tables looking intense, throwing dice and arguing loudly with each other about elves or whatever. Some of them are pretty nice – they have a geekish intensity I usually find irresistible. But I'm back with Yves now. I drape myself around him.

Bets is hesitating by the door, looking like she's at the dentist's or something. I thought she'd decided to go with the flow – what happened? For a minute I feel guilty – here I am, showing off my Yves-related happiness when she's in the middle of a serious boy-crisis. And then this little, terrible part of me goes, *Now she knows how it feels* – all that time she was so couply with Declan, when Yves wasn't even emailing me. I shake that thought off quickly.

'Zac, you and Bets should go and find that fighty game she likes.'

'Oh, yeah,' Zac says. 'They have it in the arcade room. I mean, I think they do.'

Bets gives me and Yves a worried look before she trails off behind Zac, but I know I'm doing the right thing. Zac's clearly mega into her and they need to be alone.

151

Besides, I want Yves all to myself.

'OK. What shall *we* play?' I gaze up into his eyes and wait for him to woo me with his wonderful voice.

'Er . . . We could try the new XYZ-one two three,' he says, only not exactly those letters or numbers. Quite honestly, I can't be bothered to listen because I know it's just a cover and we'll start snogging as soon as we find a quiet corner, and I can't wait.

'Sure,' I say.

He spends absolutely ages going, 'XYZ, ABC, one two three,' or whatever, at the Harry Potter lookalike behind the counter, and at last he comes back with this pink gadget and two cartridges.

'Pink?' I'm slightly shocked. I was a million miles from being a pink sort of girl when we went out together. Doesn't he remember?

Oh. Well, I suppose he's trying to be thoughtful, getting something girly for me. Anyway, it's not like we're really going to play, is it? We can catch up, get to know each other again. Oddly enough, for me, I don't just mean Kisses Etcetera either. I really want to talk to him. I want to know why he didn't try harder to get in touch with me after I left, for a start. Maybe the emails were blocked, but there had to be some other way of reaching me. I thought I could ask him this stuff in the burger bar but as soon as we got our food he disappeared to take some work call, and I ended up eating all by myself. I had a good view of him from across the street, though, and I took the opportunity to steal his kids' meal toy.

I choose a quiet corner table and we sit down. I edge along my seat, closer to him.

He starts fiddling with the computer thingy.

'Hey, Yves.' I decide to go for it. What do I have to lose? 'So I've been meaning to ask – where have you been all my life?' I laugh. 'Well, OK, the last two years.'

He acts like putting the cartridge in the gadget is the most important thing in the world.

I don't care. He's probably just nervous. It's been a long time. At least we've already picked up where we left off in the snogging stakes. That's what counts. The talking might take longer, and that's fine. Chatting's always more difficult than kissing, for a boy. For me too, if I'm honest.

I reach over and run my hand through his hair. 'You haven't changed,' I say.

'Neither have you,' he says, finally meeting my eyes.

I feel like snogging his face off – again – right now. And I almost do. But there's this small part of me that still wants to know.

'So what happened after I left?' I try to keep my voice light. 'Did everyone talk about me?'

'Yeah.' He smiles to himself, and it's extremely sexy. 'The rumours got kind of wild.'

'I bet they did.' I bet he didn't try to stop them either. Yves always loved his reputation. I keep my voice playful. 'Did you miss me?'

'Everyone missed you.'

Well, yeah. Course they did. I used to liven up the lessons; I was always in trouble. I try again, as lightly as I can manage: 'Did *you* miss me?'

He looks down again and mumbles, 'Yeah.'

OK. That's all I needed to hear! I feel lighter, like I've dropped a clothes size instantly. It's the Yves diet! I laugh. 'Never mind! We're here now, and that's what matters.'

'Er, yeah. Listen, though . . .'

I move again so that I'm almost sitting on his lap. I wind my arms around him.

He glances around at all the geeks. What? They're all involved in their dice and dragons, or whatever! Besides, he was all over me in the limo earlier. Or was I all over him? Well, it's the same end result!

I kiss his earlobe.

'Carlota' – he clears his throat – 'people are watching.' He hands me the games thing.

It's frustrating. People are so not watching. But he's probably right. We need to talk, not kiss.

But now that I know he's missed me as much as I've missed him, I can't think of a lot else to say.

I press some buttons at random. 'How does it work?'

'Not like that.' He takes it out of my hand.

'I've probably broken it,' I announce idly. 'I usually do. My stepdad won't let me near his computer. It was always a real pain, trying to send you emails. I had to

154

send them in the middle of the night.'

I hope he appreciates the efforts I went to. I think he must, because he says vaguely, 'It was always great to hear from you.'

'I hope you weren't too upset when I stopped sending you messages.'

'Er . . . oh.'

'Because there's an explanation, you know. I wasn't hearing back from you. I mean, at all. I think I've worked out why, though.'

He shifts about in his seat. 'Carlota, listen. Please don't take this the wrong way . . .'

'Take *what* the wrong way?' My heart thuds.

'It's just . . . you know, I couldn't believe it when I saw you there, in Uncle André's hotel!'

'It was an entirely random thing,' I explain, because I'm starting to think he has the edge here, and I can't have that. 'It wasn't like I *set out* to see you. It was part of our Extreme Travel. But at least we're back together now.'

'Yeah, about that—'

His phone rings, blaring a cheesy rap song like it did in the burger place. He's changed – he used to be a total techno boy! I don't know why his work keeps calling him either – can't they bug Zac instead?

He gets up and nods at me as if he's asking for permission. He cups the phone in his hand and walks around, but he doesn't move far from me this time. I can still hear him.

'Yes? OK. No, I haven't changed my mind in the last half-hour.'

I tap the games console. Useless thing. Why does everything break when I touch it?

'Yeah, I know. I miss you too,' Yves says clearly into his phone. 'I love you too.'

Bethany

I follow Zac into the arcade room in a total grump. I feel like I have no choice but to do this. I need to give Lots and Yves this time together to sort things out – he needs to tell her. And so I suppose I'm stuck with Zac and the game I waffled on about in the limo, when I was stalling for time. I wish I could have thought of an excuse for me and Lots to leave these boys behind and do something else – preferably something like going home and forgetting this whole crazy day.

The only people in the room are a couple of boys huddled by a shooting game. There are hundreds of other machines barking deep-voiced orders and twinkling their lights to tempt us.

'*Instant Kombat*'s over here,' Zac calls to me, all friendly. Maybe even flirty.

I glare at him. I know it's not his fault that his cousin's a cheating rat, but it still feels wrong, being here like this with Zac. What if he thinks he can be like Yves? I've got to say something.

156

'Look' – I stare at the machine – 'I know you and Yves have girlfriends. And I've got a boyfriend. Just so you know,' I blurt.

Then I can't look at him.

'Oh. OK. Right,' he says. He sounds startled.

There's a mega-awkward silence. I steal a glance at Zac.

He's focused on the machine. 'Yeah, my girlfriend. Another thing my dad thinks he can control,' he says quietly.

'What? What do you mean?' He'd better not try some lame excuse here. He'd better not be finding reasons to ignore her texts, leaving her wondering, worrying, counting months.

'Just that me and Claire – we're not really together. I *don't* have a girlfriend. What the tarot reader said was interesting. Because my father wants . . .'

I hope the way I'm looking at him is bothering him. I'm thinking, So it's *Claire*, is it, this girlfriend who *doesn't exist*? Right.

'Look, it doesn't matter.' He fiddles in his pockets, then puts some coins in the slot. 'Let's play.'

Now I'm looking forward to beating him up, virtually. I used to love doing that to Rowan, only now that he's hardly ever home he doesn't get on my nerves half as much. But boys who tell out-and-out *lies*, denying they have girlfriends . . . ? Well. Zac had better watch out.

'I always used to be Rin Chine, Queen of the Night,' I tell Zac as the selection screens start up. I point to the girl with a long dark plait and serious muscles.

'Good choice, your highness.'

Huh.

'You're a fair match for Thorene, King of Power.'

Yeah? Whatever.

Zac's hair keeps flopping in his eyes. He really is gorgeous. I can't believe I'm thinking like this, after the whole Claire thing. Boys trap you with their annoying attractiveness. It's nature's mean trick.

I force myself back to the screen, where Thorene and Rin Chine are bowing at each other politely, ready to kick each other's brains out.

I get to work at the special moves I perfected on Rowan.

When Thorene's lifeline runs out for the fourth time – ha! – Zac says, 'I accept gracious defeat, my queen. I can't compete.'

I have to admit, I'm really enjoying myself. 'You can't give up! You are the great Thorene. Your fireballs are second to none. Look.' I take over his side of the controls and bash my poor alter ego about for a while, sending a few super-turbo shots her way. When I stop, I notice Zac's got a strange expression on his face.

'Wow,' he says.

Double-ha! 'That's nothing. I can do it in real life

too. Well, some of it. I had karate lessons with Rowan when he was in his Jackie Chan phase.'

'Show me.'

'What?'

'Show me your Jackie Chan.'

'No way!' I love the way he's looking at me. I smile.

I'm officially a terrible person. I must stop this *now*!

'Aw. Please, Bet?'

OK . . . why not? I demonstrate a high kick into an empty space behind us. It looks impressive, though I say so myself. Even though I feel completely stupid.

'Amazing,' he says.

My stomach does that flip-flop thing and I get goosebumps.

I ignore them.

'Well, you're holding back, Thorene,' I say. 'Get on those controls and give me a proper game.'

Zac laughs. 'All right, Lady of the Night, one more go.'

'Oi! That's *Queen* of the Night, mate.'

'Oh, yeah?' He nudges me out of the way.

I nudge him back, because he's not getting away with that. 'Yeah, so-called King of Power, prepare to be defrocked.'

'Don't you mean dethroned?'

'Yeah, that too.' What's defrocked, then? Is it

159

taking your clothes off?

Help, I can't stop these thoughts.

Poor old Rin Chine loses the next round. I swear I didn't let him win on purpose, but Zac starts throwing his body around in time with his punches, and occasionally he leans very close to me. When that happens, I have trouble pushing buttons. Also, breathing.

The machine blinks: GAME OVER.

'Let's get a coffee,' says Zac, with a catch in his voice. As we walk out, I hang back slightly so that my hand can't be tempted to reach out to his.

He's got a girlfriend. I've got a boyfriend and I think I could possibly be pregnant.

How many wrongs does it actually take to make a right?

Carlota

Maybe he's talking to his mum. Yeah, that's who Yves said 'I love you' to. It has to be.

Oh, who am I kidding? Yves always moaned about his family. His mum was like mine, post-Diplomat – cold, rich, distant. It was one of the things me and Yves had in common – crap mums and a disrespect for annoying teachers. That, and the way we made sparks fly with our Kisses Etcetera.

Let's face it: there's no way he said that to his mum. Things can't have changed that much in two years. They certainly haven't for me. If anything, my mum's got worse, even though I hang around with the Boring Bees now and I haven't got into trouble at school. Well, not big trouble, not like before. But whatever I do or don't do, it's never good enough for Veronica.

Anyway, I know Yves has to be talking to a girlfriend.

Well, so what? Of course he has someone. He's gorgeous. He didn't think he'd ever see me again. Did I expect him to stay single for ever?

But it's weird because it's exactly the kind of thing I've been looking out for on his Bebo. I've seen a million messages from random girls, all littered with things like 'xoxo' and 'ur hot'. But none of them seemed like any kind of threat.

Oh, well. I'm here now, back in his life. And I know for a fact that we still start small fires when we kiss, and I bet that doesn't happen with Little Miss Insipid I-Love-You.

Yves finishes his call by saying it again, that meaningless phrase that *Teen Spice!* has never even listed in their 'Boy Talk: What They Say and What They Mean' column, because boys never say 'I love you'. Well, why should they? I've never said it either. Bets has but she didn't know what she was talking about. And Declan came up with some rubbish instead of saying it, but really, who cares about Declan?

But Yves said it. And not to me.

He sits down and picks up the game again.

I stay where I am instead of falling into him like before.

Neither of us speak.

That's when Bets and Zac walk over from the arcade room. Bets looks kind of flushed, which is interesting.

Yves waves maniacally at Zac and goes, 'You're back! Great! Look – I've got the latest handheld.'

'Any good?' Zac asks, leaning in with boy-like gadget-happy enthusiasm.

'We can't figure it out,' Yves says.

'*We*'. Me and him. He wouldn't say 'we' if he was serious about the other girl, surely?

'You were too busy on the phone,' I say, keeping my voice neutral.

Bets gives me this crazy look, like she's dying to tell me something.

Yves says, 'Carlota . . .' I can't make out his tone. The way I can't read Yves proves that he's special to me. Other boys are so obvious, they're boring.

No one says anything for ages. I wouldn't call it a comfortable silence, but I don't care.

'Let's see it,' Zac enthuses into the emptiness. 'Hey, this looks good.' He turns to Bets, all flirty-faced, and says, 'We're not into this at all, really we're not.' He smiles as if the tension at our table isn't bordering on unbearable.

Bets catches my eye and I know she knows there's

something wrong. Without saying a word to each other, we agree to go somewhere we can talk.

I head for the ladies, which is at the far end of the room. There's probably not that much need for it in the boy world of Mordor Mayhem.

Bets comes in a few seconds after me and stands by the sinks. 'Lots, are you OK?'

'He got a call,' I tell her. 'From his girlfriend.'

'Oh.' She doesn't seem surprised.

'You knew?'

'Yes. I heard him on the phone before, outside the shop. I was going to tell you if he didn't tell you himself.'

I peer into the mirror. 'I can't believe it! How can he do this to me?'

She chews her lip. After a bit too long for my liking she says, 'Yeah, it's bad. But it has been years, hasn't it?'

'Yes, but—'

'And you've had loads of boyfriends.'

'Not really! Not proper ones!' I nearly say *Not like you and Declan*. Luckily I manage to stop myself. 'Maybe she's not a proper girlfriend. He's probably just saying things to . . . well, you know. Win her over. He had a bit of a reputation at school. All the girls were crazy about him and he *loved* it.'

Bets frowns. 'He sounds like a male version of you! Declan says the whole football team fancies you, remember? They're falling over themselves to pull you. You're the talk of the changing rooms.'

She's definitely making me feel better!

'But what am I going to do? I mean, about Yves having a girlfriend?'

And then I wish I hadn't said that, because she goes even more serious. She says, 'Well, you can't snog him any more, can you?' Her face crumples a bit. 'I mean . . . you know . . . just that I was thinking if some girl, like Lauren, was snogging Declan . . . well, it's not right! I'd hate her!' Then she looks embarrassed and adds, 'Sorry.'

Oh, no! Why can't she stop thinking about Declan?

'Yves was kissing *me*, you know,' I say. 'You should say it's not right for *him*!' When I tell her eventually – today, omigod: it has to be, because of what I promised Becca – I want to make sure she blames Declan. I'm not having her forgiving him and making excuses for weak men tempted by so-called slutty women. Though she might think that of Lauren, but I can't imagine Bets thinking of a friend in that way – she's fiercely loyal to all her friends, even Becca, who totally doesn't deserve it. Bets will probably make an excuse for *her* behaviour too.

I think a bit more. It's making my head hurt. 'Bets, how do you stand it?'

'What?'

'You know. Caring so much about boys. One boy, I mean. I'd forgotten what it was like, it's so long since I've been with Yves. I mean, it's brilliant, but it's also horrible.'

Her lips flicker in an almost-smile. 'Yeah, I know.'

'I can't stand the thought of him with someone else.'

She sighs. 'Yeah, I know.'

Now I'm nearly crying, which is unheard of for me.

'God, Bets, I'm sorry.' I'm never going to be able to tell her – to break her heart like that. Stupid bloody Becca.

I look at our misery in the mirror. This is no good! We need more Extreme Travel, we need more fun! I pull a lipstick out of my bag and take a deep breath. I focus on saying the kind of thing Bets expects me to say, which is so far from the stuff I need to tell her later. 'I'm going to show him! I'm going to make him want me!' I announce. I concentrate on putting lipstick on.

'He already does,' says my loyal friend.

'Want some?' I offer her the lipstick.

'No, thanks.'

'Worried about getting it on Zac?'

'What? No!' But she's smiling now.

'So what happened with him?'

'Not what you're thinking.'

'Oh yeah? In that dark room?'

'We were just messing around.'

'Oh, *yeah*?' I feel like myself again.

'Shut up! With the game. Is that all you think about?'

'Yup,' I say. I'm not ashamed of it. 'I gave you a snogging challenge at the start of the day, remember.'

'And I told you I'm not doing it.'

I laugh. I mean, it's not a serious matter, is it? This is snogging we're talking about! 'I don't care. The challenge is on.'

'Oh, Lots.' She sort of opens and closes her mouth like she has some awful news for me, but whatever her latest worry is, I don't want to hear it. I don't want excuses! I'm back in action, and so is she!

I link my arm through hers and say, 'Come on, let's get our men!'

'Zac's not my man, Declan is,' she grumbles on the way out, but I can tell from the look on her face that she's not completely sure about that.

Bethany

Back in the café, Yves and Zac are in the middle of a heated discussion. They stop talking when they see us. Zac smiles uncertainly, mostly at me. Yves stares at the table, although there's nothing on it. He must have taken the console back.

'Let's do something else!' Carlota says breezily, like she really doesn't care one way or the other.

'OK!' says Zac.

'We don't have time,' Yves mumbles, but he looks up.

I think the boys are responding to Carlota's lightness. Sometimes I think she controls everyone around her, and the mood she's in sets the way the rest of us behave. It's impressive.

Zac examines a very posh-looking man-watch on his wrist. He has gorgeous hands. I really have to stop staring at him. 'We can be a bit late,' he says.

'Bets! Oi, Bets! Hello?' Carlota's waving a magazine at me. 'Have another go.'

I open it on a page about the dancers from this new West End musical. There's a cheesy-grinned woman pictured in a figure-hugging brown one-piece thing that makes her look almost naked, and the headline is, DANCE IS FOR EVERYONE!

Uh-oh.

Carlota lights up even more. 'Great! Let's gate-crash some West End musical and dance on stage!'

I'm dying just thinking about it.

'Lots, I don't want to get arrested,' I moan.

'So don't do it. Just watch *me*! You've got a different challenge to complete, anyway.' She makes a jokey lip-puckery face that, because of where she's standing, only I can see. Thank goodness.

'What challenge is that?' Zac asks innocently.

Snogging you, I don't say.

Carlota starts dancing around, weaving her arms about to some soundtrack in her head.

Oops. Zac's still looking at me, expecting me to answer his question.

'What about a silent rave?' I suggest quickly.

'What's that?'

It's the first thing that came to mind, to stop me from voicing what was in my head, which was filled with the idea of . . . snogging Zac. Carlota's dancing made me think of it.

'It's, you know, when everyone gathers in some public place and dances with their headphones on, in a big crowd.' They showed one on the local news once – loads of people bopping about silently in Victoria Station. Dad called me in to see it. It looked seriously weird, but sort of fun.

Zac says, 'Sounds cool.'

'Aren't you supposed to arrange it in advance or something?' Yves says, watching Carlota dance. I narrow my eyes at him without meaning to. How dare he eye up my friend when he has a girlfriend? And how dare he have a girlfriend when my friend's wild about him?

'Let's call some friends,' Zac says.

Yeah, I think bitterly, maybe they should call their *girlfriends*.

Oh, no, I realize: I'm jealous! I'm as jealous as Carlota is, and I have even less right to be! Never mind stress relief – today is turning out to be totally confusing.

'Why do we need to call anyone?' Carlota is asking, so I know she thought the same thing I did.

'Don't we need a crowd?' Zac asks.

'Yeah, I suppose,' I say. I turn to Carlota. 'I'll call

Becca and Baljit. I bet Becca's mum can bring them in her taxi.' They need to stop revising, anyway. I wonder if the John Lennon effect will work on them?

'Maybe Baljit can tell her brothers or Becca can bring her sister too.'

'No WAY!' Carlota practically shouts. Then she gets quieter. 'I mean, we really don't need to bring people in!'

'But—' says Zac.

'But, Lots—' I say at the same time. We're so compatible. Argh, stop it, thoughts!

'I'm going! Come with me.'

She sashays out of Mordor Mayhem, where Zac's driver is waiting for us with a frown on his face.

And now, as well as me, there are two gorgeous boys following her. How does she do it?

Carlota

I'm playing hard to get with Yves and I can tell it's working. The less attention I pay him, the more he twitches around, trying to catch my eye. This works every time with boys! They're so predictable really. I'm not all that sure why we bother with them. Wait, yes I am. Mwah-ha-ha!

This isn't like with the others. It all came naturally then because, well, I honestly didn't care. This time I'm having to work at it.

I'm using the Boy Snaring tricks I taught Bets –

169

ways of thinking yourself into confidence. Right now I'm thinking, *I'm better than his girlfriend. I'm more fun.* I just have to prove it to him. By the end of today Yves will be mine and Bets will be fine. There is never anything to worry about, or at least not for long.

Back in the limo, the driver looks disapprovingly at us and says to Zac, 'Where to?'

I tell him to take us somewhere crowded.

He looks at Zac and repeats, 'Where to?'

Zac says, 'Somewhere crowded.'

I laugh. I can feel Yves watching me.

'I'll take you to work,' the driver tells Zac.

I look at Zac in alarm but he sighs and says quietly, 'I'll sort it out when we get there.'

The driver winds through busy traffic. I don't even look at Yves the whole time. After a while a giant big wheel floats into view in the distance.

'The London Eye,' Yves tells me.

Maybe he really thought I didn't know that, or my Boy Snaring is working so well that he's desperate to say something – anything – to me.

But either way, I'm glad he said it, because the London Eye is perfect for the challenge.

'Stop the limo,' I say.

The driver doesn't.

'Stop the car, please,' Zac says, smiling at me. 'Yves and I can walk to work from here – it's so close. And no way would Dad sack you – you're the best babysitter he has.'

170

The driver turns up the grumble volume, but he pulls over and we get out, with me still hanging back slightly, away from Yves.

I point to the Eye and look at Bets and Zac, but not Yves. 'Ever been up there?'

Yves answers. 'I have. Loads of times.' He's definitely trying to impress me!

But only Bets is really on my wavelength. 'You can't be serious, Lots. I'm not dancing in one of those capsules with a bunch of strangers!'

'But you said yourself we can't have a rave with just the four of us!'

I bop up to the queue, but it's massive. There's a snaky bit at the top and then it goes on for miles.

'Fast track,' says Yves, flashing his cash. Huh, like money means anything. It's him I want!

But the fast-track queue's pretty long too.

I bet these tourist types are fed up with standing about craning their necks at a slow-moving wheel, waiting for their turn. What they really need is someone to liven things up a bit. There are some street performers further up, but most of them are standing about pretending to be gold statues and stuff. Bets's idea is much more fun.

We'll do it right here.

I think Bets is reading my mind. She goes, 'Oh, no, oh, no.'

'Oh, yes. Who's got an iPod?'

'I've got my phone,' Zac says.

Yves nods and blabs a bit about how many tracks he can fit on his state-of-the-art Nokia XXX-999, or whatever.

I interrupt him. 'Earphones? Actually, we might be better off without them. Then we can all dance round one phone.'

Bets shakes her head.

'It was your idea,' I remind her. 'Play something, Yves!'

'No,' says Bets again, but she also can't help laughing when I start bopping crazily to some old dance track Yves puts on, which is a lot more like the music I remember him liking than that rap thing he has as a ringtone.

At first I'm a bit disappointed that people seem to be ignoring my dancing. I get a glance or two, but that's it.

'Join in!' I call to Bets. A few heads turn then, but just for a second.

Bets wiggles a bit and grimaces. OK, this isn't going to work! Drastic measures. I grab Yves' hand and really let myself go, unhinging my hips and pretending I'm Shakira crossed with a belly dancer.

Ah, this is more like it – more like how we used to be. He moves along with me fantastically. And I know I've got him – he's definitely mine again. I can stop playing games and just be with him. There's no deny-ing that we're made for each other.

Yves spins me round and pulls his face close to

mine, all the earlier tension forgotten. Yum. He pulls away and twirls me again.

Now people are staring.

Next to us, Bets and Zac start shuffling about in the near-silence, close but not together like me and Yves. Bets looks like she wants to die . . . until Zac takes her hand and attempts moves like ours and her face lights up. She starts laughing so much that she can barely move, let alone dance, but it doesn't matter. This is all so good for Bets! I can't imagine Declan doing anything like this in a million years.

Someone comes up and throws a pound coin on the ground at my feet.

I say, 'Take it back and join in! It's free to dance!'

Now everyone in the queue is staring at us blankly. They remind me of a herd of cows in a field, complete with slow chewing motions.

Yves grins at me, changes the track on his phone to another similar one, and totally plays up to his audience. And to me.

A giggling couple towards the back of the queue have a go and the people in front of them start shifting about too. A few people point their camera phones in our direction, and I hear the word 'crazy' in a couple of different languages. Like I care! We might get in *The Guinness Book of Records* for this!

The queue slowly comes to life in a patchy Mexican wave of dancing people, with large gaps of cow-like cud-chewers here and there. But we're definitely doing it! We're silent raving! It looks ridiculous, and it's brilliant.

Yves pulls me close as we dance. The world melts into me and Yves and Bets and Zac – and a few dozen total strangers dancing with us.

When Zac goes, 'Look at the time! My father's going to kill me!' I dance away, shouting, 'Rave on!' We leave a trail of people wiggling like deranged caterpillars behind us.

Bets has the best extreme ideas!

Bethany

Zac's right, it doesn't take long to reach L'André Hotel South Bank on foot.

From the outside, the hotel is just a tall grey building. Inside, though, it's all wood and marble and old-style surroundings – even glitzier than the Baker Street decor. There's a receptionist who looks Swedish and as skinny as Carlota's mum in her black clothes. She's busy making smoochy noises down the phone, but she hangs up as soon as she sees Zac. Then she and Zac make nervous-sounding small talk for a few seconds. She's acting like Zac's like some kind of tyrant who sacks his employees for making personal phone calls, which seems highly unlikely from what I've seen this morning. I try giving her a reassuring smile.

We take a lift to the bar, which is less grand and

more like what I'm used to from occasional Sunday lunches out with Mum and Dad. There are booths with padded seats that look like they've had a few drinks spilled on them in their time, low tables dotted with beer mats, and two men standing behind the bar looking stern.

The taller one towers towards us and booms the French for, 'Zacharie, you're late!'

I'm quite impressed with myself for understanding that, but I've heard the phrase 'You're late' a lot in French at school, so really I'm cheating. The man must be Zac's father because he takes him aside and lectures him. Now I don't understand a word, but I can tell that he's annoyed.

'Dad. Hello to you too,' Zac says in English. He motions to us to come over.

I try to smile at Zac's dad but his eyes are steely.

'Bethany, Carlota, this is André himself, the man behind the myth behind the loan behind the hotel.'

Zac's dad sounds just as stern in English. 'Zacharie, where has the *tone* come from? You're starting to sound like your brothers! Do I need to remind you—?'

'Dad. Please. Not now. This is Bethany, and Carlota's a friend from Brussels.'

Carlota gets that glint in her eye. Uh-oh. 'I am actually from eh-Spain,' she lisps.

I look at her and then at the floor. There are giggles welling up inside me, threatening to escape,

175

just like at school – Becca and Baljit are always horrified at the way I get drawn in. I rarely got told off by teachers before Carlota arrived.

Just as a half-squeak escapes from my lips, I'm saved by a bleeping sound.

Zac's dad checks his pager, huffs and waves his hand at the man behind the bar.

'Very well,' he says. 'Raymond, bring them coffees and a lunch spread. Zacharie, you're in luck, I'm needed in Mayfair. But I'll see you here on my return – and working.' He gives a nod and strained smile to me and Bets. 'Pleasure to meet you, young ladies.'

He strides out.

Carlota leads us to the furthest booth, deep in a corner of the room and hidden from Raymond and the bar. She and Yves sit next to each other – well, practically on top of each other. She's not playing hard to get any more, that's for sure.

I sit opposite them and Zac slides in next to me. I pick up a beer mat, bash it on the table, examine the writing on it and turn it over several times.

Carlota whispers something to Yves and then stands up. 'I'm going for a walk,' she says casually.

'Er, uh-huh,' Yves mumbles without looking at us as he trots after her.

I feel strange, and suddenly really hungry. My head goes, *Lunch-spread, lunch-spread*. I wonder what they'll bring us to eat. I bet it's all caviar and stuff in a place like this.

'Are you OK?' Zac asks. 'You look worried.'

'I'm not worried.' I pass the beer mat from one hand to the other.

Yeah, I'm the Queen of Chilledness from the Kingdom of the Laid Back.

I put the beer mat down. 'So that was your dad?'

Um, yeah, Bethany, smooth subject change.

'Yeah,' he says. 'Sorry about him. But at least he's gone. I'm glad you can stay a bit longer.'

Me? Just me, or all of us? If he'd been speaking French, I'd know the difference. Maybe. If I revised a bit more.

'He didn't seem that bad,' I say, although to be honest his dad reminded me of one of those scary bosses on telly, like he was about to point at me and shout, 'You're fired!'

'You saw him at his best. He can be a lot worse. He's been pretty stressed lately.'

'So you and Yves work for him?'

'Yeah, kind of. Well, Yves is here for the holidays, but with me it's a lot more serious. My father wants me to be like him, follow in his footsteps. That includes not putting a foot wrong, ever. Just like him. He decided what he wanted when he was sixteen. He went for it, he got it, he expects me to do the same.' Zac frowns.

I know that look. It seems like wherever you live, however much money you have, your parents are still guaranteed to drive you crazy.

'So it's not what you want to do then?'

'Well, maybe. It's not so bad.' Zac gestures around the room. 'But not without having a life first.' He sighs. 'And not without trying something new. I'm only eighteen. I don't want my future all decided.'

I think, *I know the feeling.*

Zac hesitates, then says, 'That tarot reader today told me that I'm stifling a need to go against my father's wishes.' He laughs as if he doesn't believe a word of it, but he adds, 'Maybe I should go to university. I could do a late application – I could study something totally unrelated to hotel management.'

'Hang on. You mean your dad doesn't want you to go to uni?' I've never heard of a dad like this. Even my mum and dad, who have about one exam pass between them, talk about university like it's the Holy Grail.

'Not unless it's part-time business school. He thinks it's all a waste of time to study what he calls McSubjects when I have a guaranteed job and a good future here.'

'But why don't you just ignore him? It's *your* life!' Yeah, good one. It took bumping into an international superstar and reading John Lennon's biography to stop me stressing over my own dad's GCSE ramblings.

Zac shrugs. 'My brothers ignored him – one's

travelling in South America and the other's a professor of philosophy in Scotland. I'm his last hope. I think it'd break his heart if I took off.'

Ah, so he has two Rowans in his family.

'But dads should be ignored. They don't know everything.' I tell him the whole John Lennon story – I think he needs to hear it. 'The thing is,' I add, 'I know that on some level my dad's right. You shouldn't take huge risks, you should have back-up plans and stay safe. I totally agree with that. I've lived it, you know. No one's more cautious than me. But sometimes, maybe, I think you might have to be reckless and go for what you want.'

I take a deep breath. But it's not hard to tell him stuff, so I go on. 'Like, I've always wanted to sing, properly, in front of people. I don't want to be a pop star or anything, I just want to be able to do it without dying of stage fright, to prove I can. I've had all these great singing lessons and I love it, but I can't even bring myself to take the exams. So now I've started dreading the lessons. But, you know, if John Lennon can do it without exam passes, then maybe so can I.'

Zac keeps nodding like he understands, even though I'm not sure if I'm making any sense myself.

I realize I've talked about myself non-stop for ages. 'Anyway, next time your dad's having a go, remember that. He might be basing his whole life's beliefs on nothing, like my dad and his John Lennon thing. You don't have to listen to him.'

Zac has a gorgeous laugh. 'I'll bear it in mind.'

'You should.' I fiddle madly with the beer mat again. 'Was, er, your mum like that too? Did she agree with your dad?' As soon as I say it, I worry that I shouldn't have.

'Never!' He sighs a bit, but I can tell he doesn't mind that I've brought it up. 'The trouble is, now I have a stepmother who agrees with everything he says, and I hear it all in stereo.'

'God, snap! That sounds like my mum. She chronically agrees with my dad, like she's got no mind of her own.' Except that one moment this morning, but I don't want to think about that. 'And she's even worse around other people's dads. Like Carlota's. I swear Mum's scared of Carlota's dad, and she goes all' – I make my voice high-pitched and gushy – 'Ooh, yes, you're so right.'

Zac's quiet for a while. 'Um. My so-called girl-friend always makes a show of agreeing with Dad too. Like she wants to impress him all the time.' He gives me a sideways glance. 'That was her, you know. At reception. Claire.'

I drop my beer mat. 'She's a receptionist?' Why is he even telling me this? He sneaked that in almost as if he'd been *trying* to tell me about her!

'No, well, the thing is, she's like me – born into the hotel trade,' Zac says. 'She's the daughter of my stepmother's best friend. They practically pushed us together.'

Oh. I scoop up another beer mat to pass from hand to hand.

'But we're really not *together* together. It's just that our parents desperately want us to be. She's seeing someone else in secret – someone neither of our families would approve of. I cover for her all the time. It's complicated. Don't ask.'

Oh, I won't.

'I mean, really. Don't, because it doesn't matter, anyway. She's not my girlfriend, Bet. You have to believe me.'

Oh? *Why* do I have to believe him?

What's it to me?

My heart's going all weirdly ultra-thumpy.

The waitress arrives with two trays of sandwiches.

Zac says something business-like to her and waits for her to leave. Then he says, 'So how about your . . . boyfriend? What's the deal with him?'

'What's in these sandwiches?' I point. 'Do you eat caviar?'

Zac stares at me and blinks. 'Well, sometimes. But I think that's tuna.'

I shove a couple of sarnies in my mouth.

''S good,' I mumble with my mouth half-full. Really, the more I worry about seeming sophisticated today, the worse I get. I grab another sandwich to mask my embarrassment.

'Good,' Zac says. 'It's great to see women eat. Claire's always on ridiculous diets.'

Argh! What's he doing, comparing me to her? Also, wow, he's calling me a woman, not a girl? Does that make him a man? But he's the same age as Declan, who's definitely a boy. And now I'm comparing Zac to Declan.

But they don't compare. I don't think I've had a conversation of this length with Declan – not in months of going out with him. Well, sometimes he talks and I listen. That's how I know all about his plans for sports science at uni, and he knows nothing about my singing lessons. I'm not sure if it ever even occurred to me to tell him. Carlota would probably say that Declan and I don't need to talk – we speak the language of Kisses Etcetera. And it's true, we do. We speak it well.

I wouldn't mind a conversation like that with Zac. With that thought, I outdo my talking-with-my-mouth-full elegance by spluttering. A small piece of cress comes out of my nose. Argh!

Zac leans over and hits my back. Even that blatantly unsexy action makes me tremble all over.

'You OK?' Zac asks.

I manage to say, 'I'm fine, I'm fine.'

But Zac doesn't take his hand away completely. He rests it on my shoulder so that his arm is around me. He moves closer. I can smell coffee on his breath.

It would match the coffee on my breath, except that I've stopped breathing.

Carlota

I walk down a long corridor, trying every door I pass. But they have these fancy electronic locks and even the handles don't budge a centimetre. Omigod, this is a hotel! How hard can it be to find a room?

Yves catches up with me. 'Carlota, what are you doing?'

'Getting you all to myself!' I sound outrageously flirty, even for me! 'It's been too long.'

I know this is a good plan. One-on-one time for me and Yves, leaving Bets and Zac alone together again. It's a win-win situation.

I just have to find us a place.

Yves looks at me like he's starving and I'm a three-course dinner.

Oh, yes, I've got him all right.

'OK. I know where we can go,' he says, with this croak in his voice. 'But we have to be quick. If anyone sees us, my uncle will put me on the next Eurostar back to Brussels.'

He practically sprints to the far end of the corridor, towards the emergency exit. Is he going to use it? I love it! It's a Kisses Etcetera emergency!

But just before the exit he pulls open a door on the right and disappears inside. I reach it and see

183

it says STAFF on the door.

I think it's going to be a broom cupboard but it's not; it's a large storage area crammed with cleaning trolleys, hotel supplies and broken furniture. Including, in one corner, a bed. Well, a mattress with a tufty spring poking out of one end and a pile of towels at the other.

And Yves sitting in the middle, smiling at me in a way that makes a dozen bedsprings go *boing* in my stomach.

'It should be OK at this time of day. Anyone with a keycard can come in, there's no way of locking the door completely, but everyone knocks first, and there's no one really about right now, so . . .'

It's like the lab at the school in Brussels. Well, apart from the bed and all that. But it has the same degree of danger, the same likelihood of getting caught. Now we're really right back where we left off.

'Have you done this before then?' I don't want that twinge of jealousy in my voice! Where did it come from? How do I get rid of it?

Yves doesn't seem to notice. 'I've worked for Uncle André for a few holidays now,' he says.

That's not what I meant.

Also, it proves he's been in London loads of times and he didn't once think to look for me.

'I mean, coming to this room.'

'Oh, yeah, it's a good place to hide. The maids often jam the fire door open so it's easy to get in, and if you

184

close it behind you, people know to knock. You can smoke out of the window if you're careful.' The way he looks at me makes my face feel hot. 'Come here.'

Hey, I'm in control. I'll go to Yves when I'm ready. 'So do you have a different girlfriend every holiday? More than one? The maids?' I feel dizzy and I steady myself on a cleaning trolley. I manage not to ask the other questions in my head. Where's your girlfriend, anyway? Who is she? Does she work here? Is it a holiday thing? Is it meaningless? Unlike us? Why do you tell her you love her? You don't love her, do you? Is it just to get her into bed?

'Carlota.' Yves sighs. 'Shush. Come here.'

So I do. Because this is Yves and I've been dreaming of this moment for years. He doesn't have to say anything special to me. We don't need to play games.

We start kissing and then fall back, knocking the towels off, our hands everywhere. I really, really want him. Like mad.

But I can't get rid of those thoughts. I pull him closer, I think of her, I push him away. I think of him, I pull him back. We're doing a crazy dance, another type of silent rave.

He doesn't seem to mind.

How long has he had this steady girlfriend? It's stupid to settle down at our age, play-acting the parts of an old married couple like Bets and Declan.

We should have fun. It doesn't have to be deep and meaningful. I tug at Yves' shirt, reach under it.

Mmm.

Do I really believe that? Then why was I so jealous of Bets and Declan – or at least until I realized he'd happily cheat on her. But before that, I admit it – it just didn't seem fair that she had this long-term thing with Declan and I didn't have Yves at all.

But now Yves is here with me in the best way. I want to do this! Who cares who else he does this with? Since when have I worried about boys having girlfriends before I launch in on Kisses Etcetera?

He feels fantastic. I could do this for ever.

I know when I started being worried. It's since I realized how heartbroken Bets is going to be over the Declan thing. And I've worried even more since I began to feel so sick at the thought of Yves with another girl: now I know the truth of how it feels. Like poison twisting in my guts.

Well, it's time to sort it out.

I disentangle myself, sit up and say, 'Here's the thing, though.'

Yves moans. 'What?' He looks at me. 'Look, we don't have to do this.'

I can't believe he thinks that's the problem! Does he know me at all? 'Look, I *don't* like pink games holders and I'm *not* worried about doing any of this! I want to do it all! *Lots* of times!'

'Good.' He shrugs and gives me that delicious slow smile of his.

'But not if you're going to stay with her.' There. I've said it.

'*Merde*, Carlota.' He rolls towards me. He says throatily but kindly, 'Never mind that now. We can talk later.'

'No, really.' I may as well come out with it. What's the point of dancing around a subject instead of saying what you mean? 'Yves, are you going to finish with this other girl now we're back together?'

I need him to be mine. Only mine. It's not much to ask. We're right for each other. Why would he need anyone else? It doesn't matter if he's officially with her now. Technically, I was here first.

He sits up, adjusts his clothes and kind of shifts about on the mattress, like he's literally trying to wriggle out of it.

I don't feel a thing – I'm numb.

After a long silence he says, 'If I say yes, can we keep doing what we were doing?'

I'm no fool. 'That means no, doesn't it?'

'Carlota, come on, don't make me lie to you.'

Well, I don't need a *Teen Spice!* 'Boy Talk' article to make sense of that one.

So that's it. He prefers her to me.

'But why?' My voice wobbles. I can't believe myself. I'm pathetic. I never knew I could be like this. And I know the answer. It has to be because she's more respectable than me, more girlfriend-like. A Good Girl parent-pleaser, like Bethany, but without the personality.

Yeah – like Becca.

This sob noise comes out of me. Oh, no!

Maybe *she* doesn't go all blubby and pathetic after she's stalked a boy for ages and finally dragged him into a hotel storeroom for extreme Kisses Etcetera.

'Don't be like this, Carlota.' Yves moves over and tries to put his arms around me but I won't let him. I know what that means too. *Don't be like this, Carlota, it's not like you.* You never used to care. Kiss first, questions later, or never. *What's happened to you?*

He's right. And I know what's happened to me.

If I didn't believe in fate and magazine destiny before, then I certainly do now. It's like this whole day up to this point has been designed to help me understand how devastated Bets will feel. So that, when I tell her the truth, I can sympathize, minimize the damage and make sure she's OK. And I really will. I thought it was important before, but now I'm utterly convinced. I've got to remember that. Today is about *Bets*, not me. Even this, in some weird way.

And you know what? That's it for me and Yves. I mean really, totally, for ever. I'm not even going to dream about him any more. We're over, because he doesn't deserve me, any more than Declan deserves Bets. He probably doesn't deserve his girlfriend either, but how would I know when he hasn't told me the first thing about her? Not even whether she's nicer than me, or whether her parents can actually stand her.

I refuse to do the wobbly-voiced thing again.

I get up, saying evenly, 'I'm going.'

'Why?' Yves' face mists with utter confusion.

It's pretty simple really. 'Because I don't want to be with you.'

'Carlota!' He sounds exasperated. 'Come on, tell me what this is really about?'

When I don't say anything, he continues, 'It was so great to see you again, especially to find out that we're still, you know. So hot together.'

I can't leave yet. I need to hear this.

'Listen, I did feel kind of nervous about us kissing and stuff, at least at first, and I didn't know whether to tell you or not. That I was with someone else, I mean. But then you heard me and I didn't hide the fact that it was serious. And you got over it pretty quickly, didn't you? You were fine again, we did another challenge, we danced. *You* came on to *me* just now, remember!'

There's no point in explaining. Bets said he's a male version of me, designed to go out with tons of people and break all their hearts. Exactly the same as me – with everyone except him.

Well, not any more.

I should never have asked him what I asked him. It doesn't suit either of us.

'Meet me another time,' he practically pleads. 'I'm here for two weeks. I'm back in the summer. Being with you is so great, Carlota.' He gives me a loaded look. 'Don't worry about Aimee. Honestly, she never finds out.'

'No,' I state. I need to get Bets and go. Now. I need to stop standing here, drinking in his words. Tempted.

'OK, at least take this,' Yves says. He picks up his jacket and reaches into the pocket, taking out a silver container. He flicks it open and hands me a dark-coloured card with a crest that says L'ANDRÉ HOTEL, his name and a phone number.

'Ring me,' he says. 'I mean it. Any time.' He strokes my arm and I shiver inside.

Then he takes out a cigarette and lighter and walks over to the open window.

Great. Yves' phone number, Yves touching me like that. I've been dying for both these things ever since I left Brussels. But I don't want it now.

Nah, it's not that.

I don't *want* to want it.

Bethany

'Are you sure you're OK?' Zac asks.

I nod. I can't speak. Not without breathing.

If I was hooked up to a heart monitor in one of Dad's favourite hospital dramas right now, people would be running about shouting, 'Quickly, Doctor, her BP's through the roof!'

Zac's so close. Is he going to kiss me?

I think he might be.

'Bet . . .' he says. And then he mumbles, 'Sorry.'

Which is highly weird, because – for what? He hasn't done anything.

Yet?

His eyes search mine.

I don't know where to look.

I blurt, 'So, about your girlfriend out there—'

'But I told you, she's *not* my girlfriend. My father—'

'And your dad . . . was here too!' I'm aware that makes no sense.

And also that – if he was going to kiss me? Well, he's not now.

Zac shifts away from me, picks up his empty coffee cup and examines it. 'Do you want more coffee? I'll ask Raymond for more coffee.' He stands up and walks off, running a hand through his hair, looking thoroughly gorgeous.

I study my own empty cup. So that's it. No kiss. Probably just as well.

I wonder how it would have felt, though?

My thoughts are all over the place. My brain's gone to mush. I don't know who I am any more. Maybe I'm Rin Chine, Queen of the Night. I certainly don't feel like Bethany Royston, ordinary girl, sixteen and possibly pregnant, possibly Declan's girlfriend, plus definitely falling for – that's the polite way of saying 'fancying the pants off', isn't it? – Zac.

I wish I could discuss this with Carlota. But she's gone to Kisses Etcetera-land with Yves. And good for her, really. I've never seen her so crazy about a boy, and I'm glad her tricks worked for her. Maybe we can all go out together, her and Yves and me and Zac.

Oh my God, what am I thinking *now*? What happened to the thing I told Carlota – that kissing Yves would be wrong now she knows he has a girl-friend?

I'm officially a terrible person. No wonder Declan's going to dump me.

Course, Carlota would refer me to *Teen Spice!* as usual. I imagine a quiz called: *How bad is it to want to kiss someone who's not your boyfriend when you know you shouldn't?* I've never seen a quiz like that, but, you know. Question 1 could be, *What was the last thing your boyfriend emailed/texted/said to you? A) I love you, or B) We need to talk*. Stuff like that.

I'd get Mostly Bs, and the results would read, *What you're faced with could be a once-in-a-lifetime opportunity. Isn't today about extreme experiences? Aren't you here right now because your friend wanted to distract you from being miserable about your boyfriend? Didn't your boyfriend send you a highly suspicious text? Don't you want to forget all your worries? Our advice is to kiss him! Kiss him now!*

I reach over to where Carlota's left her bag and try a real quiz.

EXTREME SATURDAY: AFTERNOON

TEEN SPICE! MAGAZINE

 quick quiz

Is your boyfriend the **cheating** kind?
Experts say that boys who do the **dirty** on their girlfriends often share certain telling characteristics! Can you spot a **love rat** at a thousand paces? Put your boyf to the test in our quick quiz below!

1. Does he have nights out without you?
   A) Never. If you can't go out, he sits at home pining for you and gazing at your photo.
   B) Yes, sometimes.
   C) Every chance he gets, the dirty stop-out!

2. Are his mates ...
   A) All in committed, couply relationships.
   B) Mostly paired off, but not middle-aged about it.
   C) Mostly single and looking for action!

3. What's his attitude to risk?
    A) He likes his life safe and cosy, like a mug of cocoa.
    B) He buys a lottery ticket sometimes.
    C) Risk? He lives for it! He'll bungee-jump naked down a cliff-face before you can say 'Thunderballs'!

If you scored mostly As: Awww, how sweet! Have you bought each other slippers yet?!

If you scored mostly Bs: He's got the balance between fun and reliability just right. You've got a good 'un there!

If you scored mostly Cs: Be careful! These are the characteristics of boys most likely to cheat. It might not apply to yours, but keep your eyes peeled and don't say we didn't warn you!

Declan is mostly Bs, of course.
But which one am I?

Bethany

'Hey,' Zac says, putting the fresh drinks down. He sits next to me. His eyes are so dark they match the coffee.

His mouth is perfect.

Before I can change my mind, I put one arm around him and pull him towards me. And I close my eyes and kiss him, like my imaginary magazine told me to. It's a tiny kiss, though. It's tentative.

Zac pulls away immediately. 'Bet . . . ?'

'Yes,' I mumble. I can't look at him. Oh, no. Does he mind that I did that? This is awful.

'Are you sure this is OK?'

I nod, still not looking.

Then he leans over and kisses me. Just like my kiss, it's barely there. But it's still electric. It makes my lips tingle.

He says, 'Are you OK?'

'Yes.' I think, *Shut up, I want to kiss you.*

'Wow, I really didn't think anything like this could happen.' His breath on my ear makes me shiver. 'Though I was kind of wishing . . . I think you're amazing.'

I have to bite my lip to stop myself saying, 'Whatever.' I don't care about that stuff – the 'Effing gorgeous' and Carlota's theories about what boys say and what they mean. You can mean plenty without saying anything at all.

So then I lean in and kiss him again, and it's a proper kiss this time. After nearly eight months of being kissed by Declan, I thought I was a bit of an expert in Kisses Etcetera – at least the Kisses part.

Though the Etcetera isn't bad either.

But this is different. Zac has some kind of force-field he's pulling me into. I'm aching to get closer to him with every second of the kiss. It feels like a dream. It feels extreme. I hold him tight but I'm grasping, gasping, falling. Kissing, kissing.

'Oi! Lovebirds!' Carlota's over-bright voice makes us jump.

I'm not sure how much time has passed, but it felt like a blink. Does it still count as cheating if it only happens for a second?

I move away from Zac and fiddle with my hair, not meeting anyone's eye. I'm burning hot. It's not passion. It's guilt. What am I doing, what have I done? And how could I do it now?

'Bets, we have to go.' Carlota's voice sounds all professional and glossy.

'Oh.' Zac takes a deep breath. 'Well, OK, where are we going?' He frowns. 'I don't know how I'm going to clear it with Dad this time but I'll think of something. Where's Yves?'

My skin feels cold in the spot on my lower back where both his hands were.

Carlota shrugs. 'Smoking in a storeroom. Actually, I meant just me and Bets.' She's all hard-faced, like she's so not even bothered.

Zac gives me a searching look. He says quietly, 'Bet, can I call you?'

I should leave all this behind, pretend it never happened. Get back to reality.

'Sure, yeah.' I avoid his eyes. 'OK, let's go!' I charge away with Carlota following me.

I know Zac hasn't got my phone number. I know he was going to ask for it and I've just totally chickened out of this whole thing. I'm almost behaving like Carlota here, all 'kiss and run'.

I was only meeting Carlota's extreme challenge. It's all her fault.

On the way out we pass the super-elegant Claire, who has pulled the phone as far back from the reception counter as it will go. She doesn't notice us.

She's giggling into the phone and I hear her say, 'No, *you* hang up first.' If she's acting, she's really very good.

Carlota

The road widens and empties, then winds and fills with low-rise blocks of flats. We walk in silence. We don't know where we're going.

Bets keeps sneaking little looks at me. I can tell she's dying to ask me why I'm so quiet. But I don't know what to say.

Or rather, I don't think I can tell her anything without telling her everything.

And I can't do that.

Eventually she goes, 'Aren't you hungry? You missed the sandwiches.' She sounds like someone's mother. (But not Veronica, who's more likely to say, 'Well done, you skipped a meal for once in your life.')

'I had a burger before, remember?' And I'm not at all hungry, as it happens. My stomach's churning. I'd better not be coming down with Bets's stomach bug.

'And anyway, you weren't exactly eating *the sand-wiches* when I found you.'

She goes bright red but she doesn't let up. 'Did something bad happen with you and Yves?'

I keep walking. 'No.' I try to make it sound as if I truly couldn't care less, but as usual I'm a rubbish liar.

'Really, you can tell me. Was it about that girl-friend?'

'Nothing happened!'

She looks hurt. Argh, I didn't mean to snap at her!

So I try again, but when I don't bark, that pathetic wobble creeps back into my voice. 'I'm sorry. I'm just so wound up.' She'll never believe it! Me – wound up? But I think that might explain the churning. I'm not sick – I'm nervous. All the bad stuff's catching up with me.

After a while I manage to say, 'You know, Bets, I couldn't do it after all.'

'Couldn't do what?'

'I couldn't pretend it didn't matter – that he had a girlfriend. I couldn't make him see I was better than her. And I . . .'

I sit heavily on a nearby brick wall. Stress relief, where are you? I take out my knitting and Bets looks horrified.

She gives this little laugh. 'Lots, sorry, but d'you think it's OK to knit in a place like this? We might provoke an anti-knitting attack. It'll get reported in Dad's *Daily Scare*, and everyone will say, "Serves them right for knitting on a South London estate." You know.'

I try to laugh too. I feel my stomach calm down and unknot a bit. Bets is the only person I've ever really been able to talk to. I've never been one for having female friends – I've always found boys a lot more fun. But I didn't realize I was missing out on girl-talk – about boys, about everything – until I met Bets. I can tell her anything. She understands. She's my best friend.

I wind some wool around the needle, despite her warning. 'I asked Yves . . . to break up with her. For me, Bets!' I hate the sound of the words but I do feel strangely better once I've said them. 'I actually asked him.'

Bets's eyes go big. 'Wow, that's huge. There are boys at school that would swap their Nintendo DS for a chance like that! What did he say?'

'Nothing much. But he's not going to dump her.' I. Refuse. To. Cry.

'Right.' Bets goes all commanding. 'Give me a magazine.'

I try to give her a look, even though it's a bit blurry because my eyes are full of annoying tears. 'Bets, I don't feel like doing challenges right now.'

'I haven't felt like doing them all day. But they've worked out pretty interestingly so far. Just try it. You don't have to do anything.'

I sigh and put down my knitting. 'OK.' I open the

magazine at random. Proper random, not like before. I read it through the blur. 'It's about boyfriends. *Which animal is your boyfriend – wolf, monkey, stallion, puppy or ox?*'

'Hmm,' she says, rubbing her chin in pretend thought. 'We need a different magazine, like Mum's *Craft Monthly* or something. You need a nice cross-stitching challenge, I think.'

That makes me smile a tiny bit. 'This challenge is nothing to do with me, anyway. I don't know the first thing about boyfriends. I've never even had one. I've never wanted one.' Except Yves.

'Rubbish. You've had loads of boyfriends. A whole zoo.'

I hit her arm lightly. She's so lovely, trying to cheer me up. 'You know what I mean. Not properly. Not like you and Declan.'

I don't know why I said that! I shouldn't have said it. I don't want to remind her about Declan. But she just says, 'So which animal is Declan?'

I read out, '*Solid, dependable, stubborn.* I think he's an ox. Or maybe: *Loving, eager, devoted*, a puppy.' Well, I know Declan's no puppy, but I think she'd want to hear that.

'Huh, I don't think so,' she says, but her voice is light. That snog with Zac did wonders for her. I knew I was right about Bets and that kissing challenge.

I read a bit more. 'Yves is a total stallion: *Gorgeous, proud, thinks he's God's gift.* What about

Zac? I think he might be a bit of a wolf . . .'

'Lots!' Bets giggles. 'Anyway, he's not my boyfriend!'

'Well, Yves isn't mine.' I sigh even though I try not to. 'Wolves are *sexy, mysterious, loners*. What was it like snogging a wolf?'

'Ssh, Lots, I shouldn't have done that – snogged him, I mean. It's not fair on Declan.'

Declan deserves it, I think. 'But Zac's such a cutie,' I say instead. 'A cute, cute wolf.'

'And he's got a girlfriend too, but he says she's not really his girlfriend. Do you believe that? We saw her – the receptionist?'

The one smooching on the phone? 'I believe it.' But I feel it again, this jealous ache. Why couldn't Yves have said he didn't really have a girlfriend? He didn't even try to hide it.

Bets shrugs. 'Anyway, I shouldn't have done it.'

'But you're glad you did, right?'

She smiles sheepishly.

I'm definitely feeling better. An idea is creeping up on me – the challenge from this page. A solution. I put my knitting back in my bag.

Bets asks, 'Are we off? What's next?'

There's no better way to get over heartbreak than to snog someone else. Bets has proved it.

I'm a kissing genius!

'Playful, child-like, good kissers,' I quote. 'We're going to find some monkeys to snog.'

Bethany

'No way, Lots, I'm not kissing any more strangers!' Any *more* strangers! Listen to *me*!

'So we'll find someone we know. Maybe we can find Ash and Connor again if we go back to that library. They looked a bit like monkeys – all that facial hair.'

'Lots, I told you before – no way!' Ick ick *ick*!

She shrugs. 'See, that's why I don't ever want a boyfriend. It makes you *boring*, Boring Bee!'

She dodges me as I pretend to hit her.

'Seriously, there have to be some boys around here somewhere.'

I look around with slight dread, but the place is pretty deserted apart from a woman with a pushchair in the distance. They seem to be every-where today, following me about and reminding me to worry.

There's an odd rumbling sound behind us. It's sort of repetitive and accompanied by grunting sounds. Carlota turns round first.

'Bets, look!'

When I do, I can't quite believe what I'm seeing. There are groups of men mostly dressed in tight black clothes making their way towards us, leaping over the low buildings and somersaulting down ledges and steps. And all this activity is completely silent, except for some grunting and puffing as they land.

They pause by a gate that leads onto the bank of the Thames, and one man unlocks it.

We move closer as, one by one, the men congregate on the sand. I never even knew there was a beach-like area by the river, let alone that it was used by acrobats practising their moves. And yet, there they all are, taking turns to do backward somersaults against the wall.

It's an amazing sight. Carlota and I stare at them. 'They're fit,' she says.

Their muscles ripple. I have to agree.

'Parkour,' she says.

Is she talking French to me or something?

'Do you mean *Pwhooar*?'

Carlota grins. 'Yeah, that too. Nah, parkour, freerunning – it's an extreme sport. It's been on music videos and stuff – Trix videos, I think. You should know! They leap about through cities, no matter what's in their way. It's about freedom.'

'Really?' It all seems to be about freedom today. And extreme things and Trix, for that matter. 'Like us?'

'Yep, exactly like us.' Carlota looks at the muscly men as they bound. '*Traceurs*.'

'Bless you.'

'No, you idiot.' She nudges me. 'They're called *traceurs*, the people who do it. It's French. This geek

I snogged once told me that Lara Croft was the original *traceur*.' Of course, she takes the opportunity to stick her chest out again. It's all about Lara Croft and action heroines today too. Carlota keeps gazing at the men. 'I'm going to talk to the monkeys,' she says.

I know that look. 'Lots, you can't!'

'Why not?'

'They're training, or whatever. You shouldn't interrupt them. They might break their necks.'

'We're training too. We've got a new snogging challenge, and they're perfect.'

She can't really mean it.

'Are you with me, Bets? Come on, even someone as picky as you can see the opportunity here.'

'I am not picky!' I didn't even choose Declan, not exactly. He was just there when I wanted to practise my Boy Snaring.

'You are, compared to me. You're a total picky-pants.' She points to each guy in turn, with a determined expression on her face. 'Fit, fit, fit, not so much, fit, fit, nooo, fit.'

'You're right,' I say, to prove I'm not picky, and also because it's true. 'But we could, you know, just eye them up or something.'

Carlota makes a face at me. She shouts down, 'Hey!'

I try to hide behind her.

Two of the men look up and one waves slightly,

but they quickly go back to what they're doing. They seem focused, professional.

Good.

'Come on, let's go,' I say.

A group of boys on skateboards whizz past us, roaring in semicircles on the concrete.

'I'm on a mission,' Carlota says. 'I need a monkey.' She takes a step forward, right into the path of a skater boy.

There's a crashing sound and lots of swearing. The fallen skater's friends do these flashy jumps and roar back towards us.

Carlota rubs her ankle and smirks at the boy on the ground. She elbows me. 'I wonder if he's broken his leg, poor monkey. Might need a kiss better.'

'Carlota. *No.*'

The boy stands up, raps his board on the ground and swears at Carlota again. He's short, freckly-faced and weasely. He doesn't look any older than fourteen, but you can't always tell with boys. Midge-boy in our year at school was only about four foot tall till he came back from the Christmas holidays towering over all of us. We don't even know what to call him now – we barely remember his real name.

'Carlota, I know you're into extremes,' I say quietly. 'But he's too young!'

The boy turns to me, his baggy red T-shirt heaving up and down as he catches his breath. 'What's your problem? I'm sixteen.'

'See, Bets. Sixteen's legal.'

'Lots!'

The boy glares at me, then at Carlota. 'Are you psychos? Man!' He clatters his skateboard down and puts one foot on it, swearing again. 'Psycho magnet, that's me.' His friends zoom around us, smirking.

Carlota looks straight at him. 'No, we're completely sane. Ish. My friend and I have . . . a challenge to meet. For a special project.'

'Carlota!' *No NO NO!*

The boy narrows his eyes.

Carlota continues, 'I need someone to snog – no strings, you know.' She laughs. 'So what d'you reckon?'

The boy's eyes widen. I feel a fit of the giggles coming on, especially when Carlota adds seriously, 'Of course, I'd need to see some ID first. I'm not kissing any kids.'

'You *are* insane,' the boy says, putting his hand in his pocket and swearing in a string of words which ends in, 'Pretty, though.'

His friends skate closer and call out things like, 'Go for it, Shorty!' and 'Get it out!'

The boy hands his Oyster photocard to Carlota and puts his hands in his pockets as she inspects it. He's still got one foot on his skateboard as if he's ready to make a getaway.

'Fine.' She nods at me, then him. 'Mr R. Brown. Is that R for Romeo?' Her eyes are full of laughter.

He stares at Carlota. 'No. Robson.'

'Good name. Come here.'

'Woo, Robbo!' his friends shout, but they move further away. I think they might be a bit scared of us now.

Carlota puts her lips on Robson Brown's for about ten seconds. His hands move to her bum. She steps back quickly and says, 'OK, thanks.' She waves him away.

'Aw, you can't leave me like this,' Robson says, looking more like a weasel by the minute. I can't believe Carlota kissed him. 'And what about *her*?'

I jump. Me?

No-no-no-no-no-NO.

'Get lost, you're not her type,' Carlota says. She calls out, even though she's right next to me, 'Bets, do you fancy any of them?'

I can't shake my head fast enough.

'Picky-pants.' She laughs.

'Suggsy, get over here,' Robson shouts to one of his scraggly mates.

I look at Robson, then at the one who must be Suggsy. 'No way!' I adjust my voice to normal volume and remove the squeak factor. 'Look, I'm sorry and all. I'm sure you're all very nice.'

'No probs.' He twists a finger near his head, the international symbol of craziness. 'You're both in-*sane* in the *brain*. See ya.' He gets back on his skateboard and heads for his friends, landing a triumphant jump accompanied by a small, 'Woot! I'm the man.' The others shout out a few more rude things at us and then skate off.

'Let's go,' Carlota says.

'Yeah,' I say, relieved.

'It didn't work,' Carlota says.

'What didn't?'

'That kiss. It was crap.'

'I'm not surprised, Lots. He wasn't a monkey, he was a baby weasel.'

'No, that's not it, Bets. I *like* weasels. He reminded me of Anwar from Year Twelve, and I liked snogging him.'

'Oh, yeah.'

'My life is over.'

'No, don't say that!' I rack my brains for a quick weasel or monkey joke to cheer her up. 'Where do baby apes sleep?'

She gives me a look.

'An apricot.'

'And your life is over too, clearly, since you have now officially *become* your dad.' She gives a small smile. 'OK, next challenge, Bets. Make it a good one.'

There's a rumbling sound behind us that I recognize this time even before I turn round – it's the *traceurs*, back on their journey, leaping and jumping over concrete behind us.

Carlota peers at the magazine as I open it. '*Copycat Fashions. How to recreate designer looks on the high street. Copy everything but the price.'*

It's obvious what our next challenge should be.

'OK, I know what we're doing next.' The first of the men passes us, grunting. 'We're *copying* them.'

Carlota

Bets suddenly tears off after the *traceurs* like a mad thing and this terrible thought crosses my mind.

I could let her go.

She'd find her way home. And I could stay here. Go back to the hotel, tell Yves I've changed my mind. Kissing that monkey Romeo didn't work *at all*! If anything it made it worse – it made me want Yves more!

But. No. I'm not going back to Yves and sharing him with some other girl, a girl he 'loves'. I've only got to think about the whole Declan and Bets thing to know that's a bad idea, however tempting it is.

And also, how could I do that to Bets? Apart from anything else that would mean leaving Becca to tell her the truth about Declan. There are some things you need to hear from a real friend, not someone like Becca who is obviously anything but.

So I kind of pull myself together and break into a light jog after Bets.

Me and Bets aren't very sporty. We did this cross-country thing for school about a month ago and we were pretty bad at it. Becca and Baljit came in somewhere in the middle – PE is the only subject where Becca is average (and that includes Dumping on Friends, which she clearly excels at). And Baljit was being her typical ultra-nice self and not leaving her friend behind. She should have told Becca it was a Race for Maths – then they'd probably have come in first.

Bets is a bit faster than me and could have kept up with the Boring Bees, but I kept stopping and pulling her aside for chats. Also, one time, for a cigarette I borrowed from a boy in Year Twelve which I didn't really want to smoke, but which gave me an excuse to talk to him. I got some passing civilian lad to light it for me when the cross-country route went through a public park, so it was a dual-purpose cigarette. Result. I got the guy's phone number and me and Bets came in joint last.

Right now, Bets isn't doing a very good job of following the *traceurs*, though all the loud laughing she's doing can't be helping. I'm puffing along about half a mile behind her, just near enough not to lose her as she twists and turns deeper into the estate.

There's a series of aluminium sheds, garages and low-rise scrappy-looking buildings ahead. The *traceurs* jump up them like cats, *thud thud thud*, leaping from roof to roof, tumbling down at the end of the row as if they're landing on mats and trampolines instead of concrete. Bets manages to climb onto the first roof and then stands at the edge going,

'Aaaargh!'

'Bets, get down!' I call. Honestly, she's taking this too far! I do not want to end the day in a hospital!

I meant *climb* down, of course, but she starts to jump.

'Bets!'

I can't see her any more! The streets are deserted and there are no cars, let alone people. Even the *traceurs* have disappeared! I rush in the direction of the shed, practically collapsing from the effort. When I reach it I finally see Bets, hobbling away behind a garage.

She stops outside a boarded-up shop which is covered in faded posters from the last millennium. She's leaning against the wall and staring at a barely clothed woman on an advert for a supermarket when I catch up with her.

I swear as I get my breath back. 'What did you do that for?'

She just goes, 'The challenge. Wow, Katie Price's boobs are a whole different size there.'

'That's an ancient Jordan poster. And who d'you think you are? Lara Croft?'

'Not exactly,' she says sadly, rubbing her ankle.

I want to moan at her for risking her life but I end up laughing. 'Omigod! You might even be crazier than me!'

Then an engine roars and there's a loud bang in the distance. It echoes around the empty estate.

Bets grips my arm. So her wildness didn't last – she's turned back into a pumpkin.

I roll my eyes. 'It's a car backfiring.'

She's practically trembling. 'How d'you know?'

'Bets.' Trust her to get spooked now, after fearlessly jumping off a garage roof! 'OK, it's not a car.'

Her eyes go wide.

'It's a pair of fake boobs exploding in a flat several miles away.'

'Lots, it's not funny.' There's another bang, closer to us. 'Ssh!'

'Fake boobs can't hear us, you know,' I say. 'Even though I'm sure they have lives of their own. They're actually aliens – Foobs from Planet Fake Boob.'

She doesn't smile. 'How are we going to get out of here? We don't even know where we are!'

'It's London. How far from a tube or a bus can we be?'

'But we're in the middle of an estate! In South London! With people shooting each other! Guns!'

'Exploding Foobs,' I mutter.

'I'm serious, Lots! I remember Becca's mum saying that licensed taxi drivers won't even work in this kind of area. She went on and on about it. She called it a no-man's-land. And we're in it!'

Oh, no. I can't believe she's talking about Becca! Well, her mum, anyway. 'What does Becca's mum know about anything?'

'Everything! She's a taxi driver! She has The Knowledge!'

'Oh, right.' Yeah, typical. Just like Becca Know-It-All. She sounds like a total busybody, if you ask me.

'We'll never get out of here! No one will ever find us!'

I almost laugh at how dramatic Bets is being, except that she's reminding me of Becca, and not just by talking about her mum. Becca loves a bit of amateur dramatics. I think that might be what the Declan thing is all about. She's doing it for the attention – all of it. Come to think of it, it's probably the result of having a mum who calls some innocent estate in South London 'no-man's-land'.

'Come on, there's nothing to worry about.'

'Lots, I'm scared!'

I sigh. 'So let's go. If we keep walking, we'll at least be able to work out where we are. We can find the river and follow it.'

'I don't know if I can walk. My ankle hurts! I just want to be safe again!'

She looks like she's going to cry, and much as I wanted today to be perfect for her, I have to admit she's getting on my nerves now! Why is she being such a baby?

'Look, calm down. Magazine Power got us here, and it will get us out!' I announce. I can be just as dramatic as her and Becca.

I unfurl a magazine triumphantly and randomly in front of her. It's an article about celebrities and their mums, called 'Like Mother, Like Daughter'.

I read a bit of it. 'God, I wish my parents were like the Osbournes. Listen to this quote from Sharon: *Do I approve of everyone Kelly hangs out with? No, I don't. But she makes her own decisions.*'

Bets looks excited. 'Well, that's it! Mothers! That's the answer! We can ask Becca's mum to send us a taxi. I know she's working today and she's usually in central London. I'm sure she won't mind – not if I explain about my ankle.'

She wants to ring Becca's mum? Oh, no-no-no. Bad bad *bad* idea. Becca probably tells her mum everything. I've heard they have that kind of sickeningly cosy mother–daughter relationship you usually only see on telly. Becca's mum could ruin everything!

'No! Don't ring her!'

'Why not? Becca's mum's great, honestly, Lots! She's more like a friend than a mum!' Bets's eyes practically gleam with Good Girl parent-admiration. Why can't she be normal and realize that parents – all parents – are the enemy?

I struggle like crazy to keep my voice calm. 'I mean, if you really want, why don't we just get any old taxi?'

'I don't know any taxi numbers! Do you? And besides, it's the magazine's challenge! Like mother, like daughter. It means we have to do something linked to someone's mother.'

'We can go to a chemist like Baljit's mum, or be Crafty Nutters like yours, or . . .' I can't think of anything to do with Veronica. We could moan about my weight or give me disgusted looks, or something.

Bets says, 'No, this is perfect, Lots.'

She's got her phone out!

Help, help, how do I stop her?

She's pressing buttons!

'But you can't ring her when she's working, can you?' I shrug, trying to look casual instead of desperate. Yes, yes, this is it! 'She can't answer the phone! She's driving.'

'She has hands-free. Becca and her sister call her loads when she's at work and it's never a problem. I'll ask Becca to call her for us. '

My stomach sinks to the tip of my white boots. 'Becca? Are you calling Becca?'

'Yeah. Honestly, Lots, stop worrying. Becca's mum is so cool. She won't mind.'

Maybe not. But Becca will.

She wouldn't tell her now, would she? Not over the phone! I thought I had until the end of the day to tell Bets myself. It wouldn't be fair!

But Becca hates me. She's hated me from the minute I started at that school. She's been dying for a chance to get at me! As if hurting my best friend isn't enough for her!

'Bets, just give me the phone and—' And what? I don't know! I'll think of something. She just should *not* speak to Becca.

'Sssh, it's ringing,' she says.

Bethany

The ringing echoes in my ear. The pavements are empty and the silence feels eerie in the middle of a big city. I'm sure this is one of those estates you're not supposed to enter without protection.

I'm really pleased with myself for thinking of asking Becca's mum for a taxi. Well, it was the magazine's idea really. Extreme Travel is fantastic, even if I do feel terrible about Zac, and my ankle's throbbing.

I wait for Becca to pick up the phone, but Leah answers instead. She sounds cagey, like I've caught her being naughty. That's if you can still call nearly-thirteen-year-olds 'naughty'. I can't stop thinking of Leah as Becca's baby sister.

'Becca's on the landline. I was just . . . checking her phone for . . . Hang on, Baljit's here.'

Oh, I get it. Leah's been 'borrowing' Becca's phone again. Their mum, cool as she is, has declared Leah too young to have her own mobile, so she just nicks Becca's.

I think I hear Becca yelling in the background. Baljit comes on the phone.

'Bethany?'

'Hi, Bal. Is everything OK? What are you up to?'

'Um, Becca's talking to Harrison. Well, arguing.'

Her voice is a bit strained, like she's a bit unsure of me – as she often is with me since Carlota came along. 'We were going over past papers for English before he rang.'

'Oh, right.' Trust her – trust *them*. I think Baljit and Becca are the only people in Britain who can revise for *English*.

'Are *you* OK?'

'Not exactly. Listen, sorry about this but . . . we're kind of stuck. Do you think you could you get us a taxi number for South London? Or maybe ask Becca's mum to call me if she can? I'll tell you everything later, honestly.'

Carlota makes this horrified face that nearly makes me laugh. She doesn't need to worry – I can skip the parts about her and Yves if she wants me to.

'What are you doing in South London? Are you with Carlota?' Baljit doesn't wait for me to answer, she just sighs. 'OK, I'll ask Becca when she's finished talking to Harrison. You know, I think they really might be splitting up properly this time. Hey, Bethany . . .'

'What?'

Carlota suddenly shouts, 'Omigod! Bets!'

I spin round. Has she seen something? Like maybe *people with guns*?

'What?' I repeat, only this time it's aimed at Carlota.

But Baljit answers. 'Oh . . . Nothing. Just if you

want to talk – like, later – call me, OK?'

Carlota pulls her wallet out of her bag and says, 'Phew. Sorry, I thought I'd lost it for a minute there.'

'But only, you know, if you want to,' Baljit adds.

'Yeah, OK,' I say. 'See you soon.'

I hang up, thinking about how close me and her and Becca used to be. I promise myself I'll make an extra effort with them when I get home.

If I ever get home.

Oh, don't be ridiculous, Bethany!

I've got to stop all this worry – properly, for ever, not just for a few minutes here and there, like when I'm pretending to be Lara Croft. I've had enough of feeling like this! I want to be more like Carlota. Although the way she's acting right now – panicking about her wallet, irrationally twitching about me phoning Becca's mum – she doesn't seem very carefree at all. Of course, I know what this is really about. She can't stop stressing about Yves. Yves is her Declan – or, if she was Becca, her Harrison.

Although I've really barely thought about Declan . . . since Zac.

When I see Becca tonight, I might insist that she tries snogging someone else. I think it can really work, if you find the right boy.

Even though I'm waiting for it, I jump when my phone rings. It's Becca's mum, talking fast, with about fifty words to every one of mine. She asks a ton of questions and sorts out where we are using

218

her 'Knowledge', which took her months of Becca-like studying to get. Like mother, like daughter. Then she says she's been hanging around without a fare for half an hour and she might as well come and find us herself, and good-naturedly tells me off for being stuck in the middle of nowhere and being 'nothing like her sensible Rebecca'.

Becca's mum's still speaking when I whisper to Carlota, 'She's on her way.'

Carlota

'How on *earth* did you girls get here? It's very stupid, you know. I don't normally work in this area – it's not worth it . . . This is where the *vermin* work, you know, the minicab drivers, and yet here you were . . .'

Becca's mum is a nightmare. She talks non-stop, even when she's driving through impossible London traffic. We're lurching all over the road, weaving in and out of lanes, and she has not shut up once, not even when she was making rude gestures out of the window.

Bets, beside me, makes agreeable little parent-pleasing noises in all the right places.

As for me – I can't believe this! Why didn't I manage to stop Bets ringing Becca? At least she only spoke to Baljit. But Baljit might know! I'm glad I managed to shut her chat to Bets down quickly with my well-timed shouting.

Would Becca's mum know? Would she say anything about it? She's certainly talked about everything else in the world, more than once.

I take my knitting out and try a couple of rows, even though I nearly stab myself with the needle twice as Becca's mum slams on the brakes. *Teen Spice!* never said anything about stress relievers not working in a taxi driven by a chattering maniac.

I glare at the back of Becca's mum's head. She's nothing like her boffiny daughters. She has short dyed red hair and this total no-nonsense attitude. I bet she'd never take any crap from a boy – well, a man, in her case, I suppose. Bets told me she's been single for years because she's 'in love with her job'.

Maybe I should try it. Maybe I'll give up boys for ever and just work, or study.

It's hard to imagine.

'So am I taking you home to revise with my Becca?' Becca's mum asks Bets, and then she catches my eye in the rearview mirror – yikes, I think I might have looked terrified – and she laughs and says, 'Or do you want to stay out? Tell you the truth, I could do with picking up central fares for long enough to pay for Leah's new trainers. If you give me a time and a place, I can take you home later.'

I'm starting to see what Bets means about Becca's mum. She's so chilled about us staying out. I bet her Sharon Osbourne qualities are wasted on someone like Becca.

Bets amazes me by saying, 'Oh, we're fine to find our own way home.'

'Well, call me if you like. I'm heading up west now, better class of punters. How does that sound?'

'Ooh, yeah!' I say before I remember that I don't want to strike up a conversation with Becca's mum. She looks at me in the mirror again and smiles with one of those knowing smiles adults put on – like she understands me and I'm not a bad kid after all. I set my face into a scowl – she knows nothing! – and go back to my knitting.

But west is perfect! There's Ash's tickets, for a start – I'd almost forgotten about them! I'm pretty sure it's not too late, either. I bet there's something in the magazine I can use to persuade Bets to do it for a challenge.

I stuff my knitting away, swapping it for a magazine. I flick through and find a good page, quietly bending it back so it springs open in the right place. I fold the corner over to make doubly sure. Then I check the time on the tickets. We've got ages!

I pull out a thinner magazine which has the answer to *that* problem.

I'm a genius! A friend-saving genius.

Meanwhile, Bets is giving her parent-pleasing skills another polish. I can't make out the words, but I hear her voice, all silky smooth.

Becca's mum replies, 'Bethany, you've always been

221

such a sweetie.' She pauses, yells some rude stuff out of the window at a cyclist, then turns back as if nothing had happened. 'I know Rebecca's really worried about something right now.'

I sit right up. What's she going to say? Is this it? Just when I was relaxing!

'Who'd have teenagers! You have babies and you think you can protect them . . .'

I sit back a tiny bit. Snooze.

'But they grow up and you have to watch them make mistakes. She was in such a state earlier about some boy problem. Leah said something about a "love triangle" – honestly, how fast do you kids grow up? But Rebecca said—'

Uh-oh. I think Bets has heard enough of this.

'Here! Drop us here!' I yell. I'm not quite sure if we're where I want to be yet, but it's been ages and the streets are wider and more crowded and there are posh-looking shops and I don't want Becca's mum to go into any more detail!

'Lots!' Bets gives me a shocked look – like, how dare I interrupt a grown-up who might have been about to ruin her whole life!

Well, obviously she doesn't know that last bit.

'I mean, Bets, this is a good place for our next challenge!'

She gives me a look. 'But we haven't chosen one,' she says, all quiet, as if she's a bit embarrassed in front of Becca's mum.

'So choose now!' I hand her the thin magazine and she opens it quickly, barely looking.

'Clothes shopping,' she says quietly.

Becca's mum's busy anyway, shouting out of the window.

'Wow, I'm surprised we didn't get that one sooner,' I remark, taking the magazine back.

And I am surprised about that, but I'm not surprised that she got a shopping challenge that time, because I handed her the *Teen Spice! Fashion Shopping Special* – a free supplement that came with the main mag a couple of months ago.

But I'm doing the right thing for once. It's absolutely what we need. A total shopping-fest – no more boys, no more stress. Just clothes, make-up, accessories. Bliss.

Bets must think that too, because she makes a throat-cleary noise. 'Ms Bloom, Carlota's right. Would it be OK to drop us here? We've got some shopping to do,' she says politely. She's so good! 'Thank you ever so much.'

'On the King's Road? Are you sure? You girls must have more money than sense.'

We're on the King's Road? OK . . . *that's* somewhere you can go shopping. If you're about to marry Prince Harry, that is. I know someone at my Brussels school whose sister's cousin once dated him, which is how I know that.

'We're just looking,' Bets explains.

223

Yeah, that's what *she* thinks.

Becca's mum goes all wistful and says, 'I remember what it was like to be your age . . . and I'm going to trust you not to be like me – but only because I know you, Bethany, and I know your parents and you'd better not let me down. Call me again when you want a lift home. I want you to be safe! And take *care* of yourselves.'

'We will,' she says.

'I mean it.' She stops the cab.

She does this huge wink at us before she drives off, shouting, 'Behave!' out of the window.

At last she's gone, and she didn't say anything too awful about the Becca and Declan thing.

And we're going shopping.

Bethany

I feel loads better now as we amble in and out of shops. My ankle's recovered from being rested in the taxi. I'm limping a bit, but I don't think I hurt it too badly after all. And Lots is right, I was overreacting about the estate we were on. I do this all the time, blow things up in my imagination. I never even realize I'm doing it.

I try to get into it as if it was a normal Saturday shopping trip with my best friend, and not this really weird day where I'm worried about being *late* and my boyfriend's about to dump me and I've

224

reacted by snogging some boy I've just met. But something still doesn't feel right.

I think it's Carlota. She's almost twitchier than I am right now. She's flitting about sniffing samplers in this smelly soap shop we wandered into. She dips her fingers into something called shower jelly, pronounces it 'emo soap' and insists that we go into the large department store instead, for a 'full and serious makeover'. But when we get there, she frowns and says, 'No, forget this. We can do our own make-up. What we need is dresses. Cocktail dresses. Come on.'

There's a posh-looking boutique a few doors up. As Carlota pulls open the door, I realize I'm not even completely sure what a cocktail dress *is*. But Carlota knows. She's lived this whole other life of international schools and rich kids with limos – guys like Yves and Zac and . . . I belong with boys like Declan. I don't fit into Carlota's world. Sometimes I wonder what she thinks, slumming it with me and Becca and Baljit in the sticks.

This boutique is a good example. I've never been in a shop like this before. It's dead quiet and the rails are practically empty. But Carlota walks around like she owns the place.

She picks up a strappy white dress and strokes it. It looks expensive. She turns it over. It has elaborate stitching all up the back. It looks *very* expensive.

'Retail therapy,' she breathes, looking like she's

died and gone to heaven and it's lined with hand-bags, clothes and unlimited boys.

I laugh. I might have been pretending at first, but now I think I really am enjoying myself. It's a relief to be here, safe in this palace of a posh shop. Maybe you need to feel like that sometimes – on edge, full of danger – so that you can properly relax, in contrast. Maybe that's why people bother with extreme sports.

I make a face at Carlota and say, 'Robson Brown had a point about you.'

Carlota pretends to wring my neck. 'Right. Pick something randomly hideous out of the *Teen Spice!* fashion pages and I'll find you something like it.'

My eyes wander for thirty seconds before they stop, for ever. 'Lots, I don't want something hideous.' I look at a red sparkly dress, twinkling at me gorgeously. 'I want that.'

The price tag is titchy and hard to read. 'Sixty?' God, that's a lot for that tiny amount of material. It would be a tenner in Primark. It also wouldn't shimmer like that under their lighting. It's just beautiful. Carlota raises her eyebrows at me and takes the dress out of my hand, brushing past the tag with her eyes. 'Six *hundred*. But – ssh. You don't look, in places like this.'

See? She knows the rules. I've never been to a shop where you weren't supposed to look at the price tag.

An emaciated assistant appears at our side, blowing her nose as she towers skinnily over us and looks suspicious. She says, all snooty combined with a heavy cold, 'Can I *help* you?'

Carlota replies in her poshest voice. 'We're designers, browsing for inspiration.' She points to the knitting poking out of her bag. 'Can I show you our latest lines?'

The assistant looks totally horrified and glances at the door and then at the counter. I bet she's thinking of pressing some kind of panic button. But she sneezes and it distracts her from ringing 999 for a second.

Carlota uses that instant to take out her knitting. 'Er . . . it's . . .' Then she looks at me.

Here we go again! She's landing me in it, like she did on the tour bus.

Well, now I know I can do this.

I manage to keep a straight face as I let my brain go wild. And the dad-ish puns creep in again – I just can't help myself. 'It's called a "Holey Grail",' I tell the assistant. 'It's a totally new take on fashion. Everyone's going to be wearing designer holey scarves – er, *grails*, which is Swedish for "scarf" – this winter.'

Carlota nods and beams.

Never mind GCSEs, Dad can give me a job in second-hand car sales. I'll make him proud. 'I've been informed they're already taking Paris and

Milan by storm,' I add, Dad-ishly.

Carlota adds, 'Also Tring. It's in Hertfordshire, you know.'

'And talking of storms,' I say, getting into it, 'what's the opposite of a cold front? A warm back!'

The assistant's snooty eyes dart about again. She blows her nose. 'Er . . . I'm sorry but you need to speak to Naomi – Ms Turpington – and she's not back till Tuesday . . . If you come back then I'll tell her to expect you.'

Yes, and she can have the loony-catchers waiting, wielding designer straitjackets, if she's got any sense.

The assistant gives the dress I'm holding a snottily snooty look. 'Did you want to try that on?'

'Um . . . ' I say, losing my flow and turning instantly back into Carlota's humble sidekick.

Carlota steps in – this is her territory now. We're a team! 'Yes, she will. And I'll try this, this and this.' She scoops up armfuls of clothes.

'Ladies, let me accompany you . . . Ah . . .'

Carlota disappears into the back – how does she even know there's a changing room there? – and I give Ms Snotty-Snoot a sheepish grin as we follow her.

The dress fits in all the right places and swishes round and I really do look kind of film starry. If only we still had the limo. If only Zac could see me like this.

What am I *thinking*?!

Carlota tries on about six different white strappy dresses. They hug her curves – maybe slightly too much, even though she doesn't normally care and goes on about big being beautiful, which I think she's totally right about. You only have to see her to believe it. But today she puts her normal clothes back on and says, 'Hold on, I'm just off to see if they have anything in a bigger size.'

'I'll help you,' Ms S-S snoots at her.

They leave me swishing about in the mirror. After what feels like ages, Carlota comes back on her own.

'Right, Bets, we're leaving.'

'But – the dress!' I love it. I don't want to let it go. I want it to be my second skin.

'Don't worry about that, just get changed. Come on!'

'Why?' My heart sinks as I start changing.

Carlota gives me a mysterious smile. 'Don't worry. It's a surprise.'

As soon as I have my clothes on, she scoops up the red dress and walks briskly towards Ms Snooty-Snot, who's examining her nails behind the counter and looking generally a lot calmer.

Carlota practically throws my dress at her and says, 'Be sure to tell Naomi we have an appointment! Holey Grail – you heard it here first!' She power-walks out of the shop.

I scurry after her. 'Lots! Lots! What was all that

about?' I've got a bad feeling about this.

'That dress looked fantastic on you,' she says, as if that was an answer.

I sigh. I don't want to think about The Dress That Got Away.

'So I got it for you,' Carlota says as we turn the corner. 'Here!' She opens her bag, pushes her knitting aside and yanks out a crumpled shimmery ball.

My dress.

Carlota looks proud. 'It's exactly like the one you tried on – I checked the size and everything. And I got myself that white one too, in a bigger size.'

'Carlota!' Oh, no, this isn't happening. She took the dresses? She *stole* them? 'Take them back!'

She gives me a shocked, hurt look. 'Why? Don't you want it?'

I can't believe she's stolen over a thousand pounds' worth of dresses, just like that, and she doesn't even seem remotely worried!

I sort of gasp at her. 'But how did you manage that?' She's amazing! She's terrible! She must have taken them from right under Snooty-Snotty's nose. And don't they have alarms and stuff? Why haven't we been arrested? My insides cramp up, churning.

Carlota's still smiling smugly. 'Isn't it brilliant! What? Don't look at me like that. We *needed* them, and she can afford it. I think she practically *owes* me, really, with her attitude.'

I can't even reply to this. My head's buzzing. I

mean, yes, she was snooty but . . . she could lose her job and . . . she had a cold and . . . it's just wrong, whichever way you look at it. God, I hope she's got some GCSEs to fall back on.

I walk with Carlota in a daze, barely looking as she points out accessories and other stuff we *need*. I don't want to encourage her to take anything else. I can't believe this is what I'm doing with my life – me, the girl who worries about everything and nothing. It's like when mean parents say to crying kids, '*I'll* give you something to cry about.' Carlota's wringing me out today, saying, '*I'll* give you something to worry about.' I don't know what to stress about most now.

I get this uneasy feeling, like I'm being watched. Store detectives! My heart jumps in my mouth and does an unhinged salsa. But I put my head down and keep walking. And nothing happens.

Oh, God. I can't live like this, always running, running to keep up with Carlota, running away from my problems and her problems.

Carlota looks at me. 'Bets!'

'What?' I say, giving my lip a good chew.

'You're stressing for England.' She nudges me. 'Honestly, there's nothing to worry about.'

'Yes, there is.' My stomach cramps again. 'I don't want to do this – shoplifting and—'

'What are you talking about?' Her eyes are wide.

'Oh, Lots, come on.' She's like the total Queen of

Denial, my best friend. She can do no wrong – it's never her fault. 'Taking those dresses is stealing.'

'What?!' Carlota shakes her head and gives a hollow laugh. 'You thought I was shoplifting? No way – why would I do that? I might be selling Naomi my Holey Grails, remember?' She grins.

Now I'm totally confused. This makes no sense. 'You didn't steal them?'

'Course not. I've got nothing against that shop. Have you forgotten?' She taps her bag. 'Mum's credit card PIN number is my birthday. I've known that for years. I used to watch her type it in.'

Now I'm really headed for prison because I'm going to kill her, right here in front of all the King's Road passers-by. 'You could have told me! You could have paid in front of me so I knew! You could have put them in a proper shop bag! I thought I was a criminal! Or at least a criminal's sidekick, you know. An accomplice.'

'But it was a surprise! How was I to know you'd think I was a thief? I'm hurt!' Her eyes sparkle. 'God, is this all because I didn't get a bag? They're huge paper things in shops like that – it would have ruined the surprise!'

OK, so maybe there won't be store detectives following us, but I still feel uneasy. 'But, Carlota, you *are* stealing! You're stealing from your mum! You're not planning on paying her back, are you?'

She stops smiling. 'So? She deserves it. She stole

my whole life, marrying that man.' Her eyes go hard.

'Lots . . .' I don't know what to say and she won't look at me. We keep walking. My stupid anger at her has gone just like that – it feels unimportant now. I know Carlota's got problems at home; I'm not blind. And there's the whole boarding-school threat thing. But she's taking it too far, surely.

She says, 'It's all about what *he* wants. She's treated me like I'm nothing ever since he moved in. No – ever since she *met* him.'

'I bet she doesn't mean to—'

'No, she does!' Carlota starts walking even faster, so I have to rush to get close enough to hear her. 'I don't fit into her life. I'm not good enough – I'm an embarrassment. Too loud, too large . . . I've tried to be all good and sweet like you, you know, but I can't do it. I know I just remind her of . . . of . . .'

'Your real dad?' Straight away I think, *I shouldn't have said that.* Carlota's never mentioned her biological dad before, and I've never even thought about why. I'm a terrible friend. I'm always worrying about me, me, me. I should be ashamed of myself. Why have I never asked?

Then again, why has she never told me?

'She was only sixteen when she got pregnant, Bets! As old as *I* nearly am, as old as *you* are – can you imagine? It's unreal!'

That's news to me too. I knew Carlota's mum

must have been young. But – sixteen?

Like me.

Oh, God, I've been putting that right out of my mind.

I manage not to say anything. Anyway, it's not about me, not right now.

'He was only a bit older than her. They didn't stand a chance. She was practically anorexic – well, she still is – and she didn't know about me for months. And when she found out and told him, he left her. But then she didn't try to find him or bring him back! She gave up, just like that! *Abuela* – my grandmother – told me all this once. About how my mum gave up on my dad. And then, years later, she met *him* instead – the boring old Diplomat. And I know she thinks they'd have the perfect life if it wasn't for me. I'm like a permanent reminder – some other man's daughter, ruining it for them! And nothing I do is good enough for her!'

We stop at a crossing. I scrabble in my head for something to say to her but I come up blank. I let her continue.

'She hates me! I embarrass her!'

'Lots, she doesn't—'

'Well, I don't care anyway! She thinks I'm bad? I can be *worse*!'

She looks at me like she'd forgotten I was there. Then she wipes her face with the back of her sleeve and shuts down. She sniffs and says brightly, 'Right,

Bets, my turn to pick a challenge.'

'Lots, let's go somewhere and talk or something.'

'No way! Talk is for wimps. I'm all about the extreme action!' Her magazine springs open the second she pulls it out of her bag.

I peer shyly over her shoulder. I'm not sure how to be around her right now. 'Film reviews?' I say quietly.

'No,' she says. 'Next to it – the thing about reality TV stars. And there's a call for people to audition for the next series. I know exactly what we're going to do for this challenge! Ash gave me some tickets this morning.'

I'd almost forgotten about Ash and his creepy friend – it seems like a long time ago. I never even asked her what she was doing with him, once I knew it wasn't snogging. Too much other stuff happened straight afterwards.

'What tickets?'

'They're for a live recording of a TV programme. When I was chatting up Ash for you, I told him you wanted to be a singer, and he said he had these expensive tickets for us. He was wrong – they were free. But anyway, we've got the tickets, and the studio's right near here. Isn't it brilliant?'

'What sort of TV programme?'

Lots doesn't have to answer – I can tell by looking at her face that it's going to be fun, and she's going to make trouble.

Carlota

I can't believe I was going to pay loads of money for these tickets. I wonder what Ash paid for them? Whatever it was, he was robbed!

If I said that the Palookaville Productions studio looked pretty unspectacular from the outside, I'd be complimenting it. It's just a red sign pointing down some grimy stairs under an ordinary-looking town house. In fact, if it wasn't for Bets needing this, my first thought would be to forget it and get back to shopping. I'm sure I could work the magazine so that we get a shoe-buying challenge next.

We stand in a queue on the stairs for a while. There are three bored-looking men in suits in front of us and assorted studenty-looking people gathering behind us.

Then the door opens and a woman appears. She looks ancient except for the fact that she has bright orange hair in bunches. She also has a clipboard and an earpiece.

Her voice is extra-loud and twangy, and everything she says is a question. 'OK, studio audience? Come with me?'

We follow Bunches Woman into a basement which smells of damp cheese. We're taken to a large room. It's been painted bright blue, all of it, including the floor. It makes my Reverse Goth clothes look ultra-white in contrast. There's a gadgety-looking thing on each blue seat and loads of cameras and electrical stuff near a high-up blacked-out window.

Bunches Woman tells us to find a seat and I immediately head for the front – I figure that's where we've got to sit for this to work.

But she has the cheek to frown at me. 'Too much white?' she says. 'It flares on camera?' She tells us to move back a row.

Bets actually starts to move but I hold her back and stay put. Bunches Woman's too busy to notice, anyway.

After much fiddling about, Bunches Woman taps at her earpiece and announces, 'Welcome to Palooka-ville Productions? I'm Kirsty? The show you're about to watch will be broadcast live on the Pizazz Channel, which has a cult audience? And we're on the rise?'

A few people murmur. The cameras sweep the room and I see us all projected onto about five small screens and one large one.

Bets nudges me, all excited like I knew she would be when Ash first mentioned this to me. I wave into a camera and pull a face, and Bets watches me on the monitor and laughs.

'Well, you're probably all familiar with the format of our show? We've pre-selected acts who are going to do their stuff and get voted on by viewers on the web, and by our panel of celebrity judges?'

Someone at the back does a watered-down version of an American chat-show whoop.

Kirsty continues, ignoring him like a pro. 'And also you the audience? You'll each get your say through our unique vote-o-rama digital panel? You're vital to the atmosphere of our show and the cameras will pick you out at intervals, so be ready to smile, people!'

I remember that Bets and I are not quite ready. I probably shouldn't draw attention to the fact that I haven't moved back a row, but what the hell. I put my hand up.

Bets nearly falls off her blue chair in horror. 'Lots, we're not at school,' she whispers.

'Yes?' says Kirsty. 'Audience member with pressing question?'

'I need to take my friend to the toilet.' That came out a bit louder than I meant it to, but never mind. May as well get the focus on Bets as soon as possible. It should help.

Bets looks like she wants to die, twenty people behind us fall about laughing, and Whooping Boy lets out another weak call of the wild.

'Through there?' Kirsty points. 'We start recording in five minutes? If you're late you won't be allowed in? And when you come in, move back a row?'

When we get to the toilets, Bets says, 'Lots, I mean really, what the f—?'

'We're going on national telly. Well, the Pizazz Channel. But it's a start.'

'That's the craziest thing I've ever heard you say,

and that's saying something!'

'I mean it. It's what you've always wanted and I know it!'

'It's not! What are you talking about?'

'Bets, I know you, remember! I know all about the singing lessons and how you won't take the exams or sing in front of anyone. Well, you shouldn't be scared. Come on – you know it's in your blood, the whole frustrated musician thing. You get it from your dad, like the crap jokes and the fear of GCSEs!' I ignore the murderous look she gives me and continue. 'It's time you stopped being frustrated and actually did something about it. If you can't do it today, when everything's wild and mad and normal rules don't apply, when *can* you do it?'

She still looks like she wants to kill me, but I detect a slight smile twitching on the edges of her lips. I know I'm right.

'But we're just the studio audience.'

'For now. Ash told me they choose one member of the audience for a guest slot, and I've drawn attention to us already. And when you go back wearing your new dress, there's no way they'll be able to resist.'

Now she looks like she doesn't know whether to attack me or faint, but she does smile.

* * *

Bethany

☼♡ I can't believe her! I can't, I can't!
I also can't believe myself, because there's this small part of me that stood there thinking: *You're right, why not? It's my chance.*

So I change into my new dress, like Carlota suggested, and she changes into hers too, 'for solidarity'. I even do my make-up, without looking twice at the pregnancy-test box that's crammed into my huge make-up bag. Well, without looking three times, anyway.

It's impossible not to get swept up in Carlota's schemes – I've always found that. But I know there's no way this could happen anyway – why would they choose *me*? – and that's mostly why I'm not worried.

We get back to the studio, all glammed up apart from our shoes, which we can't do much about. I'm wearing trainers and Lots has white furry boots on. She looks like Lily Allen crossed with a sheep. And knowing her, it will probably catch on, at least among the cult following of the Pizazz Channel.

Almost as soon as we sit down, a skinny bloke in a zanily multicoloured shirt springs out of nowhere. He's close to bursting with enthusiasm, and he's also outrageously eyeing up every female within flirting distance. He bounds up to a woman a few chairs away from me. 'I'm Raj! Your presenter with Pizazz! What are you doing later?'

Carlota does a dramatic cough containing the word 'loser', which makes me giggle.

'And you, young ladies! You look delightful! Like strawberry meringue! Good enough to eeee-eat!'

I shut up instantly but Carlota beams at him and whispers, 'See? He's noticed you already. He's *so* choosing you!'

'People! This is so exciting! This is Pizazz! You're all lovely people! Especially you lovely ladies.'

There's a silence from us, the lovely people. Especially the lovely ladies.

Raj is undeterred, a true professional. He introduces the team of judges, who are 'ex-West End stars' that I doubt anyone's ever heard of, although there's a boy at the back who takes the opportunity to whoop-whoop quietly anyway.

Then Raj announces that the cameras are rolling, and he instantly changes completely – well, he's still over-the-top, but he's suddenly flirting with the men instead of the women. 'We have more raw talent here than you can shake a raw carrot stick at!' he says, sidling up to a man in the audience. 'Oooh-err!' I can sort of see how it might gain a cult following.

The first act comes on – a singer called Ella Fizz Gerald. She's a tall woman with huge eyes and what looks like a fruit bowl on her head. She croons some old song badly for a few minutes and the judges all tear into her as if their careers depended on it – which maybe they do, seeing as

241

they're on the Pizazz Channel.

'You killed the song!' says judge number one, a grey-haired obvious Simon Cowell wannabe. 'Dead! Murdered! Criminal! For shame! Life imprisonment!'

A dramatic-looking woman with a frilly collar does this double-handed wiggle – I think it's called 'jazz hands' – at him and disagrees. 'That's harsh! It wasn't murdered! Merely lightly strangled. When I was on stage at the Adelphi—'

'It's not about you!' the third judge, a younger man in skintight clothes, chimes in. 'Focus on Edith!'

'I'm Ella.' Ms Fizz Gerald stares at them with wide eyes and blubs a bit. She mutters, 'But there's no band. I'm better with backing.'

Then Raj says, 'Studio audience, over to you!' He starts to leap between the rows, followed by cameras and trailing leads that snake all round our feet. He bounces about talking to people, camply tapping men on the leg, saying 'oooh-errr' every other word and generally making Graham Norton look like a war correspondent.

This goes on painfully for another three or four acts, which include a pair of old men with an accordion and a ukulele. I'm quite getting into it – even laughing and stuff, especially at Jazz Hands and her wibbly fingers. And the judges are so *rude*! I start thinking about looking the channel up when I get home. Then Raj announces, 'OK, it's our patented audience slot – our wild card! Who wants to have a go – oooh-err!?'

And when I turn my head, Carlota has her hand up again.

She's never that polite at school.

Raj leaps over to a bald man a few rows behind us and says, 'You look like a fine specimen.'

The man's about to answer when a voice rings out, 'Er, excuse me, Raj, but my friend's a proper singer!' It's Carlota. 'She's had lessons and everything.'

The cameras turn to Carlota, and Kirsty suddenly appears next to her, expertly draping a pink shawl over Carlota's white-clad shoulders.

Raj's eyes eat her up while the camera's not looking. 'Is that so?' he says. He taps the man on the head and says, 'I'll deal with *you* later!' Then he says, not taking his eyes off Carlota once, 'What *divine* dresses you're wearing – you two are dressed like stars already. Are you singing together?'

'No, no!' I say, meaning that I'm not singing at all – I can't believe Carlota's actually making this happen like she said she would!

She says, 'No, Bets is the singer. I'm just her friend.'

The whooshing sound in my head blocks out most of the rest of the conversation between Raj and Carlota, but then I hear, 'Ladies and gentlemen, please welcome our audience slot singer for this week – what was it again? Bets! Oooh-err! Have a go!'

There's some applause followed by silence. Kirsty's going frantic, mouthing at me, *We're live! We're live!*

Raj launches into a distracting comedy routine and the audience rocks about laughing, which drowns out Kirsty saying, 'You have one minute to sort yourself out or Raj will choose someone else.'

Well, good. Let him.

'Go on, Bets,' says Carlota, half pushing me to get up. 'You can do it – you know you can!'

'This is nuts!' I hiss at her. 'I can't!' But there it is again – this slight thought at the back of my mind: *Why not*? I've always wanted to try. No one watches this programme anyway. The audience here all look like they've been dragged off the streets because they have nothing better to do. Even creepy Ash used the first chance he had to get rid of his tickets. I'll never see any of these people ever again. Today is a mad day that doesn't really count. I can do this. But what am I thinking? I *can't*!

'What am I singing? I've got nothing to sing!'

'Make it up!'

'I need music.'

'No, you don't. It's like the silent dancing.'

'But we had music for that! From our phones!'

'OK!' Carlota brandishes her phone. 'So sing my ringtone. I'll play it.'

She really is a nutter.

But . . . I suppose I could. I've heard it often enough. I know the words. And Ella Fizz Gerald herself said she'd have been OK with backing music.

So I stand up.

I don't really know who's watching me – there are so many lights, so bright. I could be in my bathroom at home, or on the Wii karaoke when Mum, Dad and Rowan are out.

Except that, in those cases, I don't have boys whooping in the background. Or people introducing me, or a round of applause.

I quickly block out that thought.

Then there's this hush, which is even worse. I freeze. I want to run away. I should never have let Carlota talk me into this! I shut my eyes and wish the ground would swallow me up.

But when I open them, I'm still here and Carlota's beside me.

'I'm doing the music,' she announces to the audience.

Then I hear her phone start – the intro to the plinky rock version of 'Que Sera, Sera'. It's really soft in the echoey space, but it's clear enough for me.

Oh, who cares? Carlota's not scared – why should I be?

My voice is tiny at first, as I sing the line about being little and asking my mother what I'll be, and it wobbles when I reach the chorus and my mother basically just answers, *Whatever*. My thoughts are going, *That would* so *never happen*. My mum's more likely to answer, *'Whatever your dad says, Bethany.'* I tell my thoughts to shut up and concentrate.

Carlota starts doing her unhinged dance beside me, flapping her pink shawl around. Her phone keeps warbling, and I sing along. We must look and sound completely, totally, cringe-makingly mental-ist.

I close my eyes a bit to shield myself from the dazzle and I throw myself into singing, recommending an easy life – no worries, take your chances, who knows what the future holds? I should be completely embarrassed but I'm not. I can hear my voice soar and I'm loving it. Who cares what I sound like? This is *fun*!

When the applause comes, I feel like I own the room – like a total star. This is what it's all about! No wonder Dad failed his exams to go for it.

I don't even care when the has-been Simon Cowell crew lays into me. Apparently I 'have promise' but I 'need practice' and 'what an atrocious choice of backing music'. Well, I might have 'come this close to murdering a classic song' and I'm not invited back for next week, but I don't care. Jazz Hands loved me, and she's been on stage in the West End!

I did it! I did it!

'Bets, you were amazing,' Carlota tells me on our

way out, looking serious and tying her pink shawl in a knot by the neckline of her dress.

Oh God – she hasn't given the shawl back! What will Kirsty do next time she meets a Reverse Goth who wants to go on national telly?

'Thanks, Lots. I couldn't have done it without you.' It's true. When the GCSEs are over, I'm so going to suggest starting a girl band with my friends. Baljit's got grade eight in clarinet and Becca's got musical theory, or something similarly Becca-and-Baljit-ish, so they can be in our band too. We can call ourselves Carlota and the Boring Bees! And I've cancelled my singing exam three times, but now I think I could maybe do it.

I laugh to myself as I run up the stairs.

There's a man standing by the entrance who's sort of familiar, and I shout, 'Hello!' at the back of his head as I skip down the road a bit.

I feel so free!

I did it!

'God, Lots, I'll never forgive you for making me do that,' I tell her when she catches up with me. And then, because she looks so weirdly worried, especially for her, I laugh and add, 'It was brilliant, you idiot! This is the best day of my life!' And because she still doesn't smile, I say, 'Give us the magazine. My turn for a challenge. I think I'm about ready to take over the world!'

Carlota

I knew she'd love it. She's over the moon. It's fantastic – it's everything I planned.

But that means . . . the next part of my plan is *telling* her. Time's running out.

I haven't thought about the next challenge – I didn't think beyond this one really. But Bets picks a good one anyway. It's perfect for what I need to do.

She groans. 'It's about exercise and five-a-day! It's about *health*.'

She does an elaborate fake yawn, and even though I try, I can't manage to smile at her. I'm imagining how she'll react. Right now she's so happy, but what I have to say will ruin it! I can't think straight, my head's full of this and nothing else.

Wow, this must be how Bets feels all the time, with her constant worrying.

You can't tell to look at her now. 'I can't exercise anyway – my ankle's still a bit sore! I suppose we could drink weird veggie smoothies or something. Where can we go?'

We need a place where I can tell her. Somewhere big and luxurious with lots of quiet corners. Like . . .

'Mum's health club. I've got her membership card.'

'Ooh, yeah, is it full of muscly guys? Hold on – isn't it near our school?'

'They have branches all over London. She's allowed to use them all.'

New Extreme Bets goes, 'OK, why not! Let's

wander round the gym ogling men with biceps!'

She sounds like me!

'Or we could just go to the spa bit,' I say. 'And talk.' I sound like her! It's freaky.

I find Veronica's card in my wallet and study it. I look loads like the photo on her card – I'm just curvier and more funkily dressed. I don't know why she has such a problem with me, when I'm so much like her, only fifteen years younger. Well, that's it, of course. I remind Veronica of her life before I came along and ruined it.

'It's got a list of branches. There's one right near here.'

We find the health club quite easily because it's on a main road and you can see the sign from miles away. As we get closer, I can barely talk to Bets at all. In fact, I feel super nervous all the time, like people are standing too close to me, like I'm being followed, like I need to run and keep running.

On the way in I hear Bets call out, 'Sorry!'

'Someone bumped into me, behind me,' she explains in the health club foyer. Our ears buzz from the contrast between the outside world and this total calm.

'So why did you say sorry?'

'I don't know.' She laughs. 'Maybe because *they* didn't! Oh, weird, my bag's already open.' She shrugs and takes out her phone, which makes me instantly nervous. Who's she phoning? Is she going to tell me?

How can I ask her without sounding suspicious?

She nudges me in the direction of the reception desk. 'Well, go on then, Mistress of the Blag! You need to get us in. I'll be with you in a sec.'

'OK, no problem,' I say, but it's not what I'm thinking. I want to stay with her and make sure she's not phoning Declan. Or Becca! Or even Baljit, who possibly knows.

The receptionist is a short blonde woman with long painted nails and a skinny body that my mother would admire and tell me I should aspire to – 'It's not impossible to achieve – it's about self-control.'

I glance back at Bets, but she's busy pressing buttons on her phone. Texting someone.

Who, who?

I book Ms Del Rey . . . Peters – urgh – into the club, plus one guest. I also ask for fluffy towels, robes and two clear plastic 'pampering kits', all of which I charge to Veronica's platinum card.

'We're in!' I call to Bets.

The receptionist raises her eyebrows at us ever-so-slightly. Well, who cares? I've paid now.

Bethany takes the pampering kits off me and chats excitedly about them all the way to the changing rooms. I manage not to ask her who she texted.

The changing rooms are pretty luxurious, as I would have expected from anything that involves Veronica, post-Diplomat. There are clean-looking benches and a sparkling, dry floor and the smell of flowers and pine, instead of bleach and sweat like the ones in even the classiest of the schools I've been to.

The lockers gleam. But it's maybe not exactly the kind of star-studded place Bets and me were expecting. For a start, the spa just consists of a steam room and a sauna off the main changing area. Also, something's gone wrong with their temperature control or whatever, because it's stifling hot in here even though it's a typically damp March day outside. There's a fire exit over in the far corner that's wedged open, obviously in a pathetic attempt to let some air in.

But the main evidence that this is a saddo place and not somewhere the slebs would hang out is that it's deserted instead of being filled with Veronica lookalikes. Or maybe they're all out shopping, spending their rich husbands' money, wishing they didn't have teenage daughters who made them feel old.

I strip off my glam dress and put a robe on. Bets heads for the lockers.

She pulls at the doors, which are blinking with a display of numbers. 'How do these work?'

Oh, yeah, I hadn't thought of that. 'I think Veronica has some kind of fancy electronic lock arrangement, like a PIN number. Try my birthday.'

But it doesn't work. Didn't she once moan about having to change the number every month? It sounds familiar, but I never really listen to Veronica that closely if I can help it.

'Ah well, no worries,' says the new breezy Bets.

'There's no one around anyway.'

We pile our stuff under a bench. Bets puts her trainers on top. 'Who'd dare to touch that?' she giggles.

'Good idea,' I say. But I'm tempted to. I could try to find out if she texted Declan or Becca, without asking her and making her suspicious.

We pick up our towels and I follow Bets to the spa rooms.

'Sauna first?' I ask, but Bets is suddenly hesitating by this large sign outside the rooms. It's the usual stuff – safety this, danger that, no responsibility taken by anyone at the health club for anything at all.

Why has she gone white?

'Lots, I need to tell you something,' she says.

And I need to tell you *something*, I think. 'What?'

'It's bad . . .'

It can't be worse than what I've got to tell her.

'What?'

She bites her lip. 'I can't think of a good way to say it but I've been dying to talk to you about it and . . . and now I feel I can cope with anything, so I can deal with this too, but I still need you to help me through, whatever . . .'

'What?' I just know she's overreacting again – being Bets.

'I . . . See that sign?'

'Yes.' Huh?

'I can't go in.'

252

'What do you mean you can't go in?' I read the sign again, the words jumping about in front of my eyes. *Not recommended blah blah heart condition, blah blah pregnancy, blah blah history of thrombosis . . .*

For a moment I still don't get it.

And then I do.

'Oh, God, Bets. You're not!' I don't mean to sound like this. I don't know where this is coming from, this accusing tone. 'Oh my God! Are you *pregnant*?'

And, when she doesn't deny it, my first thought is this: *Now how am I going to tell her?*

Bethany

Finally, finally, I've told her. Or she's guessed. Or whatever, but at last I know everything's going to be all right because I have Lots on my side. But she sounds strange and looks horrified, which I didn't exactly expect. Not from cool, unshockable Lots.

'Are you sure?'

'No. But I'm late.'

'How could you be?' she says. 'How is that possible?'

I give a nervous laugh. 'Well, you know . . .'

'No, I don't.'

What is the matter with her? 'Of course you know.'

She's not joking. 'No, I don't. Not *you*. You're always so stressy. You're always so *careful*.'

Well, OK. I see what she means about that. 'But accidents happen, don't they . . . ?'

I can't believe what she says next. She says, in this horrible voice, 'Not if you don't let them.'

'Lots!'

'How late are you?' She rolls her eyes, thinking.

'You were moaning to me about cramps during that stupid cross country thing they forced us to do about a month ago. You can't be that late.'

'I'm not. Two days.'

'Two days is nothing!'

'But I was sick!'

'You had a stomach bug!'

'I don't know if it was a bug! No one else I know had it, did they?'

'But you're fine now! Have you told Declan?'

'No! You know he hasn't called since—'

'Have you done a test?'

I look at the ground. Why am I feeling so defensive? 'It's the first day I've been out of the house since I . . . suspected something.'

'Well, I bought one today for the challenge!' She picks up my stuff and pulls it roughly across the bench. Her eyes widen with realization. 'Omigod! You *asked* me to buy it, didn't you? Why didn't you tell me?' She starts frantically yanking things out of my rucksack. 'Where have you put it?'

'In my make-up bag,' I mutter.

'I know, but where's your make-up bag?' She

rummages more. 'It's not here.'

'It is. I used my make-up at the studio. It should be right on the top.'

'It wasn't! It isn't!'

'It has to be.'

'Did you definitely put it back?'

Now she sounds like my mother.

'Yes, I . . .' I sit next to her and look too. She's right, there's no sign of my make-up bag. I must have left it at the studio, or maybe it fell out of my rucksack. Oh, no! I've lost my best lipstick, my new eyeliner, my pile cream . . . and my pregnancy test.

And my best friend's sanity.

'I can't believe you've lost it! I can't believe you think you're pregnant! There's no way you took any risks – I *know* you!'

'No method is a hundred per cent safe – they taught us that in PHSE, remember?'

She kicks at the ground for a while and I don't know what to say. Then she mumbles, 'Except one.'

'What?'

'There's a method that's a hundred per cent safe.'

'What do you mean?'

She looks up. 'I mean, not doing it. You can't get safer than that.'

I can't believe this, coming from her! She was always encouraging my Boy Snaring last year! 'Carlota, why are you being like this? You were happy for me when I found Declan!'

She swears loudly.

I'm stunned. Is she angry with me? Or Declan? I think back to her outburst after she bought the dresses. Maybe this is about her mother. Because I'm the same age her mother was when she had her? And her father just disappeared? That's probably it.

'It's OK,' I say slowly. 'I'm sure Declan will stick by me whatever.' That's a total lie, but I suddenly feel like *I* need to reassure *her*. It's crazy. The world has turned upside down.

She swears again. Then she says quietly, 'Why? What are you going to do?'

'Well, I don't know.' It's early days. I was going to talk it through with my best friend, who was going to help me sort it all out. Maybe it's just as well I didn't mention it before.

A tap drips in the distance.

It's so quiet here. I almost wish someone would walk in and interrupt our awkward silence. I speak tentatively. 'Haven't you ever, you know . . . had a scare like mine?' I mean, I should know this, shouldn't I? But now I think about it and I wonder how much she's ever really told me about her life. All these feelings about her mum, for a start – I still can't believe I've never heard those before. We talk all the time, but we seem to have skipped all the stuff that matters.

She says, 'No, I've never had a pregnancy scare.'

'You've never even been worried?'

'No. Aren't you listening? I haven't *needed* to worry. Because I've never done it.'

'Never done what?'

Her eyes blaze at me. 'God, Bets. Do I have to draw you a diagram? I've never had sex.'

Now I know she's gone crazy. She's rewriting her own history, becoming a born-again virgin or something.

'Lots, come on! You're always talking about it, ever since I met you. All that Kisses Etcetera. You've done it with loads of boys – you've told me!'

'Yeah, and that's exactly what it is. Kisses. Etcetera. There's loads of stuff you can do. You don't have to risk *pregnancy*! At sixteen! With some . . .' She uses about ten different nasty words for Declan. 'That's just *stupid*!'

I feel like she's kicked me. I've always suspected she wasn't Declan's biggest fan, but I didn't expect her to attack him like this! And me. Did she just call me stupid?

'I wasn't stupid! We used a condom! Why are you being like this?' My brain races. 'And anyway, Carlota, have you forgotten that you were caught with Yves? You can't tell me that didn't happen! It was the whole reason you ended up at our school! Or it speeded things up, or whatever you told me earlier. And wasn't it the reason . . . ?' The way Carlota's looking at me stops me from saying *you were still in love with Yves*. It sounds ridiculous

257

anyway. It sounds all wrong. I've got her all wrong, all this time.

'You mean you and Yves didn't . . . weren't . . . ?'

She shakes her head. 'I've always let people believe what they wanted to. Everyone loves spreading rumours. People want to think I'm totally wild and out of control. Especially my parents.' She pauses. 'Even you.'

There are hot cramps in my stomach. I feel awful. I never imagined for a minute that the rumours weren't true. They seemed right. They seemed like Carlota.

'And anyway, I don't think there's anything wrong with doing it, I just didn't want to . . . take the risk.' She sniffs. 'But I didn't try to talk you out of it, did I? You can do what you want. It's none of my business. You just don't *get pregnant*!'

It's not guilt I'm feeling. It's anger. Bubbling, rising. I can't stop it! 'You never told me you felt this way! You let me think you'd been doing it for years! You made me think I should be doing it with Declan!'

'Omigod, Bets, you made your own decisions. I never lied to you! About anything!'

And then I notice the look on her face. She looks like she's about to burst into tears.

I don't know what to do. I put my arm around her tentatively. 'Lots,' I say, my anger becoming a bubble in my gut. Pop. Gone.

'Oh, sorry!' she gulps. She tries to smile and pretend everything's OK. 'It's stress. Where's my knitting?'

'Listen,' I say, taking charge. I can deal with anything today. I've proved it. 'I'm not going in the sauna. I don't know what's going on with me, or what I'm going to do about it. But we can still use the pampering kits, can't we?' I nod towards the shower cubicles, which look gorgeous, and possibly better than our shower at home. 'I think we need it. And then we'll go somewhere and talk. Really talk, properly, about everything. Sort this all out.'

Carlota sniffs. 'Yes. OK. You're right.'

'OK.' I go back to the benches and pick up my pampering kit. 'I'm going to the showers.'

'Yeah.' Carlota's stopped looking teary but she's still not being herself. She's kind of shut down. She says in a monotone, 'You go ahead. I'll have my shower in a minute.'

'All right.' I feel really weird. We've never really had an argument before. In fact, was that even an argument? I'm not sure. It was *something*.

The shower cubicles are mega-posh. I let the strong stream of water pour over me, drowning out the worries. I can cope. And I've got to remember that it's all thanks to Carlota that I feel this way.

Carlota

☀ I wish I could talk this over with someone. But there's only one person in the world I can talk to, and it's Bets. And I can't tell her. I can't say anything. It was difficult before, but now it feels plain wrong.

I sit on the bench and wrap the robe tighter around me.

The shower hisses in the distance. She's so calm in there with her pampering kit. My whole stress-relief idea worked so well for her. Only now I think she was right to be worried. There are some things in life that don't get sorted out all by themselves. Some things you *do* have to worry about.

I'm running out of time. And everything's a hundred times worse. Maybe she actually needs Declan around now, no matter what he's like. Ugh. Maybe the worst love rat in the world needs another chance at a time like this. I wonder how different things would be if my mum had ever given my dad a chance. I could've had a real dad and Veronica could have stopped feeling ashamed of me.

How did this happen? It's all wrong. It's such a mess!

I know what I should do. I should ring Becca. I'll tell her about Bets. It'll stop her. How can she do this to her friend? She'll have to agree with me – and *Teen Spice!* – now. Bets should never know. Then at least Bets and Declan can work things out.

But would Bets want me to tell Becca? Somehow I really doubt it.

I reach into Bets's pile of stuff and find her phone. I turn it over in my hand, wondering. I want to check who she texted before, but I don't know how to do that on her phone. I wish I wasn't so rubbish with gadgets.

I press a few buttons and reach a list of names – Baljit, Becca, Declan. I haven't got any of these numbers. They're not my friends – they're hers. They barely put up with me. Bets insists we're all mates, but I know the truth. None of them have ever liked me, not really.

I can't call Becca.

I scroll down to Declan's number and press CALL before I can change my mind.

I can't believe I'm doing this but my thoughts go like this: *Maybe* he *can talk some sense into Becca and tell her not to say anything.*

Or maybe I'm not really thinking.

He answers. 'Bethany?'

It takes me by surprise, but I'm not sure why – it's her phone, after all. Maybe it's because he sounds strange. Hopeful. Does he love her? I don't think so, but what do I know, after all?

'Bethany?' he repeats.

'No, Declan, it's Carlota.'

Silence.

'Carlota?' Now he sounds confused.

What am I doing?

I hear footsteps and chattering. People arriving to

use the gym. Normality.

I hang up and press buttons frantically. Bethany's phone asks if I'm sure I want to 'delete all' and I press the button for YES, over and over – I want to delete absolutely everything, all the evidence of my stupidity. I switch it off and stuff it back where I found it.

What exactly did I think I was going to say? He doesn't even know about Bets. No way is it my place to give him news like that.

I shift away from the women getting ready around me, and I only remember I was supposed to be having a shower when Bets appears in front of me, towelling her hair and sounding far more normal than I expected, given what she's just told me.

'Are you OK? Did you change your mind about using the pampering kit? It was brilliant!'

'Uh . . . yeah.' How can she be like this? How can she even think about anything else right now?

'Never mind. Let's go and have that chat now – you look like you need it.'

'No, Bets, you need to do a test. This is serious. Don't you see? It's massive. It's . . . your responsibility to find out.' I can't believe I'm lecturing Bets! And using words like 'responsibility'! But I also can't believe she's not worrying more. 'We should go and buy another test right now.'

'Well . . . OK,' she says. 'I suppose we can talk later.'

'Yeah, we can.' And we'll have to. And I'm dreading it even more now.

We get dressed in silence, with this weird tension between us. I can't act normal around her, not when I keep thinking how much worse it will sound to her now, the thing I need to tell her.

Bets is ready first and she still seems far too relaxed. She says, 'I'm boiling – I'll wait for you over there,' and she stands over by the open fire exit, staring out calmly.

I know it's irrational, but I'm angry with her. How can she behave like this, like it's not the hugest deal in the world?

Just as I finish getting ready, she suddenly goes, 'Oh God, Lots, I can't believe it! Come here a sec!'

I pick up my bag and drag myself over to where she's pointing.

'Down there! Can you see it?'

'What?' There's a rickety metal staircase and an empty side road, dusty and full of rubbish.

'It's my make-up bag! How weird.'

She's right – I can see it too now. It's sparkling pinkly from the top of a mound of rubbish.

'Come on – let's leave this way. I'm going to get it.' She's halfway down the emergency stairs when she jokes, 'Phew – at least we've found the pile cream now.'

I don't laugh. It's not a joking matter.

'But how did it get there?' Bethany wonders. 'I can't have dropped it. We came in through the front, didn't we?'

I reach the bottom of the stairs. And then the ground twists in front of my eyes.

A dark shape looms in front of me and an arm pulls me roughly around my middle.

A cold claw grips my mouth and it's disgusting.

A gruff voice says, 'Give me your money. Now!'

I hear a muffled sound, a panicked half-scream.

Then I realize it's coming from me.

Bethany

'Let go of her!'

I spin on my heels and shout at the man who's grabbed Lots. I can't believe this is happening – it doesn't feel real.

He looks creepily familiar. Then, with a sickening thud in my stomach, I recognize him: it's Ash, the man Carlota got the tickets from this morning. I realize he was the man outside Palookaville too. Has he followed us?

Or maybe he knew where we'd be – because of the tickets Carlota got from him.

'You stay out of it,' he growls. 'Your purse was full of crap. It's hers I want!' He sniffs and wipes at his nose roughly, taking his hand away from Carlota's mouth just long enough for her to let out a horrible whimpering sound. 'Making me a frickin' laughing stock with my mate – taken for a ride by a pair of *girls*! He's been having a go all morning,

264

telling me I shouldn't have spoken to you. And he's right – I should have just got your stuff when you wasn't looking, like we normally do with stinkin' tourists. Distracted by a pretty face – Connor will never let me live it down.' His face twitches. 'Well, he will now I've got the loot. I knew where to find you. Wasn't hard, after you stole my tickets.'

'Those tickets weren't worth anything!' I blurt.

He sniffs again. 'Oh, yeah? So frickin' what? I was going to get her money anyway, specially after she told me she was loaded! Soon as she got her purse out, it was gonna be mine! Looks like I'll have to help myself now.'

He rips Carlota's bag off her shoulder, releasing her as he pulls out her wallet and checks inside, letting out a small whistle of approval. 'Yeah, that's more like it,' he says. 'I knew you wouldn't let me down. That'll make up for wasting my time today, stressing about you ripping me off, getting all that grief from Connor.'

Carlota hasn't even moved away from him, or made another sound. She's frozen, her eyes pinpricks of fright.

He drops the bag, stuffs the wallet in his pocket and grabs Carlota again, taunting, 'So, what else you got for me, Spanish princess?'

I'm not quite sure what I'm thinking, and I'm probably not thinking at all. My heart pounds and there's a hot rush in my ears as I tear towards them.

I've transformed into some computer-generated character with special moves, like Rin Chine, Queen of the Night.

I reach Ash and kick him once, sharply, in the groin.

He swears, staggering backwards and clutching himself.

Carlota gasps.

It doesn't seem like enough, so I do it again, getting maximum force behind my kick. My bag makes a crunching sound as it falls but I barely notice it.

So it turns out Carlota's right about women and power. It's oozing out of me. I beat a virtual Zac and I can beat a real man too – if you can even call Ash a real man.

I pick up Carlota's bag and mine and swing them on my shoulder. I want to get her wallet too, but Ash is getting up and he's threatening us at the top of his voice and we should go – now. I pull Carlota's arm and shout, 'Run!'

She finally moves.

Leaving Ash staggering and swearing, I run. I don't care that my ankle hurts. Carlota's footsteps thunder behind me. I rush past a woman who's standing at the end of the road going, 'You girls all right?' and I nearly crash into a clump of people gathered in the high street. I dodge around another couple of groups. Everyone seems intent on getting in our way right now.

I don't stop until Carlota begs, 'Bets! Wait!'

She's stopped, getting her breath back, looking pale and scared and terrible.

I walk over to her, feeling wobbly myself. But one of us has to stay calm.

There's a familiar lilting sound coming from one of the bags on my shoulder. Carlota's tinkly dial tone – the song I sang earlier. It feels like it's mocking us. I find the phone and hand it to Lots. She looks at it in a trance.

'It's my s-s-stepdad,' she says.

Carlota

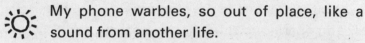 My phone warbles, so out of place, like a sound from another life.

'Aren't you going to get it?' Bethany's voice is sharp.

I stare at my handset, trying to remember how it works. 'He thinks I'm in the lo-local library. I can't sp-speak to him.' I can't even *speak*.

'If he's checking up on us, it's worse if you ignore it! Just answer it!'

She's being so tough right now. How can she manage it? I'm in pieces. 'Y-you do it.'

I hand her the phone and lean against a wall, hugging myself, trying to feel smaller and more comfortable. I wish I could stop trembling.

She huffs and takes the call like it's nothing, like

she hasn't just been terrified to within an inch of her life. Well, maybe she hasn't. But I have.

She has to hold the phone away from her ear. The Diplomat is booming, 'Carlota!'

I shudder even though it's tinny and distant. But still loud. 'Where the HELL are you?'

'Mr Peters, it's Bethany,' says the professional dad-pleaser. 'Is there a problem?'

'Because I hear . . . Oh. Bethany?'

I can make out nearly every word. He sounds angry – even with her.

'Put Carlota on the phone!'

I shake my head and my face feels wet. I touch it. Tears. Wow, I'm a wreck.

'She can't come to the phone right now,' Bets says, like an operator. 'I'll tell her you called, and—'

His voice dips up and down. I can still hear most of it. 'Tell her . . . I'll tell you what you'll tell her! . . . back home NOW, and . . . you too, young lady. NOW. . . . not in the library! . . . fraudulently . . . wife's Revivals membership card! Wallet . . . Fraud! . . . home RIGHT NOW . . . LATE . . . OR ELSE . . . new school . . . Carlota! NOW!'

My tears freeze on my cheeks.

How could he possibly know about the member-ship card? Did they trace Veronica's credit card or something? Is that possible? So quickly?

Bets seems surprised too. 'Mr Peters—'

'. . . your mother told my wife where you were,

268

Bethany. She told her . . . as if she already knew . . . any idea how FOOLISH it makes us look!'

My face burns. Bethany looks at me, then quickly away.

'Quite frankly . . . my daughter . . . no respect for me whatsoever . . .'

Bethany says, 'Mr Peters, Carlota had nothing to do with this. I wanted to go to the health club.'

I don't know why she's saying that. It doesn't help. I glare at her, but she's not looking.

'And if you started giving Carlota a little more respect then she might start respecting you more.' She takes a deep breath. 'And *frankly*, Carlota is *not your daughter anyway*!'

She presses the red button on my phone.

Suddenly the thoughts of Ash's threatening voice and his sweaty hand clamped round my mouth seem to shrink in my head, replaced with echoes of what I've just heard.

'Oh my God, Bethany.'

'I know,' she says. She seems pleased with herself.

'What. The. Hell?'

She smiles proudly, misunderstanding me.

And then I'm flooded with anger. I'm so angry that I can't see straight. 'What did he say? Did I hear him say that your mum – YOUR MUM – told Veronica I was at a health club? Bethany Royston, can I just ask you?' My head throbs. 'How the HELL did your mum know that?' I don't leave her a gap to reply. 'Huh? How?

How would your mum know that? Unless YOU TOLD HER. Did you send her one of your Good Girl texts telling her exactly where you were? Because you can't move an inch without being a dutiful daughter? Did you even stop to think that she was with my mum this afternoon and she might mention it to her? Did you think *at all*?'

She dares to look wounded, innocent – that old Bets look that's all an act. Look how she was with Ash. Look how she was with Zac. Bets, a shy worrier? I don't think so! I never did think so – I always knew she was like me! No, she's better than me! Stronger than me!

She still doesn't get it. 'But, Carlota, you should be grateful that I told my mum the truth. Think about it. What if things had got worse with Ash? At least someone knew where we were! Anyway, why did you go and tell him you were rich? You can't just go trusting random people, you know. It's your fault this happened in the first place!'

Urgh. Does she know how smug she sounds?

She's on a roll. 'It's true. You act like you own the world. You think it's OK to talk to anyone, snog anyone and act like a *slut*, but—' She stops and puts a hand over her mouth.

Omigod, I can't believe she said that!

It's true what they say about seeing red. When I shut my eyes, I see blood. When I open them, I see Bethany Royston, who is supposed to be my friend.

My voice comes out quieter than I expected, considering all the redness. 'You are totally full of shit, Bethany! It's all right for you – your life is so safe! *You're* safe, no matter what! Your parents care about you!'

She stares at me, wide-eyed. 'So do yours,' she says in a small voice.

'No, they don't! Veronica told The Diplomat what your mum said to get me into trouble, so he'd send me away! It would be better for her if I disappeared altogether today – it would save them some money!'

'Oh God, Lots, that's not true.'

'It is! He doesn't know any better – he thinks he's doing it for my own good – but *she* does! She can't wait to get rid of me!'

'I'm sure she—'

'You – you don't know anything about me! Why are you even friends with me, if you think I'm such a . . . a *slut*? Well, I know why! It's because you want someone to blame! It's my fault you're not in some boring library being boring! It's my fault you're sleeping with Declan! It's my fault you're snogging someone else to distract you from your terminally boring relationship that's always been mostly physical anyway, so why doesn't that make you a . . . a *slut*?!'

Oh, no. Oh, God. I didn't mean to call her that! Even though she said it to me! No one should use that word, ever. It's wrong. It takes girls' power away from them. I can brush that label off – I'm so used to hearing ignorant people say it about me. But no one should say it to Bets. Especially not *me*!

She looks at me like I've slapped her.

And I realize that *everything* I said to her was wrong, on so many levels. She's just saved me from that creepy Ash, apart from anything else! She's right too, about everything she said! And I'm wrong wrong wrong.

'Omigod, I'm sorry,' I say, not looking at her. I can't believe I was angry with her at a time like this. The one time in Bets's life when she really, truly has something to worry about, and I'm expecting her to think of me first? And I'm shouting insults at her for no reason? What kind of friend am I, anyway? 'I shouldn't have said any of those things. I didn't mean what I said! Any of it! I'm sorry!'

She makes a face. 'No, *I* am.' She pauses, still looking stung. 'You're right, I shouldn't have told Mum where we were. I didn't think.'

'I know you've got much, much more important things on your mind.'

'*This* is important. I don't want you sent to that school! And anyway, it hasn't really been on my mind.' Bets gives a tiny smile. 'Thanks to your stress-relief scheme.'

Yeah, well, I'm starting to think I've done the wrong thing, dragging her out like this. We should have stayed at home and talked and done a test and known for sure. I didn't even ask her properly what was wrong this morning – I just assumed I knew. And all I could think about was distracting her from what I thought was her problem – that, and trying to see Yves.

I've got to be a better friend. Starting now. I've got to be more like her. She's still worrying about me, after everything I said to her.

She says, 'Are you OK? Should we report the . . . what happened? We should report it, shouldn't we? But it might take ages and we need to get you home . . . I'll talk to your stepdad, honestly. I can fix it.'

Never mind that. 'Bets, did your make-up bag still have everything in it?'

'Yes.'

'Then we should do the test. Right now.'

'Oh,' she says. 'OK.'

Bethany

I've never seen Lots so serious about anything before. Personally, I think it's more important to get home and sort things out with her stepdad. The test – my future – can wait; it's waited all day. My problems aren't going anywhere.

But Mr Peters, with Carlota's future in his hands, really sounded like he *wouldn't* wait.

I keep telling her that I think I can sort it out with my usual Good Girl talking, but this time I'm not too sure. Maybe this time I can't. Maybe she's finally gone too far.

I definitely think we should go straight home now, though, and try. When I spoke to him, he sounded ready to send Carlota away then and there, if she didn't come straight home. And then what would I do?

But Carlota's determined that I should do the test first, and I'm treading carefully around her. She feels kind of . . . fragile now, after everything that's happened. I can't believe the way I talked to her before. I don't want to upset her again. I need to take care of her.

Everything in the street feels weird. There's an odd buzz and too many people – the crowds I passed before, when I was running away from Ash. Or I was running away from what I did to him, I suppose. I never knew I had it in me to attack a person like that, but it came naturally somehow. For a moment there, I think I almost scared myself.

We cross over to another overcrowded pavement and now it's obvious that there's something weird going on. There are two police vans parked near the tube station and uniformed officers all over the place, herding the crowds and talking sternly into oversized handsets.

Just outside the station, a man in a fluorescent orange jacket is addressing a circle of people.

I get closer and hear him say, 'Ladies and gentlemen, this is all the information available at the current time. We'll update you as soon as we can.'

This is met with stoical shrugs, except from one man, who shouts, 'You can update my arse!'

I catch Carlota's eye and whisper, 'Who'd want to get close enough to update his arse?'

She doesn't laugh, even though it's a totally Lotsish comment. She's really not herself right now.

'In situations like this, your safety is paramount. It really is out of our hands,' the fluorescent jacket man says to the rude shouter. 'Please try to understand we are acting in your interests.'

I hear some people near us asking a policeman what's going on.

'Massive security alert,' he states in a bored voice. 'All services from this station suspended until further notice. Move along, please.' He walks on, repeating the last instruction.

I suddenly realize this is a problem for us, with Carlota's stepdad expecting us home as soon as possible.

I try to reassure her. 'We'll find another station.'

But she's still only thinking about me. 'And then will you take the test? Bets, it's important!'

I resist the temptation to roll my eyes. 'Yeah, I know.'

We walk for ages, snaking randomly through the crowds, but it doesn't look good. We keep passing people who are milling about saying 'security alert' into their mobiles.

I see the entrance to Kensington Gardens and I turn in to get away from the crowds – plus I think there's a tube station we can try at the other side of the park. Carlota follows me.

I sit down for a minute on a nearby bench and Carlota perches next to me, hunching up again.

Everything that's happened today has affected her so badly. I suppose the Yves stuff alone must have been a pretty big punch in the stomach for her, and she's taken everything after that so much harder than I would have expected.

'Listen, don't worry,' I tell her. 'We're still extreme travelling. We can use the magazine to do a going-home challenge!'

Carlota stares at the ground. 'I'm not worried about getting home.'

I sigh. 'But, Lots, I heard your stepdad. He really meant it. If you don't get home right now, he'll ship you off to that place.'

'He won't.'

'But it really sounded like he *would*!'

She shrugs. 'He can't. Not if I never go home.'

'What are you talking about?' It suddenly dawns on me. 'Are you thinking of running away from home?'

She sits up straighter. 'No, Bets, *we* are. Why do we need to go back? We can get a flat together in London! I can help you look after . . . you know. You can sing professionally in bars. I can be your manager, or your babysitter, or both!'

Her eyes shine, like she's thought of the perfect solution.

She means it!

I blurt, 'But what about GCSEs?'

She doesn't answer, but her face falls.

I pick at my nail varnish. 'Look, Lots, I know you're upset. It's been a crazy day. All that stuff with Yves, and then being mugged, and your stepdad on your case again.'

She grimaces.

'But you've got to stop worrying and talk to me more. All those things you never told me – about you and Yves, about your mum . . . Well, you *should* tell me. I'm your friend! Worrying gets you nowhere except *more* worried. Honestly – I should know.'

She looks like she's going to cry again. 'But this time there is something to stress about, Bets.'

'No there isn't. We'll sort this out, all of it. I mean it. *I'll* sort it out.'

Her voice is hollow. 'You can't.'

'Course I can. I have all kinds of skills, including some I never even knew I had before today.' I count them dramatically on my fingers. 'Dad-talker-rounder. GCSE-worrier. GCSE-no-more-worrier. Friend-slagger-offer, friend-slagged-offee.' I start on my other hand, stressing the next one. 'Friend-forgiver. Stepdad-annoyer. Thief-kicker. I gave him fireballs, Lots!'

She gives a tiny smile.

I keep counting. 'Tour guide! Zac-kisser . . . Singer on live television.' That's all my fingers. 'I can do anything. Everything else I have to face – *we* have to face – is nothing.'

Her expression brightens slightly more. I think I'm convincing her.

I nod at a sign in the distance. It says PUBLIC CONVENIENCES.

'And just to prove it, I'll take that test now, OK? And I'll deal with whatever it throws at me, without stressing. But with your help.'

'Bets . . .'

'Come on.' I stand up.

And it's not long before we're standing in a corner, tucked away over by the disabled loo, waiting for the results to come up on the test Carlota bought this morning.

She read the instructions to me three times, in her new, serious, non-Carlota voice. It was possibly the weirdest thing I've ever had to do in my life, but I managed it.

Right now the flashing stick symbol on the digital display is tearing through the calmness I felt before.

'Is it supposed to blink like that?' I ask Carlota. I bite my lip.

She re-reads the instructions for about the fourth time. 'It shows it's working correctly,' she says. 'Has it stopped?'

'No.'

'Keep looking.'

'I am.' I do.

And now my heart is thumping in time with the blinks, and I'm not sure I can cope after all. This is bigger than GCSEs. This is a test I can't revise for, with only one result I want to get. This affects the rest of my life.

Carlota keeps reading the leaflet. 'It's ninety-nine per cent accurate from the first day of your expected period,' she tells me. 'I bought the most expensive one there. It's got to be the best.'

'Er, OK,' I mumble. I really never, ever expected Carlota to be like this. Ultra-responsible. Like a big sister. Not like my wild mate. It's freaking me out.

I interrupt her as she starts to read the next bit. 'OK. I think it's stopped.'

'What does it *say*?' She grips my hand and tries to read it. 'What does it say?'

My hand shakes, but it's not my fault – it's Carlota who's making it shake. And I always used to think I was the worrier out of me and her.

It's clear as anything. I read it three times to myself and once to Carlota, because saying it out loud will make it real.

* * *

Carlota

☀ 'Not pregnant,' Bets says. 'See, Lots? It's OK!' Her face lights up with mad relief. Mine should too, but it's no good.

I mean, it *is* good – it's great – but it doesn't make everything OK. She's still intent on going home, for a start.

How can I talk her out of it? Why can't she see how perfect my new idea is – the one about running away? I can't believe I didn't think of it sooner. I could have brought extra clothes with me! I should have planned this from the start, instead of getting hung up on Extreme Travel. After all, what is there at home for us? Central London has everything we need! And now we won't even need a babysitter. We can both have sparkling London careers!

Bets takes out her phone, still beaming, saying, 'Hang on – I've got a text.' She reads it and I wait, trying to push away the familiar panic building in my stomach. But she grins even more. 'It's Mum. She says the Crafty Nutters session ended early, but not to hurry home because Dad's been sick and he's acting like he's dying. See, Lots? That's even more proof! I obviously had a stomach bug! I've got to stop blowing everything out of proportion! Everything's fine! I bet there's nothing going on with Declan either. From now on I'm going to stop worrying for ever! I mean it.'

I stare at the ground.

'Anyway, our main problem now is to get home

quickly.' She fiddles with her phone. 'But don't worry. Becca's mum already offered! I'll ring Becca again.'

I take a deep breath. 'Bets – about Becca—'

'Hold on.' She taps at the phone. 'This is weird.'

Oh, no. What has she seen?

'It's blank.' She stares at it. 'My list of names and numbers – they're all gone. It's like it's been wiped. D'you think it's from when I dropped it, in that alley outside the gym? It has to be, doesn't it?' She looks at me, genuinely concerned. 'Oh God, sorry, Lots, I didn't mean to remind you about that.'

'It's OK.'

'OK, well, have you got Becca's number? Or Baljit's?'

'No.'

'I haven't got enough money for a taxi. And your mum's wallet's gone . . . God, what are we going to do?'

I take out a magazine.

'I don't think a challenge will work this time, Lots.' Bets looks worried again. 'Seriously. This time we're really stuck.'

I check I have the right magazine. 'It's not a challenge. Well, maybe it is.' I shake it until a card falls out, and I hand it to Bets. 'Your challenge is to ring Yves and ask to speak to Zac. Then Zac can take you home.'

Her eyes sparkle but she says, 'No! No way! We can't ask him to do that.'

'He'd love it. I know he would.'

'But I should never see Zac again!'

But she should. That's one of the best things to come out of today – that and her singing confidence.

'Bets, trust me, Zac really, *really* likes you. And you're great together.' Much better than her and the betraying, cowardly Declan.

This broad grin crosses her face.

'Come on, you know it's true.'

'God, Lots, you're too annoying. You know me so well, don't you? You knew you'd get me singing and you knew you'd get me snogging someone else!'

I want to do my trademark evil laugh here, but I can't quite manage it.

She sighs. 'But I've cheated on Declan, haven't I? All that time I worried about him cheating on me, and then I went and did it instead. And, you know, I don't want to face it. I want to forget it ever happened. It's better that way, don't you think? If he never knows, I mean.'

Does she really want me to answer that? All I can think about is the conversation I had with Becca yesterday.

'That's what *Teen Spice!* says,' I tell her.

'But it's going to feel weird, always knowing the truth. I'll feel guilty for ever . . .' She stares at her phone. 'Oh God, look at the time! Lots, I'm sorry! I'm being so selfish. I've got to get you home and save you from your stepdad. What are we going to do?'

I point to the card. 'I told you. You have to ring Zac. It's your challenge.'

She smiles. 'Then maybe I have no choice.'

And I'm just starting to think that maybe it's all going to work out after all when our phones both start ringing at the same time.

'The Diplomat.' I groan. 'Who's yours?'

'Declan,' she says.

Bethany

Carlota's phone's going on about not knowing what the future holds – the song I sang earlier today.

And I don't know what the future holds but I know that a minute ago just the thought of seeing Zac again made me feel all hot and cold. And guilty. And happy.

My mobile keeps ringing, displaying an 'unknown number' that I know is Declan's. I memorized it the night he gave it to me, after our second party snog.

I stare at the phone. I'm not the same girl I was this morning. I'm Action Girl now, the Friend-Saving Thief-Fighting Superhero.

Who has kind of cheated on her boyfriend.

The boyfriend who is finally ringing her.

But he's late. I've waited two days for him to call – days when I was thinking the worst, worrying myself to bits.

Well, so what? He's my boyfriend. He doesn't have to ring me every five minutes to confirm it.

Yes, but *two days*! And that text this morning? After I broke our date? There's definitely something going on.

But he's calling me now, isn't he? Before our Saturday night date, which I'm definitely thinking about going on after all. We can spend our usual Saturday night in his bedroom, with the Lynx-smelling football duvet cover and the folded pile of ironed football shirts at the foot of his bed that we forget to move and then try not to crumple.

My phone keeps ringing. Carlota's keeps singing. Our callers are very insistent.

'Are you going to answer?' I ask Carlota.

'I don't know. He just wants to give me an earful, and he can do that when I get home, can't he?'

'Yeah.' I'm relieved she's stopped talking about running away.

'What about you? Are you going to answer?'

'I don't know. No. He should have called sooner. He can wait.'

'He doesn't deserve you.'

'Maybe not. Lots?'

'Yeah?'

'So, shall we?'

'God, yeah.'

I reach over and press the button to reject her call.

Then she does the same on my phone.

I pick up Yves' card and call that number instead.

And, after that, we switch our phones off.

Carlota

I knew Yves wouldn't come. I knew it and I was still disappointed when the limo pulled up and he wasn't in it.

I felt like running away again. I nearly did it, only Bets pulled me in after her. I jumped straight out again, but only to get in the front and leave her alone back there with Zac.

Anyway, she's right – I should go home. I should face things. You can't run away for ever, not if your friend won't come with you.

Bets and Zac are giving it large with the small talk back there. I know they're flirting. There's tension crackling between them. I'm so happy for them. It doesn't matter that it'll never happen with me and Yves. Bets deserves this. And it'll help when I tell her the truth about Declan.

I still can't believe Becca's willing to risk her friendship with Bets like this, but I'm starting to think she might be right. Bets should know the truth. You can't have a proper relationship with someone if they're hiding things from you.

Anyway, I know I did the right thing today. I took Bets out of her world and showed her that she's more like me than she ever realized. That she takes as many risks, lives life as much on the edge as I do. Even if she does it in her own careful way.

It should help.

In fact, maybe I went too far. I glance at the back of the car. Right now she looks like the wild, carefree one.

And I'm every inch the scared, insecure one.

Maybe we always were like this – it's just that it looked the other way round to the outside world.

I rummage in my bag, past the magazine I'm going to use when I get home. It's the right issue – I checked. It's the one from this morning, the one with the problem page letter I told Declan and Becca about. It also has an article about Frenemies – enemies disguised as a friends.

People like Becca.

The final challenge is for me – telling Bets without breaking her heart.

I'd get my knitting out for stress relief, but I know it won't work. I find the pen Bets gave me on the tour bus and think about what to write in the magazine, so it can do the talking for me.

Bethany

Being near Zac is making me shivery all over and my mind's a total blurry blank.

'Clocks are changing tonight,' Zac tells me.

'Spring forward, ' I remark intelligently.

'Yup. Longer days,' he adds, matching me.

'Gets dark later.' I think I'm beating him in the Inane Things to Say competition. 'Does it make a difference, you know, in French?' Hey, I think I'll go in for the *Insane* Things to Say comp too.

'Huh?'

'You know, how you say *Bonjour* until a certain time, and then you're supposed to say *Bonsoir*? But *Bonsoir* isn't just "Good evening", it's also, like, "Good afternoon", but only late afternoon.'

My dad would be so proud of all the French revision I'm doing today.

Zac nods. 'Um, yeah, that's right.'

He's not even acting like I said anything nutter-ish, so I go on. 'Well, I've always wondered, at what exact time do you switch to *Bonsoir?* And is it different when the clocks go forward?'

'Yes, probably,' Zac says very seriously. 'I'm sure there are all kinds of laws about it in France. But I don't know what they are.'

'So how do you know which to use?'

'Well, I just say *Bonjour* and when people answer *Bonsoir,* I say, "Oh, yeah, right."'

I laugh. 'But you speak proper French!'

'Nah, I'm faking it, like lots of French-speakers,' he says. 'It's, like, no one knows the real difference between *beau* and *joli* either. If I want to call you beautiful and I say *Tu es belle*, you'd probably reply,

Non, je suis jolie. And the same the other way round.'

Oh my God, is he saying I'm beautiful or pretty? Or good (or crap) at French? Well, in any case. 'I would bloody not say that!' I laugh.

'Why not? You are.'

'Shut up!'

He shrugs, smiling. His phone rings and he groans and goes, 'My dad.' Then he answers, *'Bonjour, bonsoir,'* and smiles at me again before he turns away and launches into a stream of French responses to what is clearly his dad's equivalent of The Chat.

God, I really want to kiss him again.

I look out of the window at the orange light on the grey towers. Tomorrow the sunset will be at least an hour later. Today I get an extra hour to find Declan and talk to him and make things right.

Or not.

If I was more like Carlota I'd just pounce on Zac right now and not even bother giving Declan another thought. I'm sick of being me – always careful, always worrying.

Although clearly not *always*. It's been a long day.

Zac finishes his call and says, 'That went well. I only have to work non-stop for the next seventy-two hours as soon as I get back. Seventy-three, with the British Summer Time thing.'

'I'm not sure I want an extra hour of today.'

'I do,' Zac replies. 'It's been the best day.' He looks straight into my eyes.

I take a sharp breath. My insides do that flip-flop thing.

I look away.

The driver puts some music on – some techno-type stuff with French lyrics. Carlota will probably like it.

Zac shifts around on the leather. 'Listen, Bet . . . I loved everything you said to me today. You've really got me thinking. I've been thinking all afternoon. All evening.'

'About what?' I can't look at him.

'Everything.'

'Oh.'

'And you.'

'Me?'

'I mean, what you told me. You're right. I can't live like this. You know, for other people. I've got to break up officially with Claire. And stand up to Dad. I'm going to do things that I want to do.'

'Did I say that?'

'Kind of. Well, the tarot reader said some of it, but you showed me it was true.'

There's this huge long silence.

Then Zac speaks really quietly. 'Your boyfriend's so lucky.'

'What?' Yeah? Declan's lucky I don't need to have monumental conversations with him about lateness and pregnancy. He's lucky he doesn't know I desperately want to snog the boy sitting next to me.

Declan's a total lottery winner this Saturday.

'Nothing,' Zac says, but then his voice gets louder, bolder. 'Bet, I asked before and you said I could call you, but . . . for that, I kind of need, you know, your number?'

I pause too long and he adds, all flustered, 'Or you could call Yves again and ask for me. You know. Any time you're on a random adventure and you get stuck.'

I feel that magnetic pull again, tugging me towards Zac. But I can't give in to it. I don't want to cheat on Declan again, no matter how many doubts I have about him. No matter how tempting it is.

'It's not a good idea,' I mumble. 'Sorry. But thanks for . . . today. And the lift and everything.'

And I do feel sorry. Really, really sorry.

In fact, I'm about to change my mind and blurt out my number when Carlota calls out, 'Right here's fine,' and the limo comes to a stop.

We're at the top of Carlota's road.

And so is another familiar car.

I don't believe it. I look at Carlota, but she's busy chewing my red pen over a magazine, doing a quiz or something. Besides, she probably wouldn't recognize it. She doesn't know the car like I do.

It's Declan's dad's Volvo, parked up the road a bit from Carlota's, near Becca's house.

In the driver's seat I can see the shadowy outline of Declan.

EXTREME SATURDAY: EVENING

TEEN SPICE! MAGAZINE

 QUICK QUIZ: SPOT YOUR FRENEMY!

You're BFFs. You've known her for years. Your mums call each other by their first names, you've been to each other's birthday parties and done your homework together. She calls herself a mate – but is she? Try our quick quiz! If you say 'yes' to any of these questions, watch out. She could be a toxic friend, aka an enemy in disguise . . .

   – Is she suspicious of any new friends you make, acting as if you're not allowed to choose who you want to hang around with?

   – Has she ever made jealous-sounding comments about your relationship with your boyfriend?

   – Does she blow hot and cold – your best pal one

minute, barely talking to you the next?

– Has she ever hooked up with someone at a party and not cared whether or not you were left standing on your own?

– Does she seem pleased when things go wrong for you, almost as if she can't wait to rub your face in it?

Bets - Becca

Bethany

I glance at the time on my phone. I was supposed to be meeting Becca – will she mind that I'm late? And what am I going to do about Declan? He must be really serious about wanting to talk to me if he's come here.

Well, I have more important things to sort out first. If anyone can save my best friend from that new school, it's me.

Carlota puts her magazine down and glances back at me. Then she slowly gets out of the car. I've never seen her look so worried about confronting her stepdad. She's usually got more attitude than sense.

I'm not looking forward to this either, but I know we'll get through it.

I open the door, refusing to look at Zac.

'Bet, wait!'

I hesitate and let myself to turn towards him. His eyes are intense. He says, 'Bye, Queen of the Night.'

He smiles.

I smile back. 'Bye, Thorene.'

I step into the cool semi-darkness of the early evening and watch the limo cruise smoothly away.

And Zac's out of my life.

Carlota's standing at the end of her drive.

The intruder lights outside her house have switched on. I glance at the windows, but the curtains don't move and no one comes to the door.

'Bethany,' she says as I approach, studiously ignoring Declan's car and hoping he hasn't seen me. 'I need to talk to you.'

'I know – we should get our stories straight. So which parts do we tell him?'

Carlota swears, kind of at herself.

'Lots, honestly, don't stress,' I say. 'It'll be OK. I'll help you out.'

She garbles something with the word 'extreme' in it.

'What did you say?'

Carlota swallows and talks more slowly. 'The first challenge. Remember?'

'Yeah, should we tell your stepdad about the challenges?' I smile – it's a joke, obviously – but Carlota doesn't seem to think so.

'The first challenge. The secrets . . .' She's mumbling again. 'I didn't tell you. I have to tell you now.'

I feel suddenly wary. It's the way she's not looking at me.

'What are you talking about?'

She pulls a magazine out of her bag and shuffles through it frantically. 'Page eighty-five of the magazine. It wasn't about secrets – not exactly. I put that mag away – we used the others, because . . . because I didn't want you to see what it said. Not yet. And there's an article you need to read too. I turned the corner over, so—'

There's a clicking sound behind us.

Carlota shoves *Teen Spice!* at me. It's the one we started our day with.

The front door opens and I hear a roar which makes me stop thinking about how weird Carlota's acting. I'm pleased that I'm holding the magazine – it's always good to have a prop in times of stress.

Here we go.

I fiddle with the pages.

'Carlota Del Rey Peters! How long have you been standing here? You are in big trouble, young lady! *Come straight home*, I said! *Straight home!* And how long has it been?'

Carlota mumbles something about tubes and security alerts.

'Never mind that! You should have taken a taxi! I would have paid! I've been worried sick! I even called the police like I said I would, but they said to wait a while longer before filing a report, since I'd had contact with you. And the local health club said you hadn't even been there! And then we had a call from the police to say that a man had been apprehended with your mother's wallet on his person – a *man* – after someone reported witnessing a mugging of two girls! And he was only caught because of the increased police presence in the area, which was due to a major terrorist threat, and it was right where you were! Carlota, I have aged ten years in the last two hours, and I tried and tried to call you . . .' Mr Peters holds his face in his hands.

Carlota's mum appears in the doorway with her arms folded and her face displaying its usual lack of emotion.

There's a pause while Mr Peters gets his breath back, and then he throws his arms around Carlota and goes, 'You're safe, you're safe! I was starting to think I'd never see you again!'

Carlota doesn't hug him back. She's looking over his shoulder, watching her mum turn and walk wordlessly back into the house.

Carlota's face crumples. I think she might be right about her mother. Her lack of reaction, that heavy unspoken disapproval, is somehow worse than Mr Peters's tirades. I always thought Carlota's stepdad was the baddie, but he was being pretty sweet just now, considering.

But any sympathy I felt for him goes in an instant when he stops hugging Carlota and steps back.

'Bethany Royston? You've got some nerve turning up here after what you said to me today. I've never been spoken to so shockingly in my life!'

I don't know what to do with myself. So much for helping Carlota. Things were going OK before he noticed me.

Mr Peters rants on. 'I used to think you were well mannered, a good influence – it made me think I'd done the right thing sending my daughter to your scruffy school. But I know the truth about you now! I shall be forbidding Carlota to liaise with you and removing her from that *hellish* place as soon as possible!'

He puts one arm round Carlota as if to protect her from my evil powers.

'I should feel sorry for you. It's completely obvious where you get it from. The apple doesn't fall far from the tree! I spoke to your mother today, when I was beside myself with worry about my daughter's welfare and getting no reply on her phone. Your mother had the audacity to tell me not to worry, to refuse – *refuse*, mind you – to give me your number. Oh, no, your mother says, I trust Bethany. If Bethany hasn't called to say there's a problem, then there's no need to harass her. *Harass* her.'

Mr Peters takes a deep, indignant breath. 'The nerve, the very *nerve* of the woman. And I asked to speak to your father, but oh, no, your mother was having none of it, making excuses about him being unwell. When my daughter's life was at stake! Well, it figures, doesn't it . . .'

I've never had one of Mr Peters's tirades aimed directly at me before now, but having listened to him go on at Carlota, I know it takes some strength to stand up to him. I feel a sudden rush of warmth for my mum. She's far less of a slave to men than I ever gave her credit for. She stood up to Mr Peters, which is far more important than standing up to my dad, who mostly bumbles along kind-heartedly anyway. Now I want to go home.

I try to catch Carlota's eye, thinking she'll be feeling terrible about this and wanting to apologize to me, at least by giving me a sympathetic look. But she's staring at the magazine in my hands, her face sunken with misery. Does she *still* think the magazine has all the answers? *Tips for dealing with your overprotective stepdad when he finds out you've been lying and stealing?*

And she won't meet my eye. She can't possibly agree with him, can she? If I'd had my way this morning, we would have stayed in her room most of the day, revising and chatting, or gone to the local library and been home early!

He runs out of steam at last. 'I'll thank you to stay away from Carlota in future,' he throws at me.

I swallow hard. 'Mr Peters, I'm sorry if I was rude to you this afternoon on the phone. You heard about . . . what happened. I was in a bit of a state when I spoke to you. I didn't mean what I said.' There. He doesn't deserve it after that outburst, but at least I feel better about my own big mouth now and maybe I can still save Carlota.

But Mr Peters starts moaning again and, honestly, I've heard enough. I tune him out and glance down at the magazine in my hands. I'm under the security light and I can read it easily. It's open at the page Carlota picked – page eighty-five, the page from our first challenge.

The large red words of the main problem dance in front of my eyes. It says, BEZZIE BETRAYAL!

I read it quickly three times and then I read it again just to make sure I'm not imagining things.

Everything seems to stand still around me. Why did Carlota want me to read this?

It's a letter from a girl who saw a friend snogging her best friend's boyfriend and she's worried about what to do.

I read the smaller print. Some phrases jump out at me. *Should I tell my friend? She really likes him. It will break her heart.*

And well-meaning phrases from the answer: *Be supportive – she may suspect he cheated and she needs you right now. Who would benefit if you did tell your best friend what you saw? You could try to stop anything like that from happening again.*

What's going on? Is this about Declan?

Does Carlota know something about Declan? Has

he cheated on me with *one of my friends*?

I quickly flip back to the other page she mentioned – finding the place where she's turned down the corner of the page for me. It's an article called 'Spot Your Frenemy'. I skim-read it. It's about people who are jealous of you, who pretend to be your friend when they're anything but.

And underneath, Carlota has scrawled something.

My name, and Becca's. And a sad face.

I feel dizzy. What's Carlota telling me?

Is it about Becca? Is Becca not a real friend?

Why?

She couldn't mean . . . Has Declan cheated on me . . . with Becca?

My mind's reeling. I know Becca had a row with Harrison earlier. Her mum said she had boy problems. Carlota got funny about me ringing her. And Baljit – she's been weird with me. Almost . . . ultra-sympathetic. What has Becca told her?

Does Becca want to meet me . . . to tell me? To rub my face in it? The Frenemies article says, *Does she seem pleased when things go wrong for you?*

And Declan's car parked here, with him still inside. He's waiting outside Becca's house. For Becca! He's waiting for Becca to tell me so that they can go off together into the sunset!

But Becca? Of all people? She knows how it feels to have a cheating boyfriend. And I'm her friend – practically her best friend, jointly with Baljit.

Or, at least, that's how it used to be, before Carlota came along.

Maybe that's it. She's jealous of my friendship with Carlota! She's getting back at me! At me and at Harrison, all in one go! Using my boyfriend and Harrison's best friend!

I'm completely stunned.

I can't believe Becca could do this.

Carlota

☼ I wish my stepdad would leave us alone. I need to know what she's thinking. She can't have understood what I'm trying to say – the magazine's a start but it's not enough. I need to talk to her!

She's holding my magazine open. She's read both the pages; the pages of my final challenge: to get her to understand and not be hurt.

She looks confused.

My stepdad's still ranting, completely oblivious to the fact that no one's listening. To be honest, I'm kind of surprised by him so far. He hasn't been too bad. Although he's being ridiculous about Bets. And as for Mum – Veronica – well, she's so predictable. I'm not even sure I care any more.

But I care about Bets! And I can't tell what she's thinking!

Eventually The Diplomat winds down. 'I can't stand around here all night.' He gestures at me. 'Come in the house, Carlota.'

Bets doesn't say anything, so there's definitely something up with her.

This is important. I have to plead with him if that's what it takes. 'I need a minute, Dad. Please. I have to talk to my friend.'

My stepdad glares at Bets. I manage not to say anything rude to him. But I called him 'Dad'! It wasn't even planned, or cynical – it just came out like that. He does sort of behave like a proper dad sometimes, I suppose.

He must have noticed the d-word too, because he does this double-take and then he says, 'OK. Five minutes.' He shoots Bets more daggers. 'But only because it's the last time you'll ever speak to her. Some friend! Look at the trouble she's led you into. You need to choose your companions more carefully, Carlota, and make sure they share your values.'

At the start of the day, me and Bets would have caught each other's eye at that, and she might have got the giggles.

But now she takes a few steps back, away from his poisonous glare.

And then.

Then.

My stepdad looks right at Declan's dad's car.

I hold my breath as he looks back at me, but all he says is, 'Five minutes, Carlota. I mean it.'

And he leaves me with Bets.

Bethany

'Lots, tell me. What's going on?'

It's so weird. She doesn't answer me, but her eyes fill with tears.

'What's this magazine thing? About me and Becca?'

She still doesn't say anything, so I press on through my confusion.

'Is it about Declan . . . ? Do you know something . . . ? About him and . . . Becca?'

I think about how I knew it. I've known since Thursday that he cheated on me. Declan's safe and predictable. He didn't reply to any of my texts on Friday and that's completely not like him. I knew it then, and I know it now. He was avoiding me because he was scared of telling me – and he didn't know how *not* to tell me.

But he texted me today. Did he know Becca was going to say something? Was he going to tell me? Had they planned it?

I think about Declan. I think I've been lying to myself about him. Maybe he was never a magazine quiz ideal boyfriend; the perfectly balanced Mostly Bs; the boyfriend who laughs with me, listens to me ramble on about life, loves me.

Well, maybe he's not perfect. But he's still my boyfriend.

I think about Becca. I try to feel angry with her. I know I should. But I can't, because something doesn't make sense.

I look at Carlota standing in front of me looking like she's about to cry, her bag bulging with magazines and knitting needles. And a different thought pops into my head.

When I saw Carlota this morning, she was knitting. For stress relief, she said.

And she wasn't stressed about her stepdad and that boarding-school thing. She told me that at the time.

This might sound crazy, but right now I'm thinking she might have been stressed about . . . talking to me.

But why would Carlota be stressed about talking to her best friend? Because she was hiding a secret about Becca?

Or something else?

When she persuaded me to Extreme Travel, she said, 'It will take our minds right off Declan, guaranteed.'

She said *our* minds.

Carlota's stepdad looked at Declan's car strangely just now.

He looked at it as if he recognized it.

I don't want to think it, but it won't leave my head.

Carlota – and Declan.

In some weird way, that *does* make sense.

It makes perfect, twisted sense.

She has tears running down her face now, watching me.

My voice comes out stunningly even and clear.

'Carlota, you need to tell me what's going on between you and Declan.'

Carlota

I'm throwing all my sorriest words at her but nothing is getting through. I can't stand the way she's looking at me. She's like stone!

'I'm sorry! It was stupid! It was nearly the end of term and we were all in a crazy mood after school and he was there and you weren't and – it just happened, Bets! But it proves he doesn't deserve you and—'

'Wait. *What* happened exactly?'

What can I say? I can't lie to her.

'Did you snog Declan?'

It would be better to say nothing. But it's too late for that.

'I'm asking you, Carlota, did you snog my boyfriend?'

My voice is tiny. 'Yes.'

She powers on, firing questions at me. 'So you kissed him? And what else? Would you even tell me the truth about that? How long's this been going on? And you did it after school? Where? You mean, with his mates around? Or ours? Or both? Am I the last to know? Did you get all *Kisses Etcetera* with *my* boyfriend *in front of everyone*?'

So many questions. I can only hold the last one in my head. Is it worse than snogging him in private? Maybe, because then it could have stayed private, like the magazine said it should. Bloody Becca, some friend *she* is! She's a total frenemy. She doesn't *care* about how this will hurt Bets!

And me.

I try to keep calm, but my voice is trembling. 'No, it wasn't in front of everyone!' I tell her. 'We'd moved away from most people, but Becca saw us because she had a row with Harrison and stormed off towards us and . . . But then Declan drove me home and—' I realize I should change direction. 'She wasn't supposed to tell you, Bets! She's not a real friend – she went against the magazine's advice! She wants to hurt you!'

'No, she wants to tell me the truth, which is more than you do! You got *in his car*? So you snog the face off my boyfriend for some random reason – oh, God, how long have you fancied him? How long have you been *seeing* him? And the way you react when my *friend* rumbles you is to – what? – *go for a drive together?*'

She has to understand! 'I haven't been seeing him! And I didn't fancy him, not like you mean! It was just once. He was just – there! Anyway, he's not right for you. You can dump him and go out with Zac!'

'Oh, right! Was that what today was for? Finding me a replacement boy so that the long-term relationship *you wrecked* doesn't matter?'

'No! I didn't wreck it! And today was about showing you what you deserve! And . . . and . . .' I can't say *What good friends we are* because it sounds pathetic, and all wrong, and she clearly thinks I'm anything but.

But it was the only thing I could think of, up there in my room, when I first read the stress-relief article. It was what I needed, but also what she needed, and it was something I knew we'd do brilliantly together!

And I thought there was no situation I couldn't control. I thought I'd make it OK!

How can I make her see it? 'Look, I'm not like you! I don't think things through. I don't worry about stuff. I didn't *think*. I didn't mean to do it!'

'No, fine. Well, maybe you *should* worry more. And anyway, what are you telling me? Your lips just hit his by accident?'

'Kind of!'

'Oh yeah? Well, someone told me today that *accidents don't happen* – unless you let them!'

What can I say to having my words thrown back at me? 'I'm sorry! But, Bets, don't you get it? Don't have a go at me – have a go at *him*! I'm single, remember!'

I wince as I remember Thursday. Me chasing Declan with the can of silly string. Getting separated from the others, spraying him and then picking off the pieces, laughing, falling. Kissing, out of nowhere. It was so easy. Becca turning up in front of us, shouting, all the drama. Declan driving me home in silence. Kisses Etcetera in the car outside my house. Him squirming after a while and saying, 'Do you think Becca will say anything?' Me thrilled, guilty, replying, 'She'd better not.' Him saying, 'You know, this can't go anywhere.' Me replying quickly, 'As if I'd want it to. I've got a boyfriend, anyway, in Brussels.'

Declan leaving and straight away The Diplomat appearing, shouting, grounding me. Me wishing I was Bets, or Yves was here, or I was there, with him, wherever he might be. Deciding to find him and know the truth, once and for all.

'I'll probably always be single.'

'Aw, poor *you*.'

I ignore her sarcasm. 'No, what I mean is, *Declan's* the one who's cheating, not me! You shouldn't blame *me*!'

Bets's eyes narrow. I know she's about to say something to hurt me, something to end our friendship for ever.

A deep voice says, 'Bethany.'

We both turn towards the sound.

Declan.

'Bethany, don't,' he says.

She's not even surprised to see him. She's icy calm.

'Declan, don't tell me what to do. Don't say anything. I *need to talk* to you.'

And she turns away from my house.

For ever.

Bethany

I'm at the centre of a whirlwind and I'm still. Nothing can touch me.

Declan follows me, whining away. It's strange to hear his voice. The last time I heard it was so long ago, when everything was normal and he was my boyfriend.

'I wanted to tell you, but Carlota said not to. But then I heard from Harrison that Becca was going to tell you.'

I think, *Declan, shut up*.

But he doesn't. 'Carlota told you, didn't she? Look, I need to explain. It just—'

'It just happened?'

'Yes,' Declan says, all gently, as if I'm made of eggshells and he's trying not to crush me.

I feel like crushing him where it hurts. What gives him the right to drip concern at me?

'I'm sorry, but it did,' he continues in that irritating tone. 'On Thursday after school. Everyone was messing around at the bus stop and she chased me with this can of silly string Harrison gave her and—'

This time I think out loud. 'Declan, shut up.'

'I swear, Bethany, I never meant it to happen. It was just one of those things. She didn't want you

308

ever to find out. She said it wasn't necessary to – to hurt you like that.'

'Yeah, right,' I say. 'Because she read it in a magazine. She doesn't actually care.'

We've reached the local shops. I realize I'm still holding Carlota's stupid *Teen Spice!*

I throw it into the first bin we pass.

'I didn't know what to do. I talked to Harrison about it, and that's when he warned me about Becca.'

Great, I think, I'm so glad Declan turned to *Harrison*, everyone's first choice for relationship advice.

'It's been so difficult—'

'Oh, yes, it must have been very hard for you.'

'Bethany, come on. You're just angry.'

Good old sensible Declan. 'Too right I'm angry.' I kick a wall, which hurts my foot. I should kick Declan. He's hurt me far more, far deeper than Ash did. Somehow it seemed acceptable to attack Ash, who was some kind of thief. Declan's only crime was to throw our seven-month relationship back in my face and make me feel I was stupid to think he ever cared about me.

But that sort of thing is normal somehow. I can't get him arrested for it, though I wish I could. I kick the wall again.

'Look, Carlota would never do anything to hurt you,' Declan says slowly, as if he's talking to some

309

irrational person who thinks walls are the enemy. Huh, I should show him what I can do.

Anyway, since when is Declan the expert on Carlota?

I swear at him. 'She already has. Carlota hurts plenty of people. She's a liar and a cheat. She makes people think they're special, then she throws them away. She doesn't care about anyone.' I try to kick him with my words. 'She certainly doesn't care about *me*. Or *you*.'

Declan sighs as if I'm tiring him out. 'Bethany—'

'It's true. Do you think you've got some kind of bond with Carlota now? Were you waiting for her outside her house? What makes you think you're anything in Carlota's life? You know, Carlota's been out all day finding strangers to snog!'

Declan stares at me.

I laugh. Oh, yes! 'Actually, so have I. I've been dancing in the street and travelling in a limo and appearing on live television in a cocktail dress and talking to pop stars and being papped and fighting criminals. Oh, yeah, and kissing a gorgeous boy I only just met.'

Declan's brow is creased; frown lines spread over his stupid cheating eyes. 'Bethany, why are you doing this? Making up crazy stuff?'

'Yeah, maybe you're right, I'm making it all up,' I say. This morning I thought I loved him. I even thought we might settle down together – I mean,

I thought it was a possibility. Now he feels like nothing to me. Why have I been hanging onto this relationship anyway? What's in this for me?

Why have I never asked myself this before?

'And maybe you're wrong,' I add.

'Bethany, look, I don't want to play games. I decided to tell you myself, before Becca, or Carlota, or whoever. That's why I sent you that text. But you didn't reply—'

'I was on the other end of the phone most of the day. And yesterday, and *Thursday night* too.'

'OK, forget it. Just forget it!' Declan looks like he wants to attack the wall now.

I'm used to calming Declan down when he gets upset about his team doing badly, or being left on the bench.

I'm not doing it this time.

Declan takes a deep breath. 'Look,' he says. 'We'll talk another day.'

'Oh, why? What are you doing now? Do you have a date with Carlota? Because you can't go one Saturday without getting any? Because ever since you bought me my first lottery ticket, every Saturday's a *rollover*?'

'Bethany, for fu—' He gets louder, more exasperated. 'Just shut up!'

'You,' I say, 'are the one who's shouting.'

'I didn't come here to see Carlota! You told me you'd be at Becca's tonight, didn't you? I came here

311

to see you.' He moves to touch my shoulder but I shrug him off. 'I didn't have the guts to knock . . . I was sitting there waiting for you to arrive. Working out what to say.'

It feels strange, hearing Declan talk like this. We've never really talked about 'us' before. We've always just carried on, with our unspoken understanding, our boring routine.

'Then I saw you in Carlota's driveway. I waited for her dad to go . . . I thought I should face you and stop being such a wuss, since I was the cause of the row.'

'It's not all about you, you know,' I say. 'That was about me and Carlota.' Because I don't know who I feel more hurt by right now.

No, I *do* know.

And it's her.

Even though she's right. *He's* the one who cheated.

But *she's* the one I trusted.

Declan stretches out his palms at me, as if that somehow makes him innocent. 'Bethany, honestly, I'm gutted. I don't want us to break up over this. When Carlota phoned me this afternoon, I was so disappointed! I wanted it to be you. I wanted to arrange to meet you and talk to you and make everything OK again. I tried phoning back but I got your voicemail. And I knew I should talk to you in person anyway.'

I stare at him. What? 'Carlota phoned you?' Why would Declan say that? Carlota was with me all day. 'No she didn't. Don't lie to me.' But something makes me add, 'When?'

'This afternoon. She called from your phone – I thought it was you! But she said it was her and then she hung up.'

I feel another wave of that stomach-punched sickness. Carlota called Declan on my phone! I realize with a jolt that it must have been Carlota who wiped my contacts. She probably only had to touch it to break it – that would be typical of her.

Declan gives me a look of pure confusion. And pain, like this is all hurting his safe, predictable, boring head.

'Bethany, listen to me, I seriously needed to talk to you. I luh—' He looks away.

So.

Was he going to say it at last?

I take a step towards him and he leans closer. I feel his breath on my cheek.

'Bethany . . .' he says.

I reach up with one hand and pull his face down towards mine.

And I kiss him.

* * *

Carlota

I've been sent up to my room, which is fine. It's where I want to be anyway. Away from *them*. All of them.

I tear my way through about a hundred issues of *Teen Spice!* but not one of them tells you what to do when your life's a total mess.

I unravel my knitting and try to find someone to blame. Declan shouldn't have let me kiss him; he shouldn't have kissed me back. Harrison shouldn't have been all over that other girl, which made Becca storm off and find us. She shouldn't be so in love with drama that she had to make a huge fuss, and so jealous of my friendship with Bets that she'd insist on ruining it by telling her what she saw. Declan shouldn't have driven me home and allowed all the Kisses Etcetera to happen right outside my house.

My stepdad shouldn't have arrived home and seen us and grounded me. And he wouldn't have done that anyway if he didn't think I was 'out of control' – if he wasn't still angry with me for getting caught with Yves in the lab at the other school.

So Yves shouldn't have taken me there in the first place, not when it wasn't safe from teachers.

And Bets thinks my whole boy craziness is because of Yves anyway.

So there it is: this is all Yves' fault.

And then I let the tears fall.

Because there's nothing I can do.

And who cares that I'm being sent away to a new school? They can send me wherever they like. It makes no difference. Bets hates me and Yves doesn't care about me.

And it's all my fault.

Bethany

Kissing him feels so familiar and comfortable. Our kiss. We know exactly what to do. It's predictable but not necessarily boring. After all, this is Declan, the boy I've been going out with for over seven months, the boy whose room I spend every Saturday night in, the only boy I've ever slept with.

My boyfriend.

My boyfriend. The boy who got off with my best friend and suddenly stopped answering his phone to me. The boy who thinks that calling me 'effing gorgeous' and replying to my texts – usually – is enough to excuse ignoring me sometimes at school, or whenever we're out with his football friends.

I breathe in Declan's leather smell. I touch the feathery hair on the nape of his neck.

I stop kissing him.

He says in my ear, 'I'm so glad you understand. I'm glad it's OK.'

'I understand,' I tell him. 'But . . .'

Declan takes a step back. 'It's not OK?' He does this long blink.

I say, 'No.'

'Bethany, come on. It won't happen again, honestly.'

'No, it won't,' I say.

'*I* told you, the thing with Carlota – it was just—'

'I told *you*, this is nothing to do with Carlota. Or, OK, not *all* to do with her.'

'But you and me . . . we've been together ages.'

'I know.' I realize the truth. It's not him . . . it's *us*. We've got so comfortable together that we can even cheat on each other and think it's OK. 'But I don't trust you, Declan.' And I really should tell him all of it. 'And I don't trust myself either.'

He acts like I didn't say it. He pulls out a piece of paper and holds it out to me. 'I got you this, like always.'

It's a lottery ticket. Our Saturday tradition.

I leave it flapping in his hand. I say quietly, 'We both know it's over.'

I walk away, not looking back, checking the time. Becca might still be waiting to tell me what she saw. Waiting to be a real friend.

I sit on a bench, the same one I sat on when I texted her this morning. After a couple of minutes I see Declan's dad's Volvo drive past, with Declan stern-faced at the wheel. He doesn't see me, or maybe he pretends not to.

A text comes through from Becca, asking if I'm OK. I tell her I know, and I thank her for wanting to tell me the truth. I write, HAVE SPLIT UP WITH D. WILL NEVER TALK 2 C AGAIN. BUT AM OK.

She texts back immediately, YOU SURE?

I'm sure. I tell her.

She writes, MEET ME ANYWAY? GOING TO BAL'S NOW. WE'RE WORRIED ABOUT YOU. WANT TO TALK?

I text back, NO. WANT 2 HAVE FUN. WILL MEET U THERE IN A BIT.

I hit SEND and I'm about to tuck my phone in my bag when a voice next to me says, 'Bet.'

I look up.

Wow.

It's Zac.

I can't help myself, despite everything that's happened. I smile at him. 'What are you doing here? Did your driver chuck you out of the limo at last?'

'I made him turn back. I remembered that there was something I needed to do in your area.'

'Really? For work?'

'Er, yes. I needed to . . .' He looks around for a few seconds. 'Er, OK, I can't think of a good excuse.' He starts talking faster. 'The truth is I needed to see you. I'm glad I found you. Listen, can I have your phone a second? Please?'

I hand it over, watching as he scrolls through some menus and adds himself to my address book. I can't believe he's here. Today has definitely been the weirdest day of my life.

Zac says, 'There. You don't have to call me. But now you can if you want, without asking Carlota for my cousin's number. That's if, er, you'd do that, which—'

'I'm not friends with Carlota any more.'

He looks surprised. 'Why not?'

'I don't want to talk about it.' I feel bold. 'I don't have a boyfriend any more either.'

'Er . . . oh.'

I look at my phone in Zac's hand. It only has one number stored now. Zac's my only contact.

I go to take the phone from him, but instead I rest my hand over his. Just because I feel like it.

The look in Zac's eyes makes a sudden coat of goosebumps spring up all over me.

I've learned a lot today. I've learned to relax and live in the moment, I've learned who my friends are, I've learned I have the confidence to do anything I want to.

Like this, for example. He's so close. I want to kiss him and it would be so easy. It would be nothing. I wouldn't need to worry about it, not now.

So I do – one small kiss on the lips.

And it's not nothing.

So I do it again.

This time he grips my hand and stops me from moving away. He shuts his eyes and kisses me back. We launch into kissing; extreme kissing on the edge of a mountain with no guide ropes. It's dangerous, but it's safe at the same time. It's everything.

I pull away because it's almost too much and it's also too soon.

'I've got to go. I'm meeting someone.'

'Can I walk you?'

'No,' I tell him. 'Bye, Zac. I'll call you, OK?'

My feelings are so mixed up right now.

But I'm not going to stress about it.

* * *

TEEN SPICE! MAGAZINE

EX-BEZZIES FOR EVER: ARE YOU READY TO FORGIVE AND FORGET?

When BFFs fall out it can be **devastating!** But holding on to grudges can also cause **unnecessary stress**.

Ask yourself: are you ready to let go? Everyone makes mistakes! Can you see things from her point of view at all? What would you have done in her shoes?

Still **angry?** Try writing her an email and get those feelings out. You'll feel better even if you never send it!

Dear Lots,

It's me. At last.

Look, I know you're sorry. Thanks for all the messages, and the prototype Holey Grail scarf. I didn't throw it away like you suggested. I even wear it sometimes, and you could be right – it could catch on. (It certainly catches on

320

enough door handles and stuff when I wear it to school, ha ha!)

I also heard you're refusing to talk to Yves, even though he broke up with his girlfriend. What's all that about? Are you just a self-punishment junkie now, or what? I think he really likes you, you nutter! As if any lad on earth could resist you for long, huh?! (Grr, etc.) Although I have to admit that it sounds like he has at least two different girlfriends every week. He's still totally the male version of you!

Oh, do you know how I know all that about Yves? Can you guess?

Yeah, I'm seeing Zac.

It didn't happen right away. He finished with Claire the day after we met, but I didn't start seeing him properly for weeks, till I was sure about it. We chatted on the phone a lot, though. He's fantastic. He's about as un-Declan as you can get! Oh, yeah, and he's got a little half-sister now – apparently this baby was predicted by the tarot reader on Extreme Saturday! And she's chilled Zac's dad out because now he has another hope for someone to take over the family business!

Oh, hey, I think Becca and Baljit miss you even though they won't admit it. We've formed a kickin' girl band now (!!). We're called The B-Bees – no one needs to know that the first 'B' stands for 'Boring', ha ha. And we totally rock! If I say so myself, but then I am the backing singer! Becca's the lead – I love singing, but I've decided the spotlight is not-not-not for me. And I'm not going on *television again any time soon either! No one except Leah and Timster the Cat has even heard us play. Yet! But, for the record, Leah and the T-meister think we're headed for stardom.*

And Becca's finished with Harrison for EVER and she's seeing – wait for it – Leah's boyfriend's older brother. Yes, baby Leah has a boyfriend! Time didn't stop after you left, you know. Though sometimes I wish it had, so maybe I could turn it back and change what happened with us.

But anyway. 'Whatever will be, will be', eh?

Tell you what, though. In some weird way, I wouldn't be in that band, having all those laughs, if it wasn't for you.

Hey, do you know who else misses you? Your mum. So there – you can stop feeling sorry for yourself, pretending she doesn't care about you and all that s*@^. (Do you like my clean swearing there?!) Apparently she told my mum that she originally joined Crafty Nutters to 'get more involved in her daughter's life' – i.e. to make friends with my mum because of me and you being BFFs. (She also brought in a nice baby pic of you last week! You were totally rockin' the Reverse Goth babygro chic.)

So, yeah, and I've been doing a bit of psychoanalysing for you. You're going to hate it, but you're going to listen 'cos you owe me. Ha ha. Here goes. I think you should stop being angry with your mum for not tracking down your real dad, way back when you were a dot in her belly in Spain. 'Cos that's it, you know, I've decided that's your problem – you blame her, and it's not right. Your mum did what she thought was best for her and for you. You should blame him, because he was the one who left. People always blame the woman – isn't that what you told me? Course, you meant I should blame Declan and not you, and you were right (kind of, although really I blame both of you!). But anyway, I think you should cut your mum some slacks, as they say down the trouser factory!

And you should talk to her. I know she's all stone-faced and stuff, but I do think she's got a heart in there.

And why do I think that? Because your mum goes on and on about you to the Nutters. I've overheard that you've been unhappy, but boarding school's a much better environment for you and she wants you to have the chances she never had, and you'll thank her one day. Ick-ick-ickness!! Don't you think? She sounds totally like your stepdad! Your mum doesn't mention your stepdad at all at Nutters, though, which is no surprise since he still thinks my mum's the devil, ha ha.

Hey, Rowan came home for summer. And guess what? Mum refused to do his ironing! *extreme laughter*

I told Rowan about Extreme Travel – the idea, I mean, not what happened to us, though I did say it kind of changed our lives. He said it's a 'wicked concept'. He's going to tell his mates to try Extreme Travel as well as the ironing thing. He said he might do a website for it where people can upload videos of themselves doing random challenges. He kept going on about 'maximizing the thrill'. (Sounds like you all over, Lots. I can't believe you've never shown any interest in my brother!) (OMG

– you haven't, have you?!)

Listen. This doesn't mean I've completely forgiven you, but . . . after you get home for Christmas (this Friday, right? That's what your mum said), let's have another big Saturday out. (You can sneak out and my mum will cover for us again. Joke!!) Have you got the December Teen Spice*!? I have. So I'm going to pick a page at random. I'll do it now.*

OK, here we go. It's page 31. Oh, this could be a laugh. Get it, quick. What do you think?

Meet me somewhere to do with page 31. Meet me at 2.30. Don't call me – I bet we'll go to the same place. And let's have a challenge too – you can pick the page for that. But no random snogging, OK? If you pick a page about boys or kissing, choose again. Text me the page number.

See you on Saturday.

Your friend,

Bets

x

P.S. Do this quiz NOW!

CARLOTA DEL REY PETERS AND BETHANY ROYSTON: FRIENDS OR NOT? A QUIZ BY BETHANY ROYSTON (HINT: YOU'D BETTER NOT GET Bs!!!)

1. Would Carlota ever snog Bethany's boyfriend again?

   A) No way, she's learned her lesson the hard way, and she's so sorry anyway.

   B) It depends on who exactly Bethany's boyfriend is – is Bethany going out with Orlando Bloom at all?

   C) Carlota has given up snogging for ever in shame.

2. What does Carlota think of Bethany?

   A) She's the coolest.

   B) Deceptively cool, despite giving off a slightly boring aura.

   C) Bethany is fantastic, brilliant, wonderful and doesn't deserve Carlota.

3. Was Bethany overreacting?

   A) No, she wasn't. It should never have happened. Best friends' boyfriends are off-limits, whichever way you look at it.

   B) Maybe a little bit. Things were stale with

Declan and they would probably have been over soon anyway. Bethany needed to face up to it, and at a push you could say that Carlota did her a favour hurrying things along a bit.

C) No, absolutely not. Carlota is wicked and sinful.

4. Is Carlota Bethany's friend?

A) Yes, of course.

B) Stop asking stupid questions.

C) She hopes so, and she will grovel at Bethany's feet and do all Bethany's chores for ever more.

5. With friends like these, who needs enemies?

A) Carlota knows what Bethany means, and is so sorry.

B) What is this weird quiz on about now?

C) Exactly, precisely, grovel grovel grovel.

MOSTLY As: Carlota is definitely Bethany's friend, and Bethany's very lucky to have her.

MOSTLY Bs: Has Carlota learned nothing? Bethany can't believe she's giving her another chance. But something tells Bethany that she and Carlota are meant to be friends for ever, come what may, Orlando or no Orlando.

MOSTLY Cs: Carlota is definitely Bethany's friend. But she needs to chill out a bit or she's in danger of not being Carlota any more. Bethany likes Carlota the way she is, really, and doesn't want her to change for anyone. Just, you know, have a bit more respect and all. For her friends, and for herself.

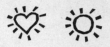

THE END

SPLIT BY A KISS

By Luisa Playa

I'm two different people. Literally. I'm split.

Jo has never been one of the popular kids . . .
until she moves to the USA. Suddenly the
coolest girls at her new high school adopt her,
and the hottest boy, Jake Matthews, notices her.
But when Jake picks her as his partner in the
kissing game Seven Minutes in Heaven, it's
not half as heavenly as she imagined!

Jo has a choice: should she carry on with Jake
for guaranteed popularity – or should she
tell him where to get off and risk losing
her new friends . . . ?

At this moment, Jo splits. She's Josie the Cool –
girlfriend of Jake, member of the in-crowd.
But she's also Jo the Nerd – rejected by the
It girls, single . . . ordinary. Will her two halves
ever come together again?

'A cute, sweet and funny read. Fans of
Louise Rennison will love it.'
Meg Cabot

MY desperate LOVE DIARY

By Liz Rettig

Kelly Ann is fifteen and desperately in love
with G – the biggest idiot in school.
Her best friends Liz and Stephanie can see
how awful G is – and also the Kelly Ann's
quietly gorgeous friend Chris is madly in
love with her. But Kelly Ann stumbles along
blindly, unable to see what's right in
front of her eyes.

Navigating her way through teenage
embarrassments, sick-filled parties and
terrible poetry, Kelly Ann is a hilariously
endearing character to root for!

'Heartfelt but at the same time fantastically
funny, this is a holiday must-read.'
Mizz

JUMPING TO CONFUSIONS

By Liz Rettig

I'm Cat – and I'm the fat, plain one in my family. When I say fat, I don't mean 'have-to-be-prised-out-of-a-hoola-hoop' fat, but when your mum and sister are practically size zero, it's hard not to feel like the elephant girl in comparison.

My twin sister Tessa is blonde, gorgeous and gets any boy she wants. Right now she's got her eye on Josh, a really fit American guy who's just moved to Glasgow.
But he doesn't seem that interested in her.
It's weird. I've never known any boy who didn't fancy Tessa. Well, not straight ones, anyway . . .

Of course! It all makes sense . . . funny that he doesn't want to tell anyone about his secret, not even me, his new best friend . . .

Could Cat be jumping to conclusions about Josh, in this wonderfully funny tale of romantic confusion?

Secrets at St Jude's

THE NEW GIRL

By Carmen Reid

A raucous, hilarious, heartwarming tale of
modern boarding school life.

Gina's mother is fed up with her staying out late,
spending too much money on clothes and too
much time IM-ing her friends. But her solution
to sorting out her wayward LA It-girl is pretty
drastic – she's sending Gina to Scotland to go
to the same boarding school she attended.

Suddenly taken from a world of malls, mobile
phones, en-suite wet-rooms, designer clothes
and sophisticated boys, Gina is forced to find her
way through games of hockey, communal meals
and showers, horrible public schoolboys and
stuffy housemistresses. Will she ever survive?
Her dorm buddies might just help, they're a
strange bunch but they seem to be good fun . . .
And there are always the boys from the local
school to keep them entertained!

THE BOYFRIEND LIST

By Emily Lockhart

The Boyfriend List was a homework assignment for my mental health. Doctor Z, my shrink, told me to write down all the boyfriends, kind-of boyfriends, almost-boyfriends, rumoured boyfriends and wished-he-were boyfriends I've ever had. Plus, she recommended I take up knitting.

In the same ten days, I: lost my boyfriend (boy #13); lost my best friend; lost all my other friends; learned gory details about my now ex-boyfriend's sexual adventures; did something shockingly advanced with boy #15; did something suspicious with boy #10; had an argument with boy #14; drank my first beer; got caught by my mom; lost a lacrosse game; failed a maths test; became a leper and became a famous slut.

Enough to give anyone panic attacks, right? I was so overwhelmed by the horror of the whole debacle that I had to skip school for a day to read mystery novels, cry and eat spearmint jelly candies.

A funny and spot-on take on the trials and tribulations of being a teenager!

VAMPIRE BEACH:
Bloodlust and Initiation

By Alex Duval

Jason and his sister have just moved to Malibu –
to a town full of beautiful rich kids whose lives
revolve around money, fashion, cars and parties.
But these teens hide a dark – and
dangerous – secret . . .

Jason gets swept along by the excitement of his
new crowd and is flattered to be included – and
also very flattered by the apparent interest of the
stunning Sienna. But when he finds out the truth
behind his new friends, Jason has to decide if
he can accept the status quo. Everyone else
seems to be able to – and it might just mean
he can get closer to Sienna . . .

'The Kate Moss of teen reads – stylish, edgy
and addictive . . . this is The OC with bite.'
The Bookseller

VAMPIRE BEACH:
Ritual and Legacy

By Alex Duval

When Jason visits a psychic he is given a warning
of great danger – and sure enough, he is soon
attacked by a mysterious assailant.
When he wakes up in hospital he discovers
that he's been shot with a crossbow.
Who would use such a weapon – possibly
some kind of vampire hunter?
Could Sienna be the one who's really in danger?

Sinister and sexy, this series is one for you
to really sink your fangs into.

'This book is hard to put down . . . a great mix
of horror, humour and romance.'
Sugar

'Outrageously addictive, super cool and as
sharp as a wooden stake right to the heart.'
The Bookseller